CW00972541

Le
Tour de Love

Lilac Mills

Copyright © 2019 Lilac Mills

This book is licensed for your personal enjoyment only. This book may not be re-sold or given away to other people. If you would like to share this book with another person, please purchase an additional copy for each recipient. If you're reading this book and did not purchase it, or it was not purchased for your use only, then please purchase your own copy. Thank you for respecting the hard work of this author.

This story is a work of fiction. All names, characters, places and incidents are invented by the author or have been used fictitiously and are not to be construed as real. Any similarity to actual persons or events is purely coincidental

The author asserts the moral rights under the Copyright, Design and Patents Act 1988 to be identified as the author of this work.

All rights reserved. No part of this publication may be reproduced, stored in a retrieval system or transmitted, in any form or by any means without the prior consent of the author, nor be otherwise circulated in any form of binding or cover other than that which it is published and without a similar condition being imposed on the subsequent purchaser.

Acknowledgments
Cover designed by: Y. Nikolova at Ammonia Book Covers

DEDICATION

To Catherine Mills, for putting up with me xxx

(and for her invaluable advice as someone who isn't the least bit

interested in cycling)

OTHER BOOKS
BY
LILAC MILLS

Sunshine at Cherry Tree Farm

Summer on the Turquoise Coast

A Very Lucky Christmas

Love in the City by the Sea

The Tanglewood Tea Shop

CHAPTER 1

Molly washed her hands thoroughly before calling in her next client, a Mr Duvall. As she dried them with a paper towel, she did a quick scan of her treatment room, making sure everything was clean and in its place. Next, she glanced down at her uniform. All was in order. She prided herself on her professionalism and it simply wouldn't do to have a stain on her white tunic. After a quick check of the very brief notes the receptionist had taken when Sue had booked the client in – broken wrist, both ulna and radius, cast removed yesterday – she was good to go.

She stuck her head around the door to the waiting room. 'Mr Duvall?'

A tall, slim guy in his late twenties stood and gave her an uncertain smile. 'That's me.'

Molly held out her hand for the form each patient was required to fill in and when he gave it to her, she said, 'Hi, I'm Molly Matthews and I'll be your physiotherapist today. This way.' As she stepped aside to let him pass, she scanned the form with practised speed.

'I see you've broken your wrist. How did you do that?' she asked as she led him into the treatment room. She didn't need to know the details in order to do her job, but small talk helped break the ice, and she liked to build up a rapport with her patients if she could.

'Came off my bike,' he said, shortly.

'Motorbike?'

'Bicycle.'

'Any other damage?' she asked, gesturing for him to take a seat.

'The bike was totalled. The idiot driver went right over it.' His tone was grim, the words clipped.

Molly gave him a sharp look. 'I meant, did you sustain any other injuries. And better the bike than you, Mr Duvall.'

'The name's Alex. And I'm seriously pissed off about the bike.'

'Halfords have a sale on at the moment,' she said. 'Maybe you could pick up another fairly cheaply—'

She stopped as her client let out a snort. Taken aback a little, because she had only been trying to help, she decided that perhaps it was best if she concentrated on his injury, especially when she spotted the incredulous look on his face at her suggestion.

'OK.' She took a breath and picked up his form again. No allergies, no health problems, and he wasn't currently on any medication, but he had suffered a broken clavicle, a dislocated shoulder, and a fractured pelvis in the past. Molly wanted to ask how he had come by so many injuries, but it was none of her business and he was not here because of any of those. It was his broken wrist he wanted physio on, so she spent the next few minutes checking the range of movement in the joint and the strength in his arm and fingers.

'When was the cast taken off?'

'Yesterday,' he replied.

Wow, he certainly didn't waste any time in booking physio, Molly thought. 'You've probably found there is a slight atrophy in the muscles of your upper arm, which could take a few weeks to recover, and your shoulder muscles may be affected, too,' she advised. 'Slip your shirt off for me.'

Alex unbuttoned his shirt and took it off.

Molly paused when she saw his torso. The man didn't have an ounce of fat on him. It was all muscle but without the bulkiness which came from excessive time spent in the gym. His abs were defined, a hint of ribs showed underneath the skin, and his chest was hairless. But what really caught her eye were the three lumps on his clavicle. Three separate breaks.

Moving around behind him, Molly checked out his back and saw there was a faint discolouration of the skin on his shoulder, another old injury. Her interest was quite definitely piqued now, as she wondered how he had come by so many injuries.

'Sorry, if my hands are cold,' she said, placing her palms on his skin and ignoring his slight flinch. She palpated his trapezius and deltoid. Both were rock hard. Too hard and full of knots.

'Before we begin the exercises, I'd like to try to loosen your shoulders a bit. Is that all right with you?' she asked.

Her client nodded, eased off his trainers, walked over to the physio table, and lay face down on it without being told. He'd clearly had a massage or two in the past.

Molly draped a towel over his waist and backside to protect his jeans, rubbed some oil onto her palms and got to work. For her size (ten) and her height (five foot two) she was strong and, as she dug her fingers in, Alex let out a groan. She was especially intent on getting at those muscles running underneath the shoulder blade, and she prodded and probed, working the knots out with ruthless determination. At each pop and crackle, Alex winced but Molly didn't stop. It was important to release as much muscle tension in the area as possible before she started work on his wrist. And once she'd taken him through the (sometimes painful) exercises, she intended to massage his shoulder again.

Not all practitioners believed it was necessary to relax the adjoining muscles and therefore only worked on the area which was causing the immediate problem, but Molly had seen the benefits time and time again, which was why she was always fully booked. It was also why Finley, who owned the practice, was always complaining that she ran over on time.

Finley wasn't a bad physiotherapist or a bad boss, but he did want to make a profit. Molly understood that, she really did, but she also wanted to do the best she possibly could for her clients and if that meant spending an extra twenty minutes on them, so be it.

With the massage finished for the moment, she wiped the excess oil from Alex's skin and asked him to sit up.

He did so, rolling his shoulders and neck. 'Good,' he muttered. 'Much better.' He looked up at her and smiled. 'Can I take you home with me?'

Molly produced a friendly, professional smile; if he knew how many times she heard that exact same comment in a week...

The rest of the session consisted of Molly putting her client through a series of joint manipulations which she knew must hurt him, although he didn't utter so much as a sigh and just sat through it stoically as she bent and twisted his arm, fingers, and wrist. Then she made him do a series of exercises.

Finally, after the second massage (the muscles in the top of his arm and shoulder had tensed up again, but not as bad as before) she reeled off her spiel about physios only being able to do so much in the time available to them and that the client must continue the exercises at home for the treatment to be effective.

'I want you to do these three times a day to start,' she added. 'No more than five repetitions of each for the first three days then gradually build them up, increasing the reps to a maximum of ten.'

He frowned at her.

'Don't worry, I'll print them out so you don't forget,' she said.

Alex continued to frown.

'Is there something wrong?' she asked.

'When can I race again?'

'Race?'

'Compete.'

'I'm sorry, what exactly are you competing in?'

'Cycling.' He said this as if Molly should have already known what he meant.

'Oh, I see. Well, it may be several weeks before you're back on your bike again,' she began.

'I'm already back on my bike,' Alex said. 'Kind of; although it's a different bike and I'm training on the turbo,' he added, by way of explanation.

'Turbo?' Molly had no idea what he was talking about. And what did he mean by saying he was back on his bike? There was no way he could grip the handlebars effectively with a barely-healed wrist.

'Turbo trainer,' he repeated. 'You can ride your bike indoors with it. It clamps around the skewer and suspends the bike on an A-frame. I've been watching real-time recordings of the Tour in my living room. It's the only thing that's kept me sane. Sodding motorist.'

'Oh.' Molly still had no idea what he was talking about, but he did look very earnest about it, whatever it was.

He must have seen the confusion on her face. Grabbing his shirt off the back of the chair he had been sitting on, he said, 'I'm a professional cyclist. I can't afford not to train, so as soon as I had the cast put on, I was on the turbo to keep my fitness levels up. It's nowhere near as effective as being on the road but it was the best I could do, under the circumstances. But now the cast is off, I can get back on my bike again.'

Molly eyed him suspiciously. 'You mean get back on this turbo thing? You'll be using that, right?'

Alex shook his head. He did up the final button on his shirt and jammed his feet back in his trainers. 'Nope. Outside, on the road.'

'But you can't grip the handlebars,' she protested.

5

'I'll take it easy, I promise. The worst bit will be changing gears.'

'But... but... you could do more damage, and it'll be extremely painful, and—' She was about to say dangerous, but Alex interrupted.

'That's what painkillers are for,' he said. 'Now, when can I race again?'

'Er...' Molly was at a loss. She'd treated sportspeople before, but no one quite like Alexander Duvall. 'You tell me,' she retorted. 'Besides, you probably won't take my advice anyway.'

'I've *got* to be race fit in three weeks,' he said.

'Why three weeks?'

'The Tour.'

He'd mentioned something about a tour a minute ago, but she didn't have a clue what it was. 'What's that?' she asked.

'Le Tour de France – the biggest, most important, most prestigious race in the cycling world.' He paused, then his face lit up in a huge grin. 'And I'm in it! *Me!* The odd boy from Spetchley who shaves his legs and spends every second of every day on his bike. Who'd have thought it?'

Molly stared at her client in amazement. The smile transformed his face and he'd gone from a rather intense, serious man, to a rather good-looking one who was full of passion and enthusiasm.

That passion disappeared as fast as it had arrived, and his face fell.

'If I'm fit enough,' he added. 'Greg won't keep me in the team if I'm not 100 per cent fit. This is only my third grand tour, and I'm second wheel to Tim Anderson. I can't not be in it!'

Molly had no idea what second wheel meant but it was clearly important to her client. 'Are you serious about this?' she asked.

He gave her an incredulous look.

'OK, I can see you are,' she added, hastily, 'but it's

going to take more than the exercises I've given you to be fit enough to race in such a short space of time.'

'I've got the legs,' he said, 'more or less, but I need to build up the road time. And I've got to be over there in just over two weeks.'

'By there, I take it you mean France?'

He nodded.

'So, I've got fourteen days, give or take?'

He nodded again.

She caught her bottom lip with her teeth and wrinkled her nose, as she considered the options. Oh, what the hell? Decision made, she said firmly, 'I want you back here tomorrow morning, seven o'clock sharp. Can you do that?'

He stared at her, his eyes wide. They were a lovely flecked hazel with long, dark lashes. Nice eyes. But right now they weren't giving any indication what their owner was thinking.

When he didn't answer she made another decision, one that could cost her her job if Finley found out. 'It's on the house,' she said, thinking he might be worried about the charges. Private physiotherapy sessions weren't cheap.

He still didn't say anything, but this time Molly guessed it might be from shock as his eyes had widened even further.

'I want to see you at six-thirty every evening, too,' she said. Her last client of the day was at five pm. If she stayed late to do some paperwork, then… She gave a mental shrug. The other two people in the practice besides Finley, a chiropractor and a sports therapist, were always out of the door bang on time, as was Sue, the receptionist. Finley wasn't in tomorrow, or the day after, so she didn't have to worry about him for now.

'Are you sure?' Alex asked, breaking what was becoming a rather awkward silence.

'I'm sure. This clearly means a lot to you.'

'But won't you get into trouble about it being on the house?'

'Not if I don't get caught,' she smiled.

'Thank you.' His expression was earnest. 'That's the nicest thing anyone has ever done for me.'

'Aww…' Molly blushed.

'I'll see you in the morning, then. Seven a.m.'

'Don't be late,' she warned.

'I won't. And thanks again.'

Without warning, he leaned in, grasped the tops of her arms and gave her a kiss, one peck of the lips on each cheek. Molly froze.

'Oops, sorry,' he said, sounding anything but. 'That's what comes from spending too much time around Italians.'

And with that cryptic comment, Alexander Duvall was out of the door, leaving Molly staring after him, her fingers raised to her face and a bemused smile playing on her lips.

CHAPTER 2

Molly was only acquainted with seven a.m. in terms of sitting at her kitchen table, staring blearily into a cup of coffee and listening to the news in the background, while trying to find enough motivation for a shower.

This particular seven a.m. saw her unlocking the main door to the offices of *Finley Stewart, Physiotherapist, BSc, MCSP, HCPC*, and hastily disappearing inside clutching a latte and a bag of croissants. The coffee was for now, the croissants for later.

It was strange, but she was quite looking forward to her first appointment of the day, even if it was gratis and very, very early.

Seconds after she had shrugged off her coat and downed half her coffee, she heard the outside door go. Hastening to see who it was, she was relieved to see a Lycra-clad Alex delicately manoeuvring a brightly-coloured bike into the reception area. The relief wasn't anything to do with the bike – although she was a little confused why he'd brought it with him – but that the noise hadn't been one of her colleagues surprising her by coming into work early.

'Will it be safe here or should I bring it with me?' Alex nodded towards the treatment room bearing Molly's name on the door. 'I don't want it going missing. I've only just been given it.'

'Good morning,' Molly said, wryly. 'Nice new bike. I'll lock the front door, shall I? It'll be safe enough in the waiting room.'

'That'll be great,' he said, then paused. 'Good morning to you too. Yeah, BeSpoke, who I ride for, let me have another one. They had to if they want me to race. They'll salvage what they can from the dead one for spares. Hang on a sec.'

She watched, perplexed, as Alex walked gingerly across the tiled floor, sounding like the claws of a very large dog. She stared at his feet as her client sat down and proceeded to take his shoes off.

'Cleats,' he explained, seeing the direction of her gaze. He held up one of the odd-looking trainer-things and turned it upside down, showing her a roughly-triangular-shaped piece of metal stuck to the sole. 'It fits into the pedals.'

'Oh?'

'More power, you see. If you don't have clip-in pedals, you only have any real power on the downward stroke. With clip-ins, as you pull your leg up, you're not just relying on momentum to carry the pedal up to the top, but you're actually dragging it up. See?'

She saw. 'OK, but how come you don't fall over when you get to traffic lights or when you have to really slow down?'

With one shoe on and one shoe off, Alex returned to his bike and sat on the saddle. He put the booted foot on one of the pedals and with a quick, almost imperceptible twist of his ankle, he clipped his shoe into the pedal. Another twist and he had unclipped it.

'It gets to be second nature, like when you're driving a car you don't think about having to move your foot onto the clutch to change gear, you just do it.'

Well, you learn something new every day, Molly thought. She checked the time. 'Shall we get on?' she suggested, conscious of the impending arrival of her workmates, and she walked into her treatment room with Alex following close behind.

Three-quarters of an hour later and her client wasn't nearly as jaunty as he had been when he had arrived. In fact, he looked a little pale and Molly guessed he was in some discomfort. She had worked him quite hard, although he hadn't uttered a sound except for a bit of harsh breathing.

After the final massage, Alex pulled his top on over his head, and Molly noticed he was favouring his left arm slightly more than he had when he'd entered her room.

'I take it you're going for a bike ride now?' she asked, hoping he was going to say "no" and that he'd brought his bike this morning because it was the sole means of transport he had.

'Of course.' He was matter-of-fact, as if it was perfectly normal to ride a bike with an arm barely out of plaster while suffering a significant amount of pain.

What was wrong with the guy?

'I've got 100 kilometres to ride today,' he said, and Molly nearly fell over in shock.

'That's over 60 miles!' she cried.

'Yep.'

'With a broken arm?'

'It's not broken now.'

'It will be if you do something as daft as cycling such a distance before the muscles and ligaments are back to full strength. And the bone has only recently set; it'll still be quite weak.'

He shrugged. 'It'll be fine.' He didn't sound in the least bit bothered and he reinforced this when he added, 'I can't wait to stretch my legs, to be honest.'

'You're mad.'

'Nah, just a professional cyclist. We're all the same.'

'You must have a high pain threshold,' she observed, as she washed her hands, noticing the bag of goodies she had placed on her desk earlier. She was dying for a coffee and one of those croissants. The early start had made her hungry.

Alex laughed. 'I'm not sure about the high pain threshold,' he said. 'It's more a case of a high level of determination and an equal measure of stupidity. One guy I know rode a tour with a broken pelvis.'

Molly grimaced.

'Can I beg a glass of water from you?' Alex asked. 'I've got two water bottles on the bike but I want to save them for later, and I want to hydrate as much as possible before I set off.'

'Certainly.' Molly filled a glass from the tap, then said, 'I've got coffee, too, if you want it.'

'Filter or instant?'

'Filter, of course.'

He hesitated, a look of longing on his face. 'I'd love one but I'm off caffeine right now.'

'I could do you a decaf?' she suggested. 'But it will have to be instant, I'm afraid.'

Alex shook his head. 'I'm good, thanks. I'll stick with the water.'

He perched on the chair reserved for patients and Molly saw him swallow a couple of painkillers before she left to fetch her coffee; even if *he* didn't need the caffeine, she most certainly did. The tablets he had just taken would soon wear off, she predicted, shaking her head in despair. Still, it was his body and he clearly knew what he was doing, although if she thought he would do himself serious or permanent damage she would refuse to treat him.

She'd offer him a croissant, she decided. He looked as though he could do with feeding up. He wasn't skinny, per se, but he was definitely on the slim side. It was all muscle though and he was clearly extremely fit.

'No, thanks,' he said, eyeing the croissant in the same way a mouse would eye up a snake. 'I've got to watch my weight.'

'Get off,' she scoffed. 'There's more fat on a pencil, as

my nan used to say. One won't hurt.'

'It will,' he insisted. 'Because I might not stop at one and I've already had my calorie intake for this morning.'

Molly, a croissant within licking distance of her lips, lowered her hand and put the pastry back in the bag. There was no way she could eat one in front of him now, no matter how hungry she was.

'You go ahead,' he said. 'I don't mind.'

But she saw the way his gaze had followed the croissant and the hunger in his eyes, so she folded the top of the bag over and placed the whole thing in her desk drawer. She wasn't bothered about torturing him when it came to his wrist, but she wasn't that much of a sadist as to wave a pastry in front of a man who dearly wanted to eat it but couldn't.

He finished his water, stood up, and reached behind him. When his hand came back into view, he was holding a credit card. 'I can pay,' he said.

Molly shook her head. 'I told you, this is on the house.'

'No really, I *can* pay. Or rather, BeSpoke can. It's their card, not mine, although they would prefer it if you invoiced them next time,' he said sheepishly.

'Invoiced?' Molly repeated. 'Oh, right. OK. Will do. Um… Actually, do you mind if we carry on the way we are, because I really do want to treat you every morning and every evening until you go to France and I don't want you or your company to think I'm saying that just to get more money out of you.'

Alex held out the card. 'They don't think any such thing and neither do I, so I insist. You can't work for nothing. But thank you, anyway. Your generosity…' He trailed off, but his eyes were on hers and she saw the depth of feeling in them. He truly was moved by her offer.

'Dinner,' he said abruptly. 'Let me take you out to dinner.'

Molly was taken aback. It was totally unexpected and although she was tempted to say "yes", she had no intention of going out to dinner with a client. It was unprofessional for one, and possibly unethical for another.

Alex jumped to another conclusion entirely when he saw her expression. 'Oh, er, forget I said anything,' he stuttered. 'I expect you've got a husband or a boyfriend, and I don't want you to think I'm hitting on you or anything.' He thrust the credit card at her. 'Please, take it.'

Molly took it, albeit reluctantly. At least she didn't have to skulk around anymore, and Finley would be delighted (astounded?) at her dedication.

'Be careful,' she urged, as Alex wheeled his bike towards the door.

'I will,' he said over his shoulder, as he put his helmet on.

'Oh, by the way, there is no husband or boyfriend,' Molly blurted. She had no idea why she felt she had to put the record straight (yes, you do, a little voice in her head told her) but she was glad she had when she saw the slow smile spread across Alex's face.

He had a very nice smile indeed, and for a moment she felt quite weak at the knees. Until she got a grip on herself, that is. But it didn't prevent her from watching him cycle down the high street, and her observation of him had nothing to do with checking how well he was using his left wrist, either.

CHAPTER 3

There were only three more days of treatment left and her work with Alexander Duvall would be done. Molly was amazed at how far her client had come in such a short space of time, and most of it was down to the man's sheer determination and bloody-mindedness. She still wasn't totally convinced that he'd regained full strength in his wrist, but there was still another week to go before the start of the Tour de France, he'd informed her. The only reason he was travelling out so early was to get acclimatised and for the pre-race training sessions with the rest of the guys.

Which reminded her, she must set her TV to record the event. She'd never been remotely interested in cycling before, but she now felt she had a vested interest in it. She very much wanted Alex to win and she told him so when he arrived for his evening session.

He stripped off down to the waist and arranged himself on the physio table. 'It's not going to happen,' he said, his voice muffled.

'I don't see why not!' Molly was indignant. 'There's no need to put yourself down like that. If you're good enough to enter the race, you're good enough to win it.'

'The tours don't work like that. It's a team effort.' He grunted when she dug her fingers into his back.

Molly worked on the muscles, his skin soft and smooth under her hands. He had a different aftershave on this evening and she kept catching tantalising whiffs of it. Resisting the urge to lean closer and bury her nose in his neck, she said, 'But that doesn't mean you can't win, right?'

'Actually, it does.'

'Why?'

'Because the sports director of each team will pick the rider who they think stands the best chance of winning, and the rest of the team, the domestiques like me, are paid to ensure he does precisely that.'

Molly took a moment to let that odd piece of information sink in. 'I take it the sports director hasn't picked you,' she said eventually.

'Nope. I'm second wheel to the team leader, though. Tim Anderson stands the best chance in our team, with me next. It's my job to help him in any way I can, from giving him my bike if his is damaged, to pulling him up the mountains.'

'Pulling him up? What, *literally*?'

Molly tapped Alex on the shoulder to signify this part of the treatment was over and that he needed to sit up.

Alex laughed. 'Not literally. It's all to do with drag and air resistance and having a team-mate to focus on.'

'You've lost me.'

'The drag bit is simple physics. Say if you were behind a car, and that car was travelling at 30 miles per hour? It would punch enough of a hole in the air that if another car was travelling closely behind, the second car wouldn't have as much wind resistance to deal with as the first and wouldn't use as much fuel in the long run. With me so far?'

Molly nodded.

'It's the same with cyclists. The guy in front moves some of the air aside with his body and his bike, so the guy behind doesn't have to work quite so hard. The men on the front of the peloton have a tougher job of it and get tired faster than the riders just behind them.'

'Wait, what's a peloton?'

'That's what the main group of riders are called during the race.'

Molly began to run him through his exercises, stopping now and again to adjust his position or to make him stretch or flex a little more.

'There's a bit more to this bike racing than I thought,' she said. 'You said you are a domestic...?' She hesitated over the word.

'Domestique. Paid to support the team's GC rider.'

'GC?'

'General Classification. Look, why don't I take you to dinner? I promise I won't bite and I can explain it all to you then. Besides, there's something I want to ask you.'

'Oh? Can't you just ask me now?'

'I was hoping to ply you with wine first.'

'Oh, no you don't. You can ask me now, when I'm sober.'

Alex hesitated.

'Is it that bad?' she quipped, then wondered if it really was something awful when she saw the serious expression on his face.

He took a deep breath. 'You remember my first session with you and I said I wanted to take you home with me?'

She nodded, wondering where this was leading.

'I still do,' he said.

'Is that all?' she laughed. 'I often get told that.'

'I mean it.'

'Excuse me?'

'I want you to come with me.'

'Go with you where?'

'To France.'

Her mouth opened and closed like a fish on a line. 'I hardly know you and you're asking me to go on holiday with you?'

'No, sorry, not a holiday. I mean, the Tour.' Alex was starting to look distinctly uncomfortable and so he should, Molly thought. They'd only just met and he was asking her to go away with him. Heck, they hadn't even had a single date yet.

Hang on, did he just say, "the Tour"? Huh! If she was going to take a few days off work, she wouldn't be spending them watching a bunch of sweaty cyclists charging up and down the roads of France. She'd prefer to spend them on a beach somewhere nice and hot, thank you very much. Besides, it was a bit short notice and she didn't know whether she'd be able to get the time off. Not that she had any intention of going...

'Er, no thanks, I... er... prefer beach holidays,' she said, thinking that what had started out as a perfectly normal day had just become quite surreal. It was nice to be asked but there was no way she was dropping everything to go off on a jaunt to France with a guy she'd met only two weeks ago. She didn't even know where he lived – oh, actually she did, his address was on his form. Not that she'd made a point of looking, but she couldn't help noticing when she'd passed the form back to reception for processing. Spetchley. Foxglove Road. Number 6. She was astounded she'd remembered it.

If it was at all possible, Alex looked even more uncomfortable. 'It's not a holiday,' he muttered. 'It's a job offer.'

'A *what?*'

'A job offer.'

'That's what I thought you said. What job? And do you mean in France?'

'France, Spain, Belgium. Wherever the cycling takes us.'

'OK, you need to slow down and explain yourself properly.' Molly was flabbergasted and more than a little mystified.

'I did mean it when I said I wanted you to come with me.' He raised a hand as Molly opened her mouth.

She closed it again – the least she could do was hear him out before she refused.

'Our physio handed in his notice a month ago. He's gone to work for Control Data. Another cycling team,' Alex added, seeing the expression Molly knew must be on her face. 'We've not replaced him and with the tour only ten days away, we're desperate.'

'Thank you very much.' Molly's voice was dryer than the Sahara on a particularly hot day.

Alex let out a sigh. 'I didn't mean it that way,' he said. 'What I mean is—' He jumped off the table and gripped the tops of her arms. 'Look, you're good. More than good – you're wonderful. And you *care.*

Which is probably just as important. You didn't need to slot me in for all those extra appointments, and the fact that you were willing to do it for free and out of the goodness of your heart means a lot. To all of us.'

Molly gave him a steady stare. 'For one thing, you *have* been paying, and for another – who is "all of us"?'

'The BeSpoke team – me, the rest of the cyclists, Chuck.'

'Chuck?'

'The sports director. Everyone is looking forward to you joining us, especially the swannies.'

'Oh.' This was all too much, and Molly felt overwhelmed. One minute she'd been bending and flexing a client's wrist, the next she was being offered a somewhat bizarre job with a bunch of people who had weird-sounding job titles. She couldn't even begin to think about what a swannie did and she wasn't sure she really wanted to know.

'Do you need a bit of time to think about it?' Alex asked, letting go of her. He peered at her anxiously.

'Yes, please.' Like a month or two.

'I'll explain tonight, yeah?'

'Yeah… er… no, actually.'

'I thought we were going out for dinner?'

'I never said yes.'

'Oh.'

Alex looked so crestfallen, Molly felt totally mean. 'Dating clients is rather frowned on,' she added, trying to let him down gently.

'That's OK then, because this isn't a date,' he announced cheerfully.

Molly's cheeks flamed. Great. She'd only gone and made a total prat of herself by jumping to the wrong conclusion. 'I still don't think it's a good idea,' she said.

'The pay is good and you'll get to see lots of great places. Can you at least think about it? Please? Over dinner?' Alex had slipped his shirt back on and was jangling his keys. She knew from previous sessions that he preferred to ride in the mornings and would usually drive to his evening appointments with her.

'But what about my job here?' she asked.

'We can talk about that over dinner.' His smile was huge and hopeful, and he tipped his head to one side as he waited for her answer.

Oh, what the hell. He'd be off on his travels in a few days and it was unlikely she'd ever see him again. Besides, they were both adults and the reason for the dinner was to discuss a job offer, so Alex was technically correct when he said it wasn't a date.

'All right,' she agreed, making her mind up in a rush and she went to her desk and scribbled her address and phone number on a piece of paper which she handed to him.

'Pick me up at eight o'clock,' she told him, 'and I expect to be taken somewhere nice.'

'You will be,' he promised and darted out of the door.

Molly watched him go with amusement. He really was very sweet and even though she understood she would probably never see him again after this, she found herself looking forward to her date much more than she should have been, under the circumstances.

CHAPTER 4

Molly hadn't eaten at Brown's Brasserie before, although she had heard of it. It was situated in a small village on the banks of the River Severn, with a pretty garden stretching almost to the edge of the water. Tables had been placed outside on the terrace, and were covered with crisp white tablecloths, shining cutlery, and sparkling glasses. It wasn't fully dark yet and the fairy lights strung through the pergola overhead created a magical feel.

Alex, Molly realised, had taken her tongue-in-cheek and totally unmeant comment that she wanted to go somewhere nice, very seriously indeed. This place looked extremely nice and she'd heard the food was good too, which was a bonus because she was starving.

When they were seated and had their menus in their hands, Molly began the conversation. During the drive home from the practice and when she was showering and getting ready, all she had been able to think about was Alex and his offer. More Alex, really, than the offer, although she was intrigued by it and it wouldn't do any harm to learn more about him. Learn more about *it*, she'd hastily corrected herself as she had towelled her hair.

'Tell me about this offer,' she suggested, eyeing the starters on the menu hungrily. Crickey, she fancied having one of each because they all sounded so tempting.

'You'd come and work for BeSpoke,' Alex said, casually as if leaving her home and her job and going to work for a company she'd never heard of was totally normal. 'Are you ready to order?'

'I think so. Shall we have a starter?'

A small frown crossed Alex's face. 'Not for me, sorry, I've got to watch my weight.'

Molly frowned in return. He was already slim, although she knew from experience how muscular he was under his clothes, but she didn't make a comment, deciding to order an extra side of something instead to make up for not having a starter. He might be watching his weight, but she certainly wasn't watching hers.

'Um, I'll have the barley-fed steak with thrice-cooked chips and salad, and a portion of beer-battered onion rings,' she said to the waitress who had come to take their order. 'Oh, and could I have a small glass of house red, please?'

'Of course, and for you?' the woman asked Alex.

'Can I have the swordfish and a plain salad. No dressing on the salad and no sauce with the fish. And a mineral water, please.'

'Go on, tell me all about this job,' she said, trying not to compare his sad salad with her chunky chips and onion rings.

'As I said, our physio handed in his notice, which was one of the reasons I came to you. Normally, I'd be at the training camp now with the guys, but with

23

our physio gone I decided to come home for treatment.'

'Home being Spetchley?'

'You remembered!' His face lit up.

'It's on your client records.'

'Oh.' He paused for a moment, then rallied and smiled. 'You looked me up?'

Molly rolled her eyes. 'The job?' she reminded him.

'Look, I understand if you're sceptical; I would be too, but as I said the pay is good and you get to see the world.'

'France,' Molly stated flatly. It was hardly the world, was it?

He gave her a grin. 'There's the Tour of Flanders, the Vuelta in Spain, the Giro in Italy, the Tour Down Under in Australia, the Tour of California, the Tour of the Alps, not to mention the ones held in Saudi, Turkey, South Africa – I could go on for ages, and if you get homesick, then there's always the Tour of Yorkshire, the Tour of Britain—' He stopped and regarded her hopefully.

'You win, that's a lot of places.' She thought for a moment. 'Does that mean I'd spend most of my time on the road?'

'Yeah, but—'

'I'm not sure if I'd want that.'

Their waitress appeared with their drinks and Molly took a grateful sip of hers, her throat suddenly dry. Alex drank his mineral water in one go, and before the waitress had a chance to move away from their table, he ordered another.

'What?' he asked Molly as her eyes widened. 'I drink a lot of water.'

'Do you drink anything else?'

He shrugged. 'Energy drinks, fruit juice, coffee when I'm not racing, vodka in the off-season.'

Molly jumped on the last. 'There's an off-season? Does that mean you're not on the road all year round?'

'October.'

'That's it? One month off?'

'More or less.'

'Hmm.' Molly found herself torn. What Alex was offering her was a once-in-a-lifetime opportunity. Most physios would bite his hand off at the chance to get paid to travel the world. But Molly didn't know if she was cut out for it. She liked the familiarity of her own house (it might be small but it was hers) and she wondered how soon the novelty of being somewhere different every few weeks would wear off. Besides, she knew nothing about cycling and she wasn't sure she wanted to learn.

She said as much to Alex.

'You know about bones and muscles and tendons, don't you? That's your trade, your profession. You don't need to know about power ratios, or tyre pressures, or Category 1 mountains, because that's my job, my profession. All of us, from the sports director down to the bus driver have our parts to play. Although, to be fair, everyone does actually know how to ride a bike. Saying that though, I do have my doubts about Tim sometimes.' He laughed to show he was joking.

'Tim?'

'Team leader – the guy we pin our hopes on.'

'Ah, I remember. You're his second wheel.'

Alex looked surprised. 'You *have* been paying

attention,' he said.

'Paying attention isn't the same as agreeing to take the job,' Molly pointed out.

Alex sighed. 'I can't believe I'm having to try so hard to talk you into it. I thought you'd have been pleased.' He seemed genuinely perplexed.

'*You* asked *me*, not the other way around. I'm not applying for a job; you're trying to persuade me to take one.'

He leaned back as their meals arrived and didn't say anything until they were alone again. Molly looked at the plain salad on his plate and the large piece of unadorned swordfish, comparing it to her steak and chips. Her steak was definitely more appetising.

'You get used to it,' Alex said, noticing the direction of her gaze.

'Do you ever eat fries, or chocolate or cake, or anything remotely naughty?' she asked, feeling rather sorry for him.

His eyes lit up. 'Cake,' he drawled. 'I have a bit of a thing for cake. Actually, it tends to be a bit of a thing for cyclists in general. There's nothing nicer than going out for a ride in Italy and stopping halfway for coffee and cake.'

Molly couldn't help smiling. 'Is that something you do often?'

'Yeah, but it's not always in Italy. It could be in France' (he waggled his eyebrows at her) 'or Spain, or Belgium – although Belgian coffee isn't the best – or whichever country we happen to be in. Cyclists get really excited when they find a new coffee shop and we have been known to plan our training rides around where the best ones are in that area.'

She gave him a quizzical look.

'You're thinking I need to get out more, aren't you?' he sighed.

'Maybe, but you do make it sound electrifying.'

'I do?'

'No.'

'Oh.' He put his fork down, his plate almost empty. Molly had hardly touched hers, and she marvelled at the speed he'd eaten his meal. He must have been really hungry.

'Is there anything I can say to persuade you to accept the job of a lifetime, a job that many people would kill for, a job where you get paid to see the world?' he asked her.

'If you put it like that…' she said, feeling incredibly guilty as she speared a chip and bit into it.

'Does that mean you'll say yes?'

She shook her head. 'I don't think so. I've already got a job and I don't particularly want to swap it for another.'

'OK. Here's the deal,' he said, placing his elbows on the table and leaning forward. 'I want to show you an email I received from Greg. He's the man who manages the team.'

'Okaaay.'

Alex got out his phone, found what he wanted and handed it to her. Molly read it. Then she read it again.

'Is this a wind-up?' she asked.

'No. He means what he says.'

'But that's double what I'm earning now.'

'Is it?' Alex looked relieved. 'I was hoping it would be more than your current salary. And that's not the best bit. All your travel expenses are taken care of, all your hotel accommodation, all your meals.' Alex hesitated, then grimaced. 'Actually, forget I mentioned meals, because unless you want to eat like a pro-cyclist, then you might want to buy your own food.' He smiled hopefully. 'It's a pretty good deal, actually.'

It most certainly was.

Molly stared down at her half-eaten steak without really seeing it. Think about this logically, she told herself, trying to count up the downsides. Apart from being away from her family and friends for months on end, what other reasons were there to turn the job offer down?

If she was honest, she couldn't really think of any. She was young, single, and had no one to answer to but herself. She was at an ideal point in her life to do something like this, because she certainly wouldn't be able to when she was married and had children.

So, what was holding her back?

Aware that Alex was studying her with concern, she lifted her gaze from her plate, her appetite suddenly gone.

'Are you all right?' he asked.

She nodded. 'I'm thinking.'

'I'll shut up then.'

And he did. He leaned back, sipped at his water and seemed to sort of switch off. Molly regarded him for a moment, wondering what he was thinking, then she went back to her deliberating.

If she didn't take this chance now, it wouldn't come again, and when else would she have the opportunity to travel the world, doing what she loved and was good at, and being paid for it at the same time? Never, she decided. If she let this slip through her fingers, she'd probably stay in Worcester for the rest of her life. Not that that was a bad thing – she loved the little city with its ancient Cathedral and serene river, and not to mention the beautiful countryside surrounding it, but she was being offered the world.

The question was, did she have the courage to take it?

CHAPTER 5

'You're planning on doing *what*?' Molly's mum was clearly appalled. 'With a bunch of men?' She spat that last word out as if "men" were the equivalent of something nasty stuck to the bottom of her shoe.

'Yes, Mum. It's the opportunity of a lifetime. How many physios get the offer to travel with a professional cycling team all over the world?' Molly had lain awake for hours after Alex had dropped her home (with another one of those weird two-cheek kisses) planning on what she was going to say to her parents. Breaking it to them gently and giving them time to get used to the idea wasn't an option, considering she intended to leave the country in a matter of days.

'How many would actually want to?' her mother countered. 'And what about your job?'

That was the second thing that had kept her from slumber last night – Finley and his reaction. He certainly wasn't going to be pleased and she felt a right heel for dropping him in it and leaving with such short notice, but if she didn't take Alex and BeSpoke up on the offer... yada, yada, yada. The argument went round and round in her head until she was sick to death of her own thoughts.

'I'll resign,' she said.

'Over my dead body,' her mother snorted.

Molly cocked her head. 'If that's what it takes, Mum,' she said with a smirk.

'Don't be cheeky. What I mean is, you've worked hard to get where you are. You can't throw it all away for a bunch of blokes on bikes.'

'It the Tour, Ines,' her dad said, over the top of his newspaper, peering at her with his glasses perched on the end of his nose.

Up to this point, he'd strategically stayed out of the proceedings, but Molly was very glad of his input now. If anyone was able to convince her mother it was a good idea to jack in her job and fly off to France solely on the basis of a verbal offer and an email, it was her father. Actually, Molly thought it best if she didn't mention the last bit. Her mother would have a fit.

'I don't care what it is, I'm not happy about *our daughter*,' her mum stressed the last two words as if her father had forgotten Molly's relationship to them, 'traipsing off to Europe with a horde of hairy men.'

Molly bit back the retort that actually pro-cyclists tended not to be hairy. Alex had told her that coming off a bike at 30 miles an hour and leaving a top layer of skin on the tarmac was bad enough, without having the subsequent dressings and bandages stuck to any body hair. Hence the seemingly narcissistic obsession with shaving, waxing, or epilation. It wasn't a vanity thing, but a pain-reduction thing.

'What if it doesn't work out, eh?' her mother continued. 'She'd be coming back to no job and no house.'

31

'I'm not going to sell my house,' Molly said. 'I'll probably rent it out. Eventually.'

'You said "eventually". Why not do it straight away if you're so set on this mad idea? Because you don't think it'll work out, either, do you?'

'It'll take time, that's all, Mum, and I don't have a lot of it at the moment.'

Ines narrowed her eyes at her. 'What do you mean, you don't have a lot of time?'

Molly grimaced. 'I'll... um... be off in two days.'

'Two days? *Two days?* Why the rush, that's what I want to know? If they want you so badly, they can wait for you to sort yourself out. It all smells very fishy to me. Tell her, Colin.'

'The Tour starts on Saturday,' he said, mildly. 'That explains the time-frame.'

Ines rounded on him and Molly cringed. Her mother in full flow was a sight to behold. 'Don't you go all boardroom-speak on me, Colin Matthews,' she began, her hands on her hips and fire in her eyes.

'I'm just saying, love, that the reason Molly doesn't have a lot of time to sort things out is because the Tour starts in a few days.' He put his paper down and gestured to the plate of toast sitting in the middle of the table. 'Want a piece?' he asked his daughter.

Molly had thought it best to get the inevitable confrontation over with as soon as possible, and had dropped in on her parents to break the news during breakfast. Her other reason for choosing this particular time of day, was that having to go to work ensured the encounter had a finite time limit. Although, no doubt, her mother would be straight round to Molly's house after work to continue the argument.

Molly shook her head. She felt a little nauseous, but whether that was from the stress of breaking the news to her mother (her father was taking it remarkably well, she thought) and the dread of Finley's reaction, or the excitement of the impending trip to France, she couldn't tell.

'I've got a suggestion,' her dad said, and both women turned to stare at him. Her mum frowned, her hands on her hips.

Uh-oh, here goes, Molly thought. Her mum had been expecting Colin's full support, and here he was about to suggest something that she guessed her mother wouldn't like. Molly, on the other hand, wanted to hear what her father had to say.

'What if you ask Finley for a sabbatical?' Colin said. 'Just for the duration of the Tour. That way, if you don't like it, you've not lost anything – like your job.'

Molly and her mother continued to stare. Gradually, Ines' hands slid from her hips to rest by her side. Her mother liked the idea, Molly could tell.

Molly's first reaction was to disagree – she'd thought long and hard all night about this job offer, and it had taken some deep soul-searching to decide it was a good idea. A great idea, in fact.

But her father's suggestion was perfect. Molly had a number of weeks holiday available to take and it would allow her a bit of breathing space to see whether she really could live out of a suitcase and work alongside a bunch of men. If she decided it wasn't for her, then she would simply return to her house and her job, and everything would carry on as before. Try before you buy, she thought; all the fun of the experience without the risk.

She was just a little miffed that she hadn't thought of this solution herself. Good old Dad!

**

Finley?' she cooed, as soon as she walked through the door. 'How many days holiday do I have left?'

'I dunno. I'll have to check.' Finley was in the office, neck deep in paperwork and he didn't look too thrilled about it.

Knowing how much her boss hated the admin side of things, this probably wasn't the best moment to approach him to ask for a favour, but as time was of the essence, she really didn't have much choice.

'Can you check now?' she asked, using a wheedling tone. 'I'll make some coffee…' As a bribe, it wasn't much, but it was the only thing she had to offer.

'When were you thinking of?' he asked, looking up from his computer screen and shuffling some invoices to the other side of his desk.

'Um… Wednesday?'

'Which Wednesday? You're going to have to be a bit more specific.'

'This Wednesday.'

Her boss frowned. 'As in the day after tomorrow?'

'Yes?'

'It's a bit short notice. Is everything all right?'

'It's fine.' Molly knew she was looking sheepish, but she couldn't help her expression. 'I've been offered an opportunity I can't refuse,' she said.

'You want to resign,' Finley stated, flatly. He leaned back in his chair and folded his arms. 'Who is it? McFee?' McFee was Finley's main rival and they were always trying to poach both clients and staff from him.

'Good lord, no!' Molly explained. 'I wouldn't dream of going to work for McFee.'

'Who is it, then?'

Molly took a deep breath. 'I've been offered the chance to work with a cycling team on the Tour de France,' she announced. 'It's the opportunity of a lifetime.'

There was that phrase again. She couldn't get it out of her head. Because that's exactly what it was.

'But that starts on Saturday,' Finley pointed out.

'Exactly. I hate to ask, but—'

'It's the opportunity of a lifetime,' Finley finished for her, with a roll of his eyes.

'Yes. Can I go?'

'What if I said no?'

Molly's face must have given him her answer, because her boss let out a long sigh.

'OK, go if you must. Take all the leave you need. Within reason,' he added, hastily. 'Anything over and above your annual entitlement will be without pay. Understood?'

'Of course.' Molly hadn't expected anything less.

'I'll square it with Sue,' he said.

'Thank you.' A huge grin spread across Molly's face. This was the best news ever. Not only was she going to France for what was, in effect, an all-expenses-paid holiday, but she was being paid twice – once by BeSpoke and the second by Finley, plus she had her job waiting for her if it all went wrong.

Result!

CHAPTER 6

Molly stepped off the little plane with profound relief. Not that she minded flying (she didn't) but the plane from Birmingham to Dinard airport was hardly of the jumbo jet variety. She had never flown in anything so small. There had, however, been a coffee and croissant service, which she had been surprised about, and she had eaten Alex's share as well as her own after arriving at the conclusion that if she was going to spend any time around cyclists, then she would have to get over her reluctance to eat like a normal person in front of them.

Taking a deep breath of foreign air, she felt a quiet sense of joy and excitement flood through her. She was here, really here. It had all seemed a bit surreal and dreamlike over the past few days, as if she was standing outside herself and watching some stranger making plans to vacate her home and job for the best part of a month. She kept thinking someone would shout "joke" at her and run away laughing.

It was only when she met Alex in the departure lounge of Birmingham airport that she had begun to think it was actually happening. He'd been standing in front of a gleaming black car (she did think the airport was taking things a tad too far on the duty-free front) and making appreciative noises when she'd spotted him.

Glad that she wasn't travelling on her own, she'd probably chatted too much, both before the flight and during it, as she tried to keep her nerves and her excitement under control. He'd seemed willing enough to talk and she'd discovered that he had a brother (older); that his parents were divorced but supportive and very proud of his achievements; that he wished he had a dog but he couldn't consider it with his lifestyle; that he had his own house but didn't get to see it as much as he'd like; and that the scariest thing he'd ever done was to give a best man speech at a friend's wedding.

The airport at Dinard was tiny, and they were through security and collecting their bags within minutes of landing. Once outside, Alex put a hand up to his brow to shade his eyes and scanned the car park.

'We're over there,' he said, pointing.

Molly followed his finger and saw a bright pink and green car with a man half-in and half-out of the driver's door, waving madly.

'Mick! Great to see you, man!' Alex dropped his bag when he neared the car and strode toward the man, slapping him on the back as the pair of them went in for a hug.

The other man pulled back after a second or two, to scrutinise Alex. Molly hung back, shyly.

'Are ya fit?' Mick asked, in an Australian accent, holding onto the tops of Alex's arms and looking him up and down.

'Finally. All thanks to this lovely lady here.' Alex

turned to her and she felt her cheeks grow warm. 'This is Molly Matthews, our new physio.'

In two strides Mick was at her side and pumping her arm up and down. His grip was strong enough to crush pebbles and she winced slightly while trying to smile at the same time.

'Sorry, love,' Mick said, and dropped her hand. 'I tend to forget what it's like to be around ladies.' Mick had an open sunny face and Molly liked him immediately.

'Mick is one of the swannies. He's been over here a couple of days, haven't you?' Alex said.

'Yeah along with Greg and Chuck, and Jakob and Keiron and Damien—'

Molly listened as Mick reeled off a list of names and wondered who they all were, what they did, and how she was going to remember them all.

'Excuse me?' she asked Alex. 'I'm sure you must have told me, but what is a swannie?'

'I'll answer that, shall I?' Mick suggested. 'Swannie is short for soigneur. It comes from the French, to be cared for, and that's what us swannies do; we care for the riders, doing anything from giving massages, to washing kit, to packing up the luggage, to helping the riders off the bikes at the end of a race. You name it, and it's usually us what does it.'

'Oh, I see.' It sounded like hard work, and Molly was glad she didn't have to do that job.

With the luggage in the boot, Alex opened one of the rear doors for her and she slid onto the backseat of the car. Alex got into the front, and soon he and Mick were discussing people she had never heard of and places she knew nothing about, so with no contribution to make, Molly relaxed and watched the

French countryside whizz past.

It looked remarkably like Devon or Dorset, she thought, though maybe a little flatter, and once they were on the motorway if it hadn't been for the fact that they were driving on the opposite side of the road and the signs were in French, Molly could almost believe she was still in England.

Snippets of the conversation from the front seat made her take notice.

'Where are we based?' Alex was asking.

'Dinan. We'll be there in fifteen minutes.'

Alex sighed, 'How far are we from the Mont?'

'About 60 kilometres. An hour's drive.'

'That's not too bad. I've heard of worse. 'Alex shuffled in his seat to look at her. 'I've known teams who have had to drive for three hours before they get to the start of a stage,' he told her.

Molly knew from her almost obsessive Googling that "stage" meant a particular day's racing. The Tour de France consisted of twenty-one race days, or stages as they were called, with two rest days in the middle.

'Why so far away? Do you have to stay in designated places or something?' she asked.

Mick laughed. 'This is your first grand tour?'

She caught him looking at her in the rear-view mirror and she nodded.

'You're in for a treat,' he said, with a smile. 'It's like the biggest bun-fight in the world with a travelling circus thrown in for good measure. There are twenty-two teams in this year's Tour. With eight riders per team, that makes 176 riders; add all the team managers, sports directors, mechanics, swannies – that's what I am – doctors, chefs, physios, drivers, and that's without the press, the motorcyclists, the tour organisers (and there's hundreds of those), the security… It's a cast of thousands, and they all need somewhere to stay. When you add in the tourists, you'll be lucky to bag yourself a tent!'

'What's this place like?' Alex asked him, adding to Molly, 'We'll be staying there for two nights, then after that it'll be a different hotel every night.'

Oh, goody, Molly thought, not looking forward to packing and unpacking twenty-odd times.

'It's all right, I s'ppose' Mick drawled. 'A typical box with a bed in it. We've been here for a couple of days,' he said to Molly. 'Me, the rest of the swannies, the mechanics and the drivers all came over by Eurostar. No fancy planes for us.'

Molly wanted to explain that the plane had hardly been fancy, but Alex interjected with, 'You're lucky they don't make you cycle it mate, just to get a feel for what us riders have to go through.'

There followed some good-natured teasing between the two, which only ended when Mick drove the car into a car park filled to bursting with assorted vehicles all in the same pink and green colours.

The hotel itself was a white, low-rise, unprepossessing building, and Molly felt a vague sense of disappointment when she saw it. For some reason (silly, she knew), she'd imagined something more *French*, like a converted farmhouse, or a chateau. Not this impersonal hotel which looked no different from any other budget hotel in the UK. In fact, from what she'd seen of the country so far, she *could* be in the UK – there was nothing remotely French about any of it. So much for seeing the world. She might as well have stayed in the Midlands!

Despite her protests, Mick insisted on carrying her

bags and Alex's too. 'Don't want him to wrench anything,' he said, 'and you're a girl.'

Molly's eyes widened in shock at the rather un-PC remark, but she let it go; she might have worse than that to contend with if she was the only female among so many men.

'Don't let her gender fool you,' Alex said, as they followed Mick into the hotel's reception. 'She's stronger than I am.'

'She's still a girl, and my old mum would turn in her grave if she knew I let a woman carry her own cases.'

'Your mum is very much alive,' Alex retorted, 'and let's see how quickly you change your tune when you've been lugging cases around for the last ten days. You'll be begging her to carry yours!'

'There you are! I thought you'd got lost!' a male voice called.

Molly followed the direction of the voice and saw a tall, thin man with a mop of grey hair striding towards them.

'Greg!' Alex exclaimed, and another round of hugs followed. 'This is Molly,' he said, stepping to the side to present her.

'Molly, this is Greg Easthope, the team manager.'

Greg held out his hand and Molly took it. 'Nice to meet you,' she said.

'You, too.' He looked her up and down. 'So, you're the girl whose praises Alex has been singing. I can see why.'

Alex shook his head. 'It's not like that,' he protested and Greg laughed.

'I'm sure it's not,' he said. 'Just make sure you keep your mind on the job.'

41

Alex winked at her to show that Greg was only teasing, but Molly wasn't so certain.

Maybe taking the job hadn't been such a good idea, after all. What if Greg thought she was too much of a distraction?

Another man joined them. Molly guessed him to be in his early forties, and he was as lean as Alex.

'This is Chuck Griffiths; he's the sports director. In conjunction with Greg, he decides on tactics, nutrition, day-to-day activities, and so on,' Alex explained.

Molly shook his hand and smiled. Not another new face and name.

'Get checked in, then go into the lounge area – the guys are all in there,' Chuck said. 'Only Elias hasn't arrived yet. He's due to fly in tomorrow morning. Maybe Molly could go and pick him up?' He raised his eyebrows.

Molly gulped and nodded, but she wasn't too keen on the idea. She'd not really driven abroad before and she really didn't want to start now. Was that even in her job description?

As if sensing her reluctance, Alex said, 'It's a small team and everyone mucks in, and since you're not needed on the physio front much yet.'

'It's OK,' she said, meaning anything but. At least she was getting to experience new things, she told herself. That was partly why she was here, right?

Mick was waiting for her and Alex to check in, their bags at his feet. 'No worries, the car's got a Satnav. Just plug the airport in and the car will guide you in. It'll practically drive itself.'

Molly smiled weakly, not believing a word of it. She was bound to get lost, and that was assuming she actually managed to get out of the car park – how did you cope with the gear stick and the handbrake on the wrong side, anyway? She guessed she would find out in the morning. Maybe they'd let her have a little practice before they shoved her out onto the main road?

Feeling rather overwhelmed, she wanted nothing more than to go to her room, freshen up and have a lie down. She needed time to assimilate everything. It had been a long day already and she still had the rest of the afternoon and the evening to get through, despite feeling out of sorts and rather tired.

'Right, sign here and hand over your passport to reception; you can pick it up in the morning,' Chuck said as Molly exchanged her signature for a key card. 'You've got a room to yourself,' he added.

Wasn't that normal, she wondered.

'It's because you're the only female on the team,' Alex explained. 'Greg didn't think you'd want to share with one of the swannies. Talking of swannies, give your key to Mick and he'll drop your case off in your room. I want you to meet the guys. You might as well get acquainted now, considering you might have your hands on their legs this time tomorrow.'

'I thought the race didn't start until Saturday?' she said.

'It doesn't, but we'll be going out on a few rides between now and then to keep the muscles loose.'

'Oh, I see.'

'Here they are!' he exclaimed, and once more she hung back while Alex and the others did the hugging, back-patting thing. One of them moved in for a two-cheeked kiss and Alex laughed, glancing over his shoulder at her and mouthing, 'Italians!'

Everyone was laughing and talking at once, and the sense of excitement and anticipation was so palpable that Molly could almost taste it. It reminded her of a group of kids on a school trip, all high spirits and noisy enthusiasm.

'Guys, this is Molly Matthews,' Alex said to the rest of the team. 'Be nice to her; she's got the power to make grown men weep. I wouldn't upset her if I was you.' He rolled his shoulders and winked theatrically.

There followed a chorus of "Hi, Molly" and lots of smiles and nods. She wondered if they'd be as happy and laid back once the racing started. For all their bounciness now, it might be a different matter after a few days of enormous physical effort. She might not know all that much about the race itself (although she had tried to do some research and had watched endless clips of past races on YouTube), she knew what terrible strain a race such as this would put on their bodies and the kinds of problems and injuries it could cause. She was under no illusion that she wouldn't earn her salary – she would. And she intended to start as soon as she had a shower and a few minutes to herself.

She was about to do exactly that, when Chuck patted her on the shoulder. 'Don't look so worried,' he said. 'Just do your job and you'll be fine. Henno, he's the team doctor, and I are more than happy with the work you've done on Alex's wrist. We'll talk later, yeah, and I'll introduce you to Henno. In the meantime, get to know the guys. I'll make sure you have access to all their medical records.'

It was best if she got started right away, she decided, because the quicker she was up to speed, then the sooner she'd be able to start earning her salary.

Her first victim would be Alex and the thought made her heart miss a beat.

CHAPTER 7

Maybe prodding and poking several assorted men wasn't the best prelude to dinner, she told herself after she'd chased most of her meal around her plate. Not that treating clients had ever affected her appetite before... but that was the excuse she had given herself this evening and she was sticking to it.

Late afternoon had seen Molly "interviewing" each cyclist (they were still waiting for the elusive Elias, but she'd tackle him tomorrow) as to their medical history, previous injuries and any concerns.

As planned, she'd started with Alex, hoping her familiarity with him would steady her nerves. However, she discovered that once she'd changed into her tunic and black trousers, she was far less anxious than she thought she'd be.

Even the tour bus didn't faze her. OK, it did a bit, but that was only because she'd been expecting a bog-standard coach and not a kind of headquarters on wheels. Aside from the seats (leather, individual, reclinable and swivel-able), it had an enormous fridge, a small hob, a microwave, more cupboards than she had in her own kitchen at home, two showers and a loo, along with a partitioned-off area behind which lay a treatment table and several pieces of equipment that she identified as ultrasound machines and electrical muscle stimulators. This was more like it! She knew what she was supposed to be doing in this space, she understood what her purpose was, and she relaxed a little more.

'You should have seen to Tim first,' Alex said as he made his way down the aisle towards her and into the back of the bus.

'I should?'

'Yeah. He's team leader. Everything revolves around him.'

'Oh. Sorry. I didn't realise.'

'That's OK, the guys understood.'

'I'll know for next time.' Molly watched with detached, professional interest as Alex took his top off, (ignoring the thumping of her heart at the sight of him; she was still just a bit nervous – she'd soon settle down.) scrutinising every move of his arm, wrist, and hand, and studying the flex of the muscles in his shoulder and across his chest. She'd done a good job on him, even if she did say so herself. She couldn't take all the credit, to be fair; most of the healing was down to Alex's sheer determination to be race fit. She'd merely helped him on his journey.

After a brief check over, she sent him away with more exercises to do in his room, and a hope that she'd see him later at dinner. Then she turned her attention to the man the team were here for – Tim Anderson.

He was slight, fairly short, and wiry. He reminded her of the flat-racing jockeys she used to see being interviewed on telly (her granddad had been a bit of a horse-racing buff, although she suspected the closest he'd ever got to a horse was seeing one pass him by, going over 30 miles an hour on the rails at Worcester racetrack).

As she ran through Tim's medical history with him – Chuck had given her a laptop with all the riders' details on, but she wanted to form her own opinion before she looked at it and prior to her meeting with Henno – she felt quite capable and professional and very much in her comfort zone, despite the unfamiliar surroundings.

After he left, she spent a few minutes going through his electronic file and tweaking his ICP. Her predecessor had left detailed notes as well as the Individual Care Plan, and aside from a slight adjustment or two, she agreed with Tim's treatment going forward. Molly, aside from treating existing injuries and weaknesses, was well aware of the need to try to prevent new ones occurring. She could do nothing about accidents, but she could work to help riders to correct their postures, and so on.

By the time she had worked her way through another five riders (she'd do Elias tomorrow), it was time for dinner. Realising she hadn't eaten since those croissants on the plane, Molly was starving, and after a quick change out of her uniform, she joined the others in the dining room.

'I'll have your report later, yeah?' Chuck said to her, and she was to discover that this would become part of her evening routine.

She hadn't realised just how many people BeSpoke had, and seeing approximately forty men seated at several tables, she felt anxious once more. Introductions were made again, although Molly couldn't recall the names of most of those she had already met earlier, so these new ones stood next to no chance. And there were so many different nationalities too, although from what she'd gathered BeSpoke was a British team.

'Am I glad to see you,' one of the swannies (Damien, she thought his name was, although she couldn't be sure) said in a Yorkshire accent. 'I thought I would have to rub Pietro's veiny legs for him!'

Pietro (broken clavicle – twice – tendency towards saddle sores, Molly recalled) gave the swannie a finger. 'No, the relief is all mine,' he joked. 'You have got hands like a butcher. If you never touch me again, I will die a happy man.'

'I'll remember that when Molly is treating a dislocated shoulder and your legs are cramping so hard that you're crying like a three-year-old who wants an ice-cream,' Damien retorted and the rest of the guys laughed.

'Pietro does scream a bit,' Tim said. 'It's pitiful.'

'And what makes you think he won't scream when I get my hands on him?' Molly asked, deadpan.

There was a pause, then the room erupted into laughter.

'She'll fit in,' someone said, and Molly agreed that she just might.

Mick tapped an empty chair next to him and she sank into it gratefully, noticing that the riders were all grouped together on one large table along with Chuck and Greg. She caught Alex looking at her and she sent him a small smile.

'He's a good bloke, is Alex,' Mick said softly, noticing the small exchange. 'But do yourself a favour and don't go getting involved; not with him or any of the riders. Not until after the Tour, at least. He doesn't need the distraction. Anyway, it's not the done thing to get too familiar with the riders.'

Molly blinked in surprise. She had no intention of getting involved with anyone, thank you very much! No matter how attractive she found him.

Ah… She blinked slowly at the sudden realisation.

So, she really did think Alex was attractive, did she? It was nice of her subconscious to let her in on the secret. She'd had her suspicions, but until now she had managed to pass her erratic heartbeat and tingly feelings off as excitement or nerves. The fact that these things occurred more often when Alex was actually around was something she had chosen to ignore.

It didn't matter if she did think he was attractive or if he did make her heart beat a little faster, it didn't mean she had to act on it. She was a grown woman and perfectly capable of keeping her feelings under control. Besides, she was a professional and was determined to act like one.

When dinner arrived, Molly had found she had lost her appetite a little, but she forced herself to nibble on the watermelon and spinach salad, and tackled some of the rice and chicken main course. The food was well-cooked and very tasty, but all through the meal she kept catching sight of Alex out of the corner of her eye and remembering Mick's less-than-subtle warning. Was how she was beginning to feel about the rider really that obvious, or would Mick have said the same thing to any other woman who joined the team?

The dessert of yoghurt and fruit went down a little easier, and she was impressed by how healthy everything was. This was better than booking into a spa for a week.

But, crikey, those riders couldn't half pack their food away, she thought. For such slight men (all of them were slender and some of them weren't very tall, either) they ate like they wouldn't see another meal for days.

Mick caught her staring. 'You've not seen anything yet,' he warned. 'Just wait until the racing starts. Six thousand calories a day they'll be taking on board.' He laughed. 'It's like babysitting a pride of lions. They do as little as possible for hours on end except stuff their faces, then ride like the blazes for four or five hours. It's either all or nothing with this lot. You'll never see anyone chill out like a professional cyclist.'

Molly was bemused.

'They need all the rest they can get, see?' he continued. 'There's this unwritten rule – don't stand if you can sit and don't sit if you can lie down. It doesn't apply to us lot, of course. The support staff run around like blue-arsed flies. Be prepared for eighteen-hour days when racing starts. This is the calm before the hurricane, so you better make the most of it.'

Henno, the team doctor, told her more or less the same thing later, after dinner. German, dark-haired, tall, serious-looking behind his horn-rimmed glasses, the man spoke perfect English with only the slightest of accents. He had appeared at the end of the meal and Mick vacated his seat to make room for him. Another man had arrived with him, and as they ate their dinner, Henno explained they'd been on an exploratory drive to the start of Stage 2.

'I don't follow,' Molly said.

'It's all about the detail,' the doctor said. 'I always like to know where the pharmacies are located and which ones are open late, just in case. I won't have time to do it for the rest of the stages, but I thought I'd make use of these couple of days before the madness begins. Now, Chuck tells me you've examined all the riders except Elias. Tell me what conclusions you have arrived at.'

Goodness, but this felt a little too much like a test for Molly's liking, but she did as she was asked, consulting the hand-written notes she had made during each examination.

'Good, good,' Henno nodded when she'd finished.

After that, they were both required to join Chuck and Greg to discuss the next two days of practice rides and the riders' associated medical care.

Finally, after what seemed like hours, an exhausted and dazed Molly made her way to her room to drop into a fitful slumber.

It didn't last long.

Tap, tap, tap.

Molly sat up, pulling the covers up to her chin. Was that someone at the door? She checked the time. Eleven-fifteen p.m.

'Alex?' she muttered, only half awake, but there was no answer.

Another tap. 'Molly? It's Damien,' a male voice hissed loudly.

What on earth did he want? She hoped it wasn't anything she wasn't prepared to give. Had she given the wrong impression at dinner? God, she hoped not! The only physical contact she intended to have was with the riders, and that would only be in the course of her job (she deliberately pushed all thoughts of

Alex Duvall out of her mind).

'What is it?' she asked.

'I'm doing a beer and chocolate run. Do you want anything?'

Molly heaved a sigh of relief, clambered out of bed, and padded to the door, opening it a crack. 'Chocolate run?'

'Yeah, we don't like to do it in front of the riders.'

'Why not?'

'Have you *seen* what they eat?' Damien retorted. 'It might be good for you, but I miss a good burger and fries. And beer. I don't want water, the isotonic drinks, the fruit teas or the juice. I want a beer.'

'Are you allowed?' Molly would have sold her soul for a glass of wine at dinner, but nothing even remotely alcoholic had been served.

Damien shrugged. 'As long as we don't get drunk and it affects our job. I'll only have one, anyway. Do you want anything?' he repeated. 'Crisps? A pastry? There is a little shop about ten minutes away that stays open all night.'

I wouldn't mind you bringing me a bottle of wine, she almost said, but changed her request to, 'Some chocolate, crisps, and cola, if they have any, please.'

'Give me half an hour, then come to my room. All the swannies will be there and a couple of the mechanics. I warn you, though – those guys will bore your socks off, unless you're into tyre pressure and gear ratios. And don't get them started on power metres!'

Thirty minutes later saw Molly sitting cross-legged on one of the beds in Damien's room, surrounded by swannies and mechanics and a vast array of chocolate, savoury snacks, sodas, beers, and assorted sweet and savoury pastries.

'Mmm, this is wonderful,' she enthused, her mouth full of caramel chocolate. She hadn't realised how hungry she was until she'd bitten into it, but she vowed that she wouldn't make a habit of eating hardly any dinner only to fill up on junk food later.

'I'll come with you to pick up Elias,' Mick offered. 'and if you're not needed later when the riders are out on a practice run, you're welcome to join us for a spot of lunch and some coffee and cake, if we can get away.'

'I'd love to, thank you.'

'Make the most of it, though, because all hell will break loose on Saturday, then it's every hand on deck,' one of the mechanics pointed out. 'There'll be no time to do anything except keep the riders and the bikes racing. You'll be up to your neck in massages and support tape.'

Great – she couldn't wait!

CHAPTER 8

Mick insisted that Molly drove to the airport, and although she was apprehensive about being in the wrong side of the car and on the wrong side of the road, having Mick there was a real comfort. She'd left Henno doing his "rounds" after each rider had been weighed (to check hydration levels, apparently), had eaten a hasty breakfast of oats and fruit, before dashing off to pick up Elias.

Then it was back to base-camp, as Molly thought of their hotel, an examination of the newcomer with Henno, then the riders were off for a cycle to loosen up and keep their muscles and minds ticking over.

A team car followed them, its roof stacked with bikes, and Molly watched it go. Chuck and Greg were in the front, Henno and a mechanic in the back.

She wondered what to do with herself until the riders returned, and briefly considered a quick walk around the little town of Dinan.

However, she was soon roped into doing something, as Mick showed her how to prepare food and drinks for the riders both for before the race and for afterwards, when the cyclists would come back hungry and dehydrated. Each swannie was responsible for a rider, and Mick's was Alex, although he was keen to stress that every one of the staff had to be flexible and be prepared to do anything and everything at a moment's notice.

By the time she'd taken it all in, the riders were back and Molly, alongside Henno, checked each one over carefully, followed by a massage for each rider and a series of stretches and flexes, before some substantial snacks.

Finally, by late afternoon, Molly had a couple of hours to spare.

'How far is it to the town centre?' she asked Mick.

'Ten minutes at the most, if you factor in parking.'

'Oh, I wasn't thinking of taking a car, I was going to walk.'

'A half hour, then.' He shrugged, 'I'd come with you, but Chuck wants to do a final kit check.' He groaned. 'It'll take hours – do you know how much kit there is? No, how could you? Trust me, it's a lot; bib shorts, jerseys, tights, leg warmers, arm warmers...' He was still muttering about clothing as he wandered off towards the car park and the enormous lorry.

Tights? Leg warmers? Molly giggled to herself.

'What are you laughing at?'

Molly took a quick breath and whirled around to find Alex standing behind her. 'Um, tights and leg warmers,' she said. 'They sound like throwbacks to the 1980s. You'll be telling me you wear leotards next.'

'We do wear this all-in-one bib thing, like a pared down vest with long shorts or trousers attached. It's very fetching.'

She shook her head.

'Thankfully the jerseys, (you'd call them T-shirts

56

with full-length zips) cover up the worst bits, but you're going to catch glimpses of all of us wearing one sooner or later,' he warned. 'You might want to prepare yourself.'

'I'll look forward to it,' she promised, trying not to think of a semi-clad Alex. His current nearness was disconcerting enough without imagining anything else.

'What have they got you doing now?' he wanted to know.

'I'm free for the next couple of hours,' she said, 'so I thought I'd take a walk into Dinan and have a look around. From what everyone's been telling me, it will probably be the only chance I'll get to see France, apart from through a car window travelling down the motorway at 50 miles an hour.' She glared at him accusingly.

'It'll get better when we're on the mountain stages,' he said. 'No motorways, but lots of steep, winding roads. It's pretty.'

'Hmmm. Anyway, I need to get going if I'm to make it back before dinner.'

'Hang on. Wait there. I won't be a minute.' He dashed off, and Molly narrowed her eyes, wondering what he was up to.

When he returned, he was wearing a pair of jeans, trainers and a T-shirt, and was waving a set of keys at her.

'No thanks,' she said. 'The walk will do me good.'

'I'm not walking,' Alex said. 'Anyway, it's a bit too far to walk.'

'Mick said it would take about half an hour to walk to Dinan. That's not too far.'

'We're not going to Dinan. I've got somewhere far

nicer in mind. Not that Dinan isn't nice,' he hastened to add, 'and you should go and see it if you can, because they say it's the prettiest town in Brittany, but I've got somewhere far more impressive to show you.' He leaned in, close enough for her to smell the soap he'd showered with after his ride and the cologne he'd splashed on. Underneath both was the slight masculine scent of the man himself. It made her feel all giddy.

'If anyone asks, tell them I wanted to recce the start and I asked you to drive me,' he whispered.

Anyone would think he wasn't allowed out, Molly thought, then paused. Maybe he wasn't.

'Are you allowed?' she asked.

'Of course, I am.' He shrugged one shoulder. 'Here, you drive.' He handed her the keys and she took them reluctantly. The sojourn to the airport had been enough for her for one day.

'Where are we going?' she asked once they were in the car.

'I told you, to the start of the race.'

'Mont Saint Michel?'

'The very same.' He had his phone in his hand. 'Turn left as if we're going to the airport,' he instructed, 'then turn off onto the N176.'

'How long will it take to get there?'

'About an hour.'

'Oh.' At the very, very least, they would be AWOL for around two hours. Concern briefly flashed across her mind, but she pushed it to one side. Alex must know what he was doing, and dinner wasn't for another four-and-a-bit hours yet as the team really did eat quite late, she thought, being far more used to eating her evening meal and the dishes having been washed, dried, and put away by six-thirty.

They chatted about nothing much in particular as the car ate up the miles, crossing over a suspension bridge spanning a stretch of sparkling water dotted with small boats, and speeding along non-descript roads until, after about fifty minutes, Alex guided her off the main road and down a smaller one which was surrounded by flat fields with only the odd farm building to break the monotony.

Eventually, they drove through a small village which boasted a couple of hotels, restaurants and campsites, and Molly was surprised at how busy the place was.

'It's for the Grand Depart,' Alex explained. 'The start of the Tour de France. By tomorrow, you won't be able to move, so it is either now or never.'

'What is?'

'That.'

Oh, I see, Molly thought, as they came out of the other side of the village. In the distance was a massive mound and a long, straight road leading towards it. She couldn't see it all that clearly, and she realised the reason was because distance and summer heat had blurred the Mont into a purple-grey lump rising out of a pancake-flat landscape.

'Cars aren't allowed any further,' he said, pointing her to a large parking area and a waiting open-sided bus. 'We could walk it, but…'

'You want to save your energy?' She smiled at him, and he grinned back.

'You've heard about the famed sloth of us cyclists, then?' he said climbing aboard and taking a seat.

'I have, but I don't blame you for not wanting to walk from here. It looks a fair distance away.' She squinted at the Mont and was just able to make out the building on its summit and the spire of a church. As the little bus drew closer, Molly exclaimed in delight.

'It's like a fairy-tale castle! Do you know what it reminds me of?'

'No?' Alex was laughing at her excitement.

'A huge cupcake, with a swirl of buttercream, going into a point at the top.'

Alex peered through the non-existent window. 'You're right, it does, a bit. If you screw your eyes up.'

You're humouring me,' she said, and he laughed again.

'I promised you'd see places,' he said. 'And when I bring you to one of the most iconic places in Normandy, all you can do is compare it to a cupcake. Let's see if you still feel like that when you reach the top.'

Molly swallowed. 'We're going up there?' The closer they got to the huge lump of rock, the higher it seemed, and she seriously didn't fancy walking up it. 'It'll take ages,' she added.

'We've only got an hour or so,' Alex said, 'so maybe another time?' He looked up at her hopefully as he stepped off the bus and reached back, holding out his hand to help her climb down.

She took it and felt a surge of electricity through her palm, up her hand, and into her chest.

Molly shot Alex a look. Had he felt it, too?

For a second, they stood there, hand-in-hand, facing each other, neither of them saying a word. Then someone jostled Molly and she moved to one side, letting her hand slip out of his in what she hoped was a natural gesture. Heat crept up her neck and into her face, and she knew she was blushing, so to hide her embarrassment, she rooted around in her bag for her sunglasses.

'It floods,' Alex said, abstractly.

'What does?'

'This.' He gestured to the causeway they were standing on. 'At high tide, the Mont is cut off.' He was staring at the landscape, not meeting her eye, and Molly wondered if it was deliberate or whether it was because he was genuinely fascinated by the huge walls which held the encroaching sea at bay.

Despite her awareness of the man by her side, Molly couldn't help but be impressed by the sight in front of her – an iconic medieval abbey perched on a rock in the middle of tidal mudflats, with salt marshes all around. This was more like what she expected France to be.

Once inside the massive walls with their circular turrets, Molly felt she was on a film set, with the higgledy-piggledy buildings, tiny, narrow cobbled streets, brightly painted shops, restaurants and museums, with many of them displaying wooden-beamed facades. Planters and hanging baskets filled with colourful flowers were everywhere, and their scent mingled with the smell of the sea. And with the smell of Alex. Every now and again she'd catch a whiff of his aftershave and the clean, muskiness of his skin, and her heart would flutter and catch.

Stop it, she told herself. You've no right to feel… whatever it is you're feeling. She had a job to do, they both did, and neither of them could afford to let a silly attraction get in the way. Actually, she guessed the attraction was probably all on one side – hers – and she vowed to keep it under control. She would have no choice, considering they worked together.

The Mont was heaving, people cramming into narrow streets barely wide enough to fit three abreast. She jerked in a quick, panicked breath when Alex grabbed her hand, and she shot him a confused look until she understood he was simply being practical; getting separated in this bustling throng wouldn't be good.

The heat was surprising, as the narrow streets and alleyways trapped the sun's rays, the ancient stone soaking it up and bouncing it back at her. Sweat trickled uncomfortably down her back and she winced, her hand hot and damp in his, but she clung on to him regardless, delighting in the feel of his fist wrapped around hers. They could be any young couple enjoying the scenery.

'I don't think we've got time to walk up to the abbey,' he said. 'We'll save that for next time.'

There would be a next time? The thought set her heart fluttering again, and she stamped it down with hard determination. He was just being nice, it was the kind of thing one just said. He didn't mean it. Besides, she was well aware there would be no time between now and the end of the Tour to do anything other than race stuff. This was a hiatus, a tiny moment of calm before the storm of the race began.

From what Henno had told her, she would be working eighteen-hour days, and would be too tired to think straight by the end of twenty-one of them. Yesterday, when the doctor talked her through a typical day and what to expect, she'd had a brief thought that this wasn't what she'd signed up for, that Alex had maybe glossed over the sheer hard, unrelenting work. But she was here now (the opportunity of a lifetime, remember?) and she was determined to make the most of it. Three weeks, that was all; not long in the scheme of things, and maybe she would love it, take to the lifestyle like the ducks in Barbourne Park's pond took to water.

But if she didn't, all was not lost – she had a job and a house to return to and would chalk this up to experience.

Alex's hand was still hot in hers, his grip firm.

She tried to ignore how it made her feel.

CHAPTER 9

Subdued didn't describe how Molly felt today. And last night, too. Having been soundly told off after her sojourn to the Mont, by Chuck, Greg and, to a certain extent, Mick too, she'd almost felt like telling BeSpoke where to stick their job. It was only Alex's insistence that it had been his idea (it had) and that Molly wasn't to know that Alex should be conserving his energy and making sure he was hydrated (she did, deep down), and his subsequent assurance to her that it would all blow over by tomorrow, that she decided to sleep on it.

Alex had been right, more or less. Friday morning, the day before the Grand Depart which was the start of Stage 1, had seen everyone treating Molly exactly the same as they had yesterday morning, although she did catch Mick giving her the odd speculative glance when he thought she wasn't looking.

It was Molly herself who was having trouble moving on and acting as though nothing had happened. Apart from the remonstration, nothing *had* happened. She and Alex had wandered around the lower streets of the Mont for a while, sat outside a café, their table facing out to sea, and had some drinks (water for him, coffee for her) and soaked up

64

the atmosphere along with the faint but welcome breeze coming off the water, and had chatted.

Then they had taken the shuttle back to the car park and Molly had driven to the hotel.

Absolutely nothing had happened, apart from the hand-holding. And the telling off.

'Sorry.'

Molly glanced up from her job of ensuring the fridge and the cupboard on the tour bus were stocked to the brim with water, electrolyte drinks, gels, nutrition bars and all the other stuff the riders would need after the race, to see Alex lurking in the aisle, silhouetted by the sun shining through the bus's front window.

'I didn't mean to get you into trouble,' he added.

She smiled to take the sting out of her words. 'So you keep saying. It doesn't matter.'

'Are you OK?'

'I guess… yes.' This last was said with more determination.

'For a moment, I thought you were going to go back to England,' he said.

Molly had seriously thought about it. 'It never crossed my mind,' she lied. 'Anyway, who would massage Tim's skinny legs if I left?'

'Who, indeed?' Alex let out a sigh. 'I'm sorry,' he said for about the thirtieth time.

'Stop apologising. It's done. I've put it behind me.' And she had – sort of. Ish.

Oh, who was she kidding? She was still smarting, feeling like a kid who'd been told off by a teacher. She was hugging a vague sense of injustice to her chest, keeping it close and letting it warm her irritation whenever she thought about it. Which she had done, frequently throughout the course of last night and today.

But eventually, she let it go as the excitement and nerves began to build.

There were meetings after meetings, Chuck and Greg at the heart of them all, checks and more checks performed, as everyone cranked up to fever pitch.

Eventually, before dinner and after Molly and Henno had gone over each rider with a fine-toothed comb, ensuring all were as fit and healthy as they could possibly be, another meeting was called with the riders, and Molly and Henno were asked to join.

'Tomorrow is the Grand Depart,' Greg began, as he stood in front of a large screen connected to his laptop, and was greeted by heckling and cat-calling.

'I wondered why we were here,' Pietro, one of the riders, drawled in his thick Italian accent.

That was one thing Molly had definitely not been prepared for – the huge variety of accents. She hadn't really considered it before she'd arrived, having naively assumed that with BeSpoke being a British team everyone would, in fact, be British.

Not so. Alex had informed her that there were at least twelve different nationalities in the team and that this was quite normal for professional cycling. He had told her to think of it like a premier league football team, where a team would buy players from all over the world. Cycling teams didn't actually buy riders, but they did negotiate contracts and someone who had ridden for one team last year, might well be riding for their main rival the following year. Then there were the other staff, who tended to fluctuate as the needs of the team dictated. Cycling was, she discovered, quite a small insular world, where everyone seemed to know everyone else, and loyalties changed by the season.

When Greg had brought the meeting under control, he went on to remind the riders of what they could expect during the stage and what tactics should be employed.

Most of it went over Molly's head, and she was beginning to echo Pietro's words (silently, of course) when the sound of her name brought her to attention.

'Henno and Molly, that's what you need to be aware of.' Greg pointed to a map on the screen. 'These flashpoints, here,' he tapped what looked to be a sharp bend in the road, 'and here.' He pointed to another one. 'Everyone will need to slow down and there will a bottleneck. It's the perfect place for a crash. I don't want it to be any of you.' He glared at the assembled riders. 'But you might well be caught up in it if there is one.' He glanced at Henno and Molly. 'Henno will ride in the team car behind the riders, Molly will go on ahead with the swannies. Henno, you know the issues if any of them come off – shredded skin and collar-bones are the most likely injuries here, because there won't be much in the way of speed. Molly, you'll meet the guys at the finish and deal with any immediate injuries. Have you got everything you need?'

She nodded. The rear of the team bus was as well-equipped as her treatment room back home. Better, in fact, although not as spacious obviously.

'Make sure you don't forget to order the ice,' was the last thing she heard as Greg went on to talk about cross-winds and echelons and Category 4 climbs, and the rest of the meeting went over her head.

'What did he mean about not forgetting to order

the ice?' she asked Henno, once they were free to go.

The doctor sighed. 'I forgot to mention it,' he said. 'Sorry. I have so much on my mind I keep forgetting you are so inexperienced.'

Molly was about to tell him exactly how inexperienced she wasn't, when Henno added, 'All the riders have an ice bath after each and every race. It helps with the inflammation.'

'I know all about ice and inflammation,' she began but the doctor cut across her.

'You don't know about this kind. The Tour de France has been called the greatest endurance race in the world, and for a good reason. Until you see for yourself the condition those riders are in at the end of a stage, then you won't appreciate what they have put their bodies through to get there. After the warm down sessions on the turbos, every rider will have a massage and an ice bath, plus any treatment needed.' He shuddered. 'It's brutal. Those guys will do anything to keep riding, to stay in the race. They'll insist they are fine when they clearly are not and they will try to hide injuries from you. One rider a couple of years back competed in a Grand Tour with a broken pelvis. That is the level of their commitment and determination. And our job is to keep them in the saddle. But,' he held up a finger, 'they may confide in you, tell you things they wouldn't tell me, and certainly wouldn't tell Greg or Chuck. You'll have to use your judgement, about whether to pass it on.'

Molly wasn't sure she liked that idea. Although she wasn't a doctor, she still felt she was bound by patient confidentiality and she wasn't comfortable about breaking a confidence.

Henno leaned forward and gazed earnestly into her

face. 'If one of them tells you something which might compromise the race, you have a duty to inform me,' he insisted. He took her elbow and guided her towards one of the chairs in the lobby.

'Look, he continued. 'Loyalty between team mates runs high, it has to, this is a team race, after all. If one of them is under par, for whatever reason, it could compromise the team leader's chances. And they are here to support him and only him. Every effort they make, every gruelling, punishing kilometre they endure, is to maximize his chances of winning the race or a stage. And to gain the maximum exposure for their team's sponsors,' he added wryly.

'Do you think Tim will win?' she asked.

'Unlikely,' Henno replied. 'He's too far down the GC rankings to be a serious contender, although he might win a stage if luck is on his side and the conditions are right.'

'GC?'

'General Classification,' Henno said. 'Hasn't anyone explained any of this to you? Chuck?' He paused. 'Alex?'

'Not really. A bit,' she admitted. This was all so new to her, no wonder she hadn't been able to take it all in. Not even her repeated visits to Google-land compared to the reality of being here, and with all the different terminology, the names the acronyms, the sheer intensity of it all.

'At the end of the first stage the winner, who is the rider with the fastest time, will wear the yellow jersey,' Henno said. 'This means he is the leader of the race. By the end of the second stage, there may well be another winner of that stage, but that rider doesn't necessarily get to wear the yellow jersey. He might not be the leader of the race overall. It is dependent on times. Whoever has completed both stages in the shortest time is the race leader, and he will wear the yellow jersey.' Henno barked out a sudden laugh, making Molly jump. 'Until he loses it to someone else. Riders compete to win a stage, and they also compete to wear the yellow jersey. It is not unheard of for a rider to be the race leader having never won a stage. This is because he has completed all the stages so far in the shortest time. He then is top of the General Classification board. He is the one most likely to win the race as a whole, at that particular point. You will hear things like, "he's slipped down the GC from fourth to seventh" or something similar.'

'But the most important thing is the yellow jersey?' she clarified.

'Correct.'

'And you don't think Tim or BeSpoke will win it?'

He glanced around to make sure no one was in earshot and shook his head. 'No. It is unlikely. This race attracts the top riders in the world. Tim is good, damned good, and he's won many other races, but he probably will not win this one. The best we can hope for is a stage win.'

'So why does he bother; why does Bespoke bother?' Molly wanted to know.

Henno patted her on the arm as he stood up and she craned her neck to see his face.

'Because it is their passion, the sole reason they get up in the morning, whether they are riders or not.'

'Is that why you are here, because you love cycling?'

He smiled. 'Yes, and because they pay well. You will see – there is nothing like the exhilaration of the race, the challenge, the nobility of the riders, the dedication, the bloody-mindedness. And I get to be a part of that.' Another pat on her shoulder. 'I warn you, you will be bitten by it too. It creeps into your blood, like malaria, and once you are infected, there is no cure for it.'

She watched him walk away, his long legs reminding her of a stork, and she wondered what she had let herself in for.

But it wasn't yellow jerseys, or broken collarbones, or ice baths that filled her thoughts as she drifted off into an exhausted sleep some hours later, it was Alex, as she had first seen him with his wrist barely out of a cast and grim determination on his face, and she began to have an inkling of just how driven he was, of how much he loved cycling.

Her last indistinct thought was how can I ever compete with that?

CHAPTER 10

The noise was incredible. Horns blaring, music playing, loudspeakers all proclaiming different messages, sirens from the police motorcycles, and the laughter, screams, and shouts from the thousands of people crammed onto the end of the walkway, where yesterday the press had been setting up their various stands and the shuttle buses had turned around on the large concreted areas either side of the road.

Molly, with a newly issued security pass, had been ushered by Mick into this vast mass of people, cars, motorbikes and riders, with the words, 'Make the most of this. You won't be at the start of any other stage, but Alex,' he gave her a sideways glance, 'thought you might appreciate it today.'

One by one the riders cycled slowly to the end of the walkway, dodging cars and bikes and people, and Molly stood on tiptoe, trying to spot the pink and green BeSpoke jerseys among the throng, pleased that she was starting to get to grips with the terminology.

As she looked around her, she saw the towering mass of the Mont rising up behind and she shivered, remembering the feel of Alex's hand in hers. She glanced up at it, thinking what a majestic backdrop it made to the start of the race. Several helicopters hovered and droned overhead and she wondered what it would be like to be up in one now, looking down at the incredible sight below. She watched as one of them circled close to the gold statue of the Archangel Gabriel which perched on the very top of the abbey's spire, his wings outstretched and his sword held aloft, and she wished she had the same view. It must be spectacular. It was certainly impressive enough from down here as the statue glittered in the sun. Even though she had her sunglasses on, Molly cupped a hand over the top of them to reduce the glare and peered into the distance.

What a fantastically bright day! The sea behind shimmered and glittered, as did the river which ran beside the Mont and flowed into the Atlantic, and the air was already warm. It was perfect, or it would be if 176 riders didn't have a 188 kilometre race ahead of them in the heat of a Normandy summer, and she worried that she'd not stocked the bus with enough water and other drinks, even though she knew both the onboard fridge and several cupboards were stuffed to their limits.

She paused as a thought struck her; two days ago she would have been more interested in the carnival mood of the start of the Tour de France and would have soaked up the atmosphere like a proverbial sponge, than she would have been interested in the riders. But right now the only thing on her mind was what state her team would be in when they passed the finish line. *Her team?* Yes, they were *her* team.

There they were! All eight BeSpoke riders with Tim in the lead, were working their way to the end of the causeway. Caught up in the heady atmosphere,

Molly jumped up and down, waving frantically. Mick laughed at her antics.

'You're a breath of fresh air,' he told her, 'but I bet you five euros you won't be as bouncy by stage ten.'

Molly didn't care. This might be her one and only time to ever be at a Grand Depart for the Tour de France and she intended to enjoy every second of it, despite her concern for the riders' welfare.

As BeSpoke came closer, Molly searched their faces, looking for one in particular. They appeared so different in their helmets and glasses, and it took her a moment to realise which one of the eight was Alex. He wore number 121, Tim was 120, and she made a note of both of them. Tim might be the team leader, but it was Alex who she was more interested in, although she told herself it was merely because she'd known him first and for longer than any of the others. She and Alex had a rapport, which was perfectly natural considering she had been treating him for nearly a month. It was to be expected. There was nothing unusual about it.

Honestly.

She watched as the riders slowed right down, almost coming to a halt as they circled around to line up in a raggedy group with the other teams, most of whom were already there. As Alex turned his bike, she stared at him intently, praying he would notice her.

She only wanted to wish him good luck. There was no other reason.

But when his gaze swept casually over the crowd and he finally spotted her, a huge grin spread across his face. At least, Molly hoped it was her he was smiling at and not someone else, because she couldn't really see his eyes behind his glasses.

'This isn't the *actual* start,' Mick told her, as BeSpoke and the other riders moved slowly away leaving Molly feeling strangely bereft. Luckily Mick hadn't noticed Alex's reaction when he saw her – oh, wait. Maybe it was Mick who Alex had been smiling at and not her? Yes, it had probably been Mick...

'It's all the way up there,' the swannie said, pointing back down the causeway. 'See those two arches either side of the road?'

Molly peered into the distance. She hadn't noticed the large, brightly-coloured inflatable arches either side of the road before, but she and Mick must have walked underneath them earlier. There had been so much going on and so much to see, from giant tyres on the backs of trucks advertising Pirelli tyres, to a huge carnival model of a cyclist on a bike wearing a yellow jersey and helmet, that she hadn't really had a chance to take everything in. There had been an enormous procession of what seemed to her to be carnival floats, followed by numerous tour cars, most of them with a bristling array of bikes on their roofs, and cyclists were simply everywhere, so it became hard to tell who was actually in the race and who were spectators who had brought their bikes along.

'That's the official start,' Mick said. 'You can't see him from here, but the Race Director is at the front in one of the official race cars and he will lead the riders out. Orozlo Myback are in the very front,' Mick added. 'They earned that place by winning the Tour last year.'

"The Tour" – although most people seemed to refer to the race as "the Tour" as if it was the only one. Alex had already explained that there were loads of these races, but this was the largest, most important, and most widely known, so perhaps people were right to call it "the Tour", because it was the one race that every cyclist wanted to win. Or be a part of, she said to herself, thinking of Alex and the other domestiques who would sacrifice their own chances of winning for the good of their team and its leader.

'Look!' Mick nudged her and pointed skywards. In the distance was a phalanx of eight small jets, and streaming out behind them was blue, white, and red smoke – the colours of the French flag. Cheering filled her ears as the jets passed low overhead, and Molly found herself cheering madly along with everyone else.

Slowly the assembled cyclists began to move and such a huge roar went up from further down the road Molly guessed that the race must have officially started, and when her heart began to pound, she realised she was getting caught up in all the excitement. Even though she understood it to be a remote possibility indeed that BeSpoke would win, she was rooting for them with every fibre of her being.

At this rate, she wasn't going to get through the next three weeks without becoming a nervous wreck!

'We've got to get ahead of this lot and meet the riders at the finish,' Mick said, leading her quickly through the crowds of people and heading for the place they had parked the car. 'Normally we'd go straight there from the hotel, but as this is the Grand Depart...' he smiled widely, his eyes sparkling, '...we get to see it. You are to come in one of the cars with me,' he added. 'Jakob and Damien will travel with us, too. Mees, Keiron, and a couple of the other swannies will drive straight to tonight's hotel and set everything up.'

'Can they pick up some ice?' Molly asked, thinking of running eight freezing cold baths later.

'We've already got some. There's a freezer in the truck,' Mick informed her and Molly blinked in surprise.

'There is?'

'Yeah and four washing machines, so if you want your smalls washed...?' He grinned cheekily at her and winked.

Molly rolled her eyes. She'd see to her own smalls, thank you very much, she thought.

They got to the car to find Damien and Jakob already waiting for them. Molly slipped into the back seat.

'How long will it take?' she asked as the car manoeuvred into the stream of other race traffic and they became part of the convoy. Amazed at how many people lined the road, she stared out of the window, mesmerised at the waving, the flags, the banners, and the terrific noise.

'Four, to four-and-a-half hours,' Jakob said, looking at her through the rear-view mirror.

Molly swallowed. Dear God...

'Although we should arrive in one hour and forty-five minutes,' he added. 'Maybe.'

Oh, he meant *the race* would take four hours! For a second there, she thought he meant it would take the car four hours to get to the finish line, and her first horrified thought was that four hours in the car could be trebled on a bike... She vowed to pay more attention during meetings in the future – she'd almost made a total fool of herself!

After a short while the convoy thinned out, and the spectators became fewer, then non-existent as the car turned onto the motorway, but Molly was paying scant attention to her surroundings – her attention was firmly on the TV screen secured to the dashboard.

'Is this live?' she asked, seeing an aerial view of the French countryside with the bunched cyclists scooting along a road below the helicopter. The shot zoomed in on a field with tractors arranged in the shape of a bicycle and the commentator was joking that there must be a tractor factory nearby. The scene then switched to the road again, focusing on a couple of the riders, the ones at the head of the race.

'Yeah, love, the whole thing is televised. Handy for us, eh? We don't miss anything.'

Molly thought it was wonderful, until she noticed that the driver, Damien, was studying the screen too, and her mouth was suddenly dry and her hand crept down to the buckle of her seatbelt, making certain it was fastened correctly.

'There's Tim,' Damien shouted, making her jump, and she leaned forward hoping Alex was nearby.

He was right in front of Tim, along with three other BeSpoke riders, but then another aerial shot changed the view and she lost sight of him in the mass of bodies and bikes, although she could still make out the pink and green of BeSpoke's jerseys.

Ignoring the view from the car window, Molly was entranced as the pretty French countryside unfurled on the screen. Mile after mile of farmland, a patchwork of bright yellow rapeseed, the lush green of pastureland, the darker green of corn, were interspersed with orchards and golden wheat fields. And along the way, farmhouses were dotted around, and the race passed through tiny hamlets and lovely small villages. Occasionally people had gathered along the road, to wave, clap, and cheer, but more often than not the roads were empty and the riders had them all to themselves.

'Do the authorities close all the roads between the start and the end of a race?' she asked.

'Sort of, but not all at once. It's like a great beast rolling along,' Mick said. 'Advance police motorbikes, about a half an hour out from the stage leaders, will stop the traffic. Before the riders get there, another wave of gendarmes will leapfrog over them and stop the traffic at the next point, and so on. It's amazing to watch, and to be fair to the race organisers, they've got it down to a T. Once the riders and all the cars have passed through, the last police will open the roads again, then will head to the front of the race and start the process all over again.'

Molly was fascinated and for the next few minutes she tried to watch the police motorcycles whenever the coverage showed them.

'That wind is coming from behind,' Jakob observed. 'It is keeping the peloton bunched up.' He worried at his lip.

'Is that bad?' Molly wanted to know.

'Yes and no,' Mick explained. 'No, because our team is keeping up with the peloton and being in the middle means our riders don't have to work quite so hard, and yes, because there is more risk of a crash. The best place to be is at the front, where Orozlo Myback and the other GC teams are. BeSpoke doesn't have that kind of punch yet. They could get

Tim to the front but keeping him there would be a challenge. We'd use up our domestiques too fast, for no real gain – not this early in the race. Today will be about the riders getting their cycling legs in, doing a bit of testing to see how strong the other teams are, and just getting to the end without a mishap.'

'There's no chance of Tim winning this stage?' she asked. There was so much to learn, so much to take in. These men had been doing it for years, but she was having to take a crash course in it, and she wished there was a book called "Le Tour de France for Dummies" or something similar, so she could gen up on it all. She had never for one minute thought things would be this complicated when she'd agreed to take the job.

Talking about "complicated" – there was Tim again, with Alex and two other BeSpoke riders just in front of him. A little frisson of restlessness shot through her every time she saw Alex, and she realised that her reaction to him was complicated indeed. The lovely afternoon with him yesterday had made her see just how much she liked him, and not only because he was good-looking and she fancied him. It was also because he was a lovely man inside and out, fun to be with and easy to talk to – she felt as though she'd known him for years. Yet there was also the added anticipation of discovery – what was his favourite meal (when he wasn't watching what he ate?); did he like the beach? How about long walks through bluebell-carpeted woods?

Oh dear, this simply wouldn't do, would it? She was letting the whole romance of being in France and being part of such a famous event get to her. But even as she was chiding herself, she was wondering if it had been Tim who had walked into her treatment room all those weeks ago instead of Alex, and if it had been Tim who had asked her to take a job with BeSpoke, would she have agreed to come?

Another shot of BeSpoke, who were near to the front and off to the side, drew her attention. Alex was ahead of the rest of the team, and as she watched she saw him make an odd gesture with his elbow, almost as if he was nudging a person who was standing too close to him.

She looked closer as he did it again.

'I think Alex has got a problem,' she said, as one of the other BeSpoke riders edged around him, and Alex dropped back slightly.

All three of her car companions leaned forward to stare at the screen, including, Molly was scared to see, Damien.

'Why?' Damien demanded. 'I can't see anything wrong.'

'I think he is having a problem with his left arm, possibly stemming from his wrist, the one he broke.' Molly bit her lip. He seemed fine last night, his grip strong, the flexibility in the joint within normal parameters. There was no stiffness, no inflammation, so what had she missed?

'What makes you say that?' Mick wanted to know.

'He kept doing this.' Molly jerked her elbow the same way Alex had. 'He's stopped now,' she added, then said, 'What?' when the three men erupted into laughter.

'You had me super worried,' Jakob said, chortling.

'What?' she asked again, as the chuckling continued.

Mick took pity on her and explained, 'Riders do

81

that when they want someone else to go ahead of them. See? Alex has dropped back to ride alongside Tim. He's probably checking up on him, or, knowing Alex, they could be chatting about the footie score or the weather.'

'Really?' Molly checked to make sure Mick wasn't winding her up.

'Really. There's not much happening at the moment, no breakaways, no crosswinds, no cobbles no mountains, so the riders can relax a little. There is a nasty sharp right-hand turn up ahead though, and things might get a little tasty when they negotiate that.'

He was right. The overhead shot showed a straight bit of road then a right-hand turn. All the riders were forced to slow down to negotiate it, but before that there was a little bit of jostling at the front as the lead teams tried to get in the best position for the turn. Even Molly, with her limited understanding of anything to do with cycling, could see the advantage of going into the turn at the front of the peloton.

'*Oh, there's been a crash,*' the commentator cried, and Molly gasped.

A melee of bikes and riders were on the ground, others were half-on and half-off their bikes, and the rest were attempting to skirt around the blockage.

'There's Tim,' Mick said. 'He's okay. I can see one… two… three…four of our guys with him, and none of them seem to have gone down. They were far enough behind it.'

'*Let's view that again, and maybe we can see what happened,*' another of the commentators said, and the screen went back a few seconds to just before the crash. '*There! It looks like a touch of wheels. Ricci from*

Fastrakk went down hard. What do you think, Eamon?'

'Yeah, Norris that's what it looks like to me,' the second commentator said, then the screen reverted back to a live feed, and Molly saw that the road was clear of riders, all except for two, and neither of those belonged to BeSpoke.

Molly felt sorry for the cyclists, one of whom was still on the ground and nursing his arm (possibly a clavicle injury, she thought, from the way he was holding himself), and the other was staring angrily at his bike, apparently unaware of his shredded jersey. That was going to sting in a bit, Molly guessed, seeing bleeding flesh through the tear at the jersey's shoulder. Nevertheless, she was thankful that neither of the men was Alex. Or Tim, she added hastily.

The screen then re-joined the peloton, which was powering through a village. Lots of people were lining the streets and Molly almost envied them being so close to the action. She felt both in the middle of it and rather removed, the sensation being quite odd. A part of it all, yet so distant…

Another awfully sharp bend appeared, this time to the left, just as the lead riders were coming out of the village, and once again there was jostling for position. And when the camera closed in on some of the men as they pedalled around the corner, she saw the irritation on some of their faces. Tempers were becoming frayed, and although she fretted about how this might affect Alex, Tim, and the others, she could also understand how this made for more interesting viewing from the point of the people sitting at home and watching the event live on their TV screens.

More villages, more flat, straight stretches of road, and then they were through a village called Céaux, and gradually, almost imperceptibly, the gradient began to rise. Actually, she only knew this because the commentators brought up a line graph of the day's course, showing the peaks and troughs of the terrain. Most of it, as she had surmised, was relatively flat.

Finally, the peloton crested a slight hill and the countryside spread out below them, and to Molly's eye, the landscape still looked remarkably Norfolkish (she'd been there once on holiday when she was a child).

'That's the Selune river,' Norris, one of the commentators was saying as the peloton swept across an old, arched, stone bridge, and then they were on another very long, very straight road. There was talk of wind speed and direction, and the possibility of crosswinds stretching the peloton out, and all the while Molly sought out the pink and green colours of BeSpoke and one rider in particular. Not that she was able to spot him that often, but when she did, she felt like giving him a little cheer of encouragement.

A few more kilometres later and the sparsely populated countryside began to give way to houses and shops, as the race swept through more pretty villages, and Molly began to feel that she might truly be in France after all.

Then the helicopter showed a view of the sea on the left and she realised the riders were following the coastline (she was pretty sure their own car was nowhere near the coast as they had taken a more direct route to the finish). As the race powered through seaside towns, suddenly Mick was saying that they were nearly there and Molly realised that the riders were only half-way through the race, the TV screen telling her there were still another 90 kilometres of racing left, but they themselves were nearing the finish line.

She had traversed diagonally across Normandy and was now on the other side of the coast, and she had hardly noticed the journey, having been too caught up in the drama of the race. Who knew cycling could be so fascinating?

CHAPTER 11

Utah Beach, one of the five beaches in Normandy where Allied troops landed during summer 1944 and part of the D-Day Landings, was a vast open area which was currently filled with coaches, trucks, cars, and people, as far as the eye could see. Damien appeared to know where he was going and he headed unerringly towards the left, and after a considerable amount of weaving in and out of people and traffic, he pulled up next to the team bus. One of the two BeSpoke trucks was already there and so were a couple of mechanics. A large tent had been erected behind the vehicles and Molly could see BeSpoke staff carrying what looked like unfinished bikes into it, and she realised they were the turbos which were used both to warm up the riders before the start of each stage and to warm them down afterwards.

With a groan, she got out of the car and arched her back. She could do with a visit to the loo, a cup of tea, and something to eat, in that order.

'Use the one on the bus,' Mick said, when she asked about the facilities. 'There are porta-loos but they'll be rank by now. Just don't tell Greg or Chuck, as the bus dunny is strictly for the riders.'

She did as he advised being as quick as she could, and when she emerged Jakob was holding out a coffee towards her. She took it gratefully, along with the sandwich he also gave her.

'We eat now,' he said. 'When the riders come in, you won't have time.'

Molly could only describe the area at the end of the race as organised chaos, with staff (both from the various teams and the Tour officials) mingling freely with milling spectators, and there were members of the press everywhere – it seemed like there were thousands of them and they had their own tents too, a huge one with a buffet in it and another equipped with loads of workstations. She even spotted both the BBC and ITV, which made her feel a little homesick for a moment. Stop being so silly, she told herself; she'd only been here a few days but she felt as though she'd been here for far longer. So much had been crammed into such a small amount to time that now, with the building anticipation and excitement of the end of Stage 1, home felt a very long way away indeed.

With little to do until the riders came in, which wouldn't be for at least another hour or more, Molly went for a walk. This morning, while she had been getting ready for the day ahead, she'd looked up Utah Beach on her phone and was interested to discover that there was a museum built on the edge of the grassy dunes and the beach so, with some time to kill, she decided to pay it a visit.

Constructed on the very beach where the first American troops landed on June 6, 1944, the Utah Beach Museum recounted the story of D-Day, from the preparation of the landing to the final outcome and success, and Molly found herself fascinated. There was a huge collection of objects, vehicles, materials, and other paraphernalia, and she stood in front of a B26 bomber, lost in sadness and gratitude for the sacrifices of so many soldiers.

It was a humbling experience and she was reluctant to leave, aware that an hour didn't do the museum justice, but it was time to return so she hurried back to the BeSpoke bus. After checking she wasn't needed yet, she positioned herself in front of one of the many huge screens dotted around the place and watched the race from there. Deliberately, she tuned out the arrival of the carnival floats advertising the various sponsors of the events and concentrated on the TV and on trying to spot BeSpoke riders among the surging and ever-changing peloton. Apparently, there had been a breakaway of three riders. Molly worked out that this meant that a few riders had managed to escape from the main group and had surged ahead. But by the time Molly's attention was back on the race, these three were being reined back in, as the mass of the peloton bore down on them at speed.

She wondered what it must feel like to be ahead of the pack for several kilometres, maybe with your hopes raised that you might be able to stay in front of the rest and therefore have some kind of a chance of winning the stage; only to look over your shoulder and see a solid wall of cyclists coming closer and closer, until you were sucked back into the group and your hopes were dashed. It must be heart-breaking, she thought, although the commentators were quite blasé about it, joking that the three riders had done their bit for raising the visibility of the companies that sponsored them by having their share of TV coverage.

'There's the Flamme Rouge,' Norris's disembodied voice on the TV screen told her as the riders passed underneath a huge, red inflatable arch. *'Indicating there is a kilometre to go, of course, and now we see the sprinters jostling for position. Cambert has done his bit for Braconti-Alba and is dropping back to let Del Ray do his job.'* The commentator's voice grew louder and higher pitched as he became more excited.

Molly's heart was in her mouth, as the riders at the front of the group powered around a right-hand bend and—

'Oh, there's been a crash!' Norris yelled. *'Del Ray is down, Frontera is down, and bang goes their chances of winning this sprint. Who else is out of the running? Danny Penman, by the look of it. That's going to mix things up, isn't it?'*

Seven riders were either on the ground or hanging onto their bikes, while the rest of the contenders picked their way around them gingerly, trying not to get caught up in the mess. Molly tried to catch a glimpse of any BeSpoke riders, but the camera switched back to those few fortunate leading cyclists who had managed to avoid the crash and were now furiously peddling towards the finish, their bikes wobbling dangerously from side-to-side, their mouths grimacing in pain and effort.

Then they were over the finish line, and Molly suddenly realised that BeSpoke wouldn't be far behind them and she needed to be somewhere else – now!

She returned to the tour bus and the other BeSpoke vehicles to find her team being led towards the turbos, where the riders would warm down on the stationary bikes in order to let the lactic acid leach from their overused muscles.

Henno joined her.

'Any injuries?' she asked and he shook his head.

'No, thankfully. There was a near miss on one of the stretches and I thought Carlos might have gone down, but he's okay.'

'Alex?'

Henno glanced at her out of the corner of his eye. 'He is fine, I think.'

'Good. I was worried about his wrist. I'm still not convinced it's back to full strength.'

'Ice it,' Henno instructed, and Molly nodded.

'I intend to,' she said, watching as the mechanics darted in to relieve the riders of their bikes and the swannies grabbed helmets and gloves, and anything else the riders didn't need and steered them towards the turbos.

Molly scrutinised each rider as they walked past. They were clearly stiff and possibly sore, but she could see no outward signs of anything more serious, and she breathed a sigh of relief. Alex, as the only BeSpoke rider with a fairly recent injury, claimed most of her attention and she studied him carefully.

He looked exhausted, sweat trickling down his face, making tracks in the dust coating his skin. He was clearly thirsty too and he hastily gulped down the electrolyte drink Mick gave him.

'There's no podium stuff to do, more's the pity, so once they've done the doping bit, we can get moving,' Mick said to her, catching her eye.

'Podium stuff?'

Mick shrugged. 'Anyone who has won anything gets to stand on the podium at the end of each stage and will have a jersey, a bunch of flowers, and a kiss from a really tall, pretty girl and will have to speak to the media. Everyone else buggers off to the next hotel.'

Molly didn't ask about the doping – she already knew. Henno had filled her in on the Tour organisers' requirements that riders be tested for illegal substances on a regular basis, and that it was part and parcel of the daily routine of the race.

One by one, the BeSpoke team completed their warm down and headed to the bus to have a swift shower and to change into clean kit, while the mechanics loaded the bikes into the lorry, and the swannies packed everything else away. Molly, as previously instructed, joined the guys on the bus, along with Chuck and Greg, and Henno went off in one of the team cars. It might seem like total and utter pandemonium, Molly thought to herself, but everyone seemed to know what they were doing and simply got on with it. And now she felt that she was in the same position of being able to get on with it, too.

Mindful of Tim's status, and aware that there were no other problems which meant that another rider would take precedence over the team leader, as soon as everyone was aboard the bus and it began to roll, she called him through to the rear of the coach to check him over.

'Apart from everything,' she said, 'is there one part of you which hurts more than the rest? Anything you have any concerns about?'

'Nah, thanks, I'm good,' he said, and she instructed him to strip down to his underwear and lie on the table.

She began working on his legs first, knowing that they were probably aching like the devil by now, before moving up to his back and his shoulders, paying particular attention to his neck.

'There, that should do you for the time being,' she said to him after a while. 'You'll have an ice bath when you get back, then I'll give you some ultrasound treatment after that.'

Tim got off the table and rolled his shoulders. 'That feels better,' he said, and she asked him to send Alex in.

While she waited, she washed her hands thoroughly, listening to the sounds of the last few team members having their showers, and thinking it was really odd to be travelling at 30 miles an hour and having a shower at the same time.

'Hi,' a voice said.

She looked up to see Alex standing in the doorway and her heart did that funny little lurching thing it seemed to be fond of doing whenever she saw him.

'Hi,' she replied, feeling suddenly quite shy.

'Where do you want me?'

'On the table. You know the drill.'

He smiled, a wry movement of his lips, and he removed most of his clothes before hopping up onto the table.

'How's the wrist?' she asked.

'OK, I guess.'

Mindful of what Henno had told her about cyclists having a tendency to play down their problems, she regarded him levelly. 'Just OK?'

'Yeah?'

It sounded more of a question than an affirmation to Molly's ears, so she said, 'I'll take that as a "no", then, shall I? Let me have a look.'

He held out his arm and Molly felt his wrist, bending the joint and turning his hand and arm this way and that. Alex bore it all without a murmur. She checked his other wrist for comparison. The one which he had broken felt a little warmer to the touch and although he had a full range of movement in it, she couldn't be sure he was masking any pain he might be feeling.

'Massage now, ice on the wrist now. Ice bath and treatment later,' she instructed, indicating that he should lie down for her to get to work on the kinks and knots in his calf and thigh muscles. Like Tim, he winced a bit when her strong fingers dug deeply, but she was satisfied it was a perfectly normal reaction and not anything to worry about.

She massaged his back and shoulders, then asked him to turn over so she could rub the front of his thighs and those huge powerhouse muscles which had transported him over 188 kilometres of undulating French countryside at an average speed of 40 kilometres an hour. The calculation took her mind off the fact that he was lying on his back staring at her. It also helped to take her mind off the fact that, despite herself and her best intentions, she was no longer viewing him as a patient, but as a…

What exactly was she viewing him as?

Unable to answer the question in her head, Molly dug a little too deeply and Alex yelped.

A chorus of catcalls came from behind the sliding door separating the front of the bus from the rear compartment.

'Sorry,' she said, mortified. She hadn't made that kind of silly mistake since she was a student. That would teach her to lose concentration. For the remainder of the session (which wasn't long, thankfully) Molly forced herself to focus on what her hands were doing, rather than who they were doing it to.

'All done,' she said, patting him on the top of his arm to signal for him to get up. And when he rolled off the bed, she sidled past him in the confined space and went to the tiny sink to wash her hands again, ensuring she didn't have to look at him.

It was only when he had returned to his seat up front and she had another victim on the table that she was able to bring her thudding heartbeat under control.

But as she pummelled and stroked another man's muscles, the only thing she could think about was the feel of Alex's warm skin and the look in his eyes.

Unless she was very much mistaken (and that was a very real possibility) she thought Alex might be just as attracted to her as she was to him.

The question was, what was she going to do about it and how was she going to last almost three weeks without letting her feelings show?

CHAPTER 12

The hotel was just over an hour's drive away, and another hour or so from the start of Stage 2. By the time the bus pulled up in front of a remarkably similar hotel to the one the team had been staying in for the past few nights (déjà vu, anyone?) Molly had assessed all eight riders and had given them a swift massage to take the edge off their aches and pains.

It was gone six p.m. and she was starving, but apparently dinner wouldn't be until nine o'clock. The riders had eaten steadily on the bus (high carb, high protein finger-food), but she'd had nothing since the sandwich earlier, and before she'd get a chance to refuel her own tank, she had further treatments to perform.

After she'd instructed the swannies to run cold baths – not that they needed instructing as this was a regular task of theirs – and they had brought her equipment in from the bus, she called the riders into her room one at a time. Her twin-bedded room had been relieved of one of its beds and a foldable physio table was in its place. It felt distinctly odd to have a succession of riders through her door knowing that this was where she would sleep later. The lines between her personal and private life had blurred considerably since she'd arrived in France and she was beginning to understand that she wasn't, in fact, going to have much of a private life for the duration of the Tour.

Which might be why she was standing in front of Alex (she'd saved him until last because she wanted to give the cold compresses time to do their work before she examined him again), wishing she could kiss the worry from his face.

'On a scale of one to ten,' she asked, taking hold of his hand and rotating it. 'How much pain are you in?'

'Eh? Oh, um, one?'

He seemed uncertain, so she took his response as a baseline and doubled it, which wasn't too bad, considering the hammering he'd given the joint.

'So, if it's a one, what's the problem?' she asked.

'We've got two more flat stages, tomorrow and the day after,' he began, shrugging. 'They should be okay. Stage 4 is hilly, but not too bad and Stage 5 is the time trial. But it's Stage 6 I'm worried about.'

Molly had studied the course (she'd had no choice, having been forced to sit in on the team meetings) but the reality of it had yet to make itself known to her. 'What about it?'

'Pavé,' he said, with dread in his voice.

Molly had heard the term mentioned but wasn't sure what it meant. 'And that is…?'

'Cobbles,' he explained. 'Kilometres of them. They rattle your bones so hard, you feel the effect for days. It's especially bad on your hands, wrists, and shoulders.'

'Ah.'

'Yeah...' He stared into space, and Molly realised she was still holding his hand.

She let go and took a deep breath. Concentrate, she told herself. This is a professional consultation, nothing more, nothing less. Get on with it and stop being so silly.

Alex was frowning. 'I'm worried about the strain on my wrist and I don't want to let the guys down, Tim especially. He's relying on me for the mountain stages.'

'Your wrist isn't quite as strong as you've led me to believe, is it?' she demanded, and he shook his head.

'I thought it was, but today...' He trailed off.

All business now, Molly took hold of his hand again. 'Henno and I will do everything we can,' she promised. And she meant it – she would keep Alex in the saddle if it was the last thing she did.

Molly was exhausted after Alex left and she flopped down onto her bed with a deep sigh. Her room felt strangely empty now that she was on her own, so she reached for her phone for company.

Several texts between her and her mother later, a WhatsApp call to Finley, and some Snapchat photos sent to a couple of friends, Molly began to feel a little better. All that she needed now was a quick shower, a change of clothes, and a spritz of her favourite perfume, and she was transformed. A good meal followed by a decent night's sleep and she was certain she'd be ready to face Stage 2.

Dinner was another healthy affair, and although she might have seriously considered selling her granny for a portion of creamy mashed potatoes, she tucked in with enthusiasm, telling herself that with all the fruit, salads, and vegetables she was eating it was like being on a travelling health farm for three weeks.

'Fancy joining us for a run in the morning?' Mick offered, after she'd asked him to pass her the fruit salad and yoghurt, which was deliciously topped with golden honey and nuts.

'A run?' She hadn't jogged for ages and hadn't thought to bring any kit with her, although she had packed a bikini in the (now-ridiculous) hope that she'd have a chance to soak up some rays. She smiled at the notion; her week-earlier self hadn't any idea whatsoever of what she had been letting herself in for, because if she had, she might have run screaming in the opposite direction. And missed out on such a wonderful experience, she added silently, suddenly and inexplicitly very delighted to be exactly where she was right now.

The fact that she'd just caught Alex smiling at her had absolutely nothing to do with the abrupt soaring of her mood.

'I've got trainers with me, but nothing else,' she said. 'What sort of time were you thinking of?'

'About five-thirty.'

Molly nearly spat out her fruit salad. 'No chance! I intend to be tucked up in bed at that ungodly hour. But thanks for the offer.' And she was genuinely pleased he'd thought to ask her; she was really beginning to feel like one of the team despite her inexperience in the world of professional cycling.

After dinner, Molly and Henno were instructed to join the team meeting with Chuck and Greg (Molly was beginning to think of the sports director and the team manager as a single unit – Chuck-n-Greg), to dissect the day's racing and plan for the following stage.

She found that she understood a little more this time, having watched the race unfold live on the TV, and what she wasn't sure of she made a note to ask either Henno or one of the swannies about later.

It appeared that Stage 2 was going to be much the same as Stage 1, except she wouldn't be there at the start of it but would drive straight to the finish at Abbeville. Another flatish stage, it would begin in Le Havre, where they were now, and would consist of three Category 4 climbs (she really must ask what that meant) and a sprint finish. All in all, it was 190 kilometres of racing.

Later, after the meeting and not yet ready to turn in for the night, Molly wandered into the bar area of the hotel, to find Henno already there. The riders had retired (they needed as much rest as they could get) and the swannies were having a pre-midnight beer in someone's room, to which Molly had been invited but had declined.

She had fancied a vodka and lime instead and a quiet moment to herself to reflect on the day. Instead, she got a gin and tonic and the company of the team doctor. Henno gestured for her to sit with him and, feeling she couldn't refuse, she joined him.

'What's a Category 4 climb?' she asked, for something to say and feeling a little awkward.

'The easiest of the uphill slopes. The categories go all the way from four to one, which is the hardest, although there are a couple of climbs that are even harder than that. Tim is a climber,' Henno said. 'That's his speciality. Today, tomorrow, and the day after are for the sprinters – flat, fast, with the kind of mad finish you saw today. The mountain stages where the nastier climbs are will leave the sprinters behind.

They haven't got the power or the stamina for those gradients. Alex is a climber, too,' he added.

Molly shot him a quick look but Henno was examining the contents of his glass.

'Want another?' He gestured to her drink and she shook her head. One was enough, the drink being far stronger than she would have expected if she had been in an English pub and she had no intention of getting squiffy.

Henno came back from the bar with another shot of something and sat back down.

'BeSpoke is a climbing team,' he began. 'And a race like the Tour de France will usually be won on the mountain stages. It is the job of the domestiques to pull their team leader up the climbs, to use their energy to put him in the best possible position to win the stage. They will exhaust themselves in the process,' he warned. 'But it's not the ups that are the problem for us.'

He pointed to himself then to Molly. 'It's the downs. Riders can get up to speeds of 120 kilometres an hour on some of the downhill stretches.' He paused and shuddered. 'I've seen some hideous crashes. If anyone comes off at those speeds, it is not going to be pretty.'

'Is this what Al— Tim does? Ride at 120 kilometres?' Crikey, that was about 75 miles an hour. Too darned fast for her liking.

Henno didn't seem to notice her almost-slip. 'Yes, he is super quick. Descents are his speciality. But he is not as good as, say, Mateo Rohjas from Kontrol Data or Oscar del Ray from Espanda. Those guys are at the top of the sport.'

Molly wanted to ask about Alex and how good he

might be, but she dared not show any more interest in him than she did in any other rider (apart from Tim, because as the race leader, everyone showed an interest in him). It would not do at all, and anyway Alex had given no indication that he was interested in her as a woman.

Had he?

CHAPTER 13

Stage 2 was almost a repeat performance of Stage 1, without the chaos of Mont Saint Michel, as Molly and the others travelled directly from the hotel to the finish at Abbeville, a town which boasted a magnificent Gothic-style church, a museum of fine art, several more impressive churches, the Château de Bagatelle, and a convent.

She had fleeting glimpses of the town as they made their way to the finish line, and as soon as they had parked the car, Molly checked to see how much time she would have before the first of their riders were likely to roll in. If she was quick and didn't linger anywhere too long, she might just have a chance to experience some of the fantastic history around her.

Leaving the wide-open and tree-dotted Boulevard Vauban and the busyness of the end of the stage behind her, she swiftly dived in the surrounding streets, heading for the town centre and its fifteenth-century church. As she walked, she smiled to herself in delight. This was almost like a pit-stop tour of Northern France she thought, and she vowed to return to the area one day when she had more time. It was sobering to think that this part of what was now a peaceful and calm land, had seen some of the worst fighting in World War 1, and although Abbeville itself was never occupied by the Germans (according to some quick research on the Internet) the town lay on the banks of the very river which had given the area and the battles its name, the Somme. During the journey from their hotel outside Le Havre, whenever she had glanced out of the car window, she saw a signpost for a war memorial.

One day, she promised herself, she would visit some of them, but for now she barely had time to take in the Église Saint-Vulfran, an impressive gothic church in the heart of the town. Apparently, Louis XII of France had married Mary Tudor, who was the sister of Henry VIII, there.

The church was free to go in, so after a quick check of the time, she slipped inside and marvelled at its serenity. Soft light bounced off golden columns and arches of creamy stone, interspersed with the glorious colours of the stained-glass windows, and she wished she could stay there for the rest of the day. However, she needed to get back and, terrified she might have missed something important, she tore herself away and retraced her steps.

Molly then spent the rest of the time before the riders came in alternating between viewing the race on whatever screen she could manage to find, checking that the stocks in the cupboards and fridge were full (she'd already restocked everything before breakfast but she checked again, anyway), and making sure all the equipment was ready for the post-race examinations. She also managed to grab a bite to eat, remembering how hungry she had been yesterday. Actually, there were loads of places for a snack as an assortment of food and drink stalls had been erected to cater for the needs of the spectators. As usual, the press had their own buffet tent, but Molly wasn't sure if she would be allowed in, so she ate Ficelle Picarde from a stall instead, a traditional Picardy dish of rolled up crepes filled with ham, grated cheese, and mushroom sauce, covered in crème fraîche and baked in the oven. She had two of them, and probably could have eaten a third but the smell of rich coffee drew her to another stall, where she simply had to buy a slice of Opera cake to go with her cappuccino.

Licking the crumbs from her fingers and hoping none of the rich buttercream or chocolate glaze was smeared around her mouth, Molly made her way back to the tour bus and watched the first of the riders come in.

No last-minute crash this time, thank God, although her heart almost stopped at the frantic speed and the seemingly utter disregard for anyone else that the lead riders showed as they threw themselves at the finish line. Then she waited for her team to join her on the bus and repeat yesterday's process. It was Groundhog Day but with better food and a glimpse of history, she chuckled to herself.

It was after they had arrived at their next hotel and everyone retired for the night that things began to deviate from yesterday, and Molly wasn't sure it was a good thing or not.

PJs on, face washed, and teeth brushed, Molly was about to get into bed when there was a gentle knock on her door. Thinking it was probably Mick or Keiron trying to entice her to another feast of sugar, fat, carbs, and salt, (aka, sweets, chocolate, crisps, and other assorted goodies which were denied the riders) she opened the door with a smile on her face.

When she saw who it was, the smile disappeared, to be replaced by uncertainty.

'Sorry,' Alex said. 'Were you expecting someone else?'

'Um, no, not really. It's just that Mick or one of the others often goes out for snacks about this time, so I thought…'

Alex glanced over his shoulder, then turned back to her. 'Can I come in? Standing out here is a bit…'

A bit *what*, Molly wondered, but instead of asking him what he meant she opened the door wider and stepped to one side to let him in.

Furtively, he had another quick look down the corridor, then darted inside.

'Do you want to tell me what this is about?' she asked, folding her arms across her chest and feeling rather self-conscious that she wasn't wearing a bra underneath her kitten-emblazoned pyjama top.

He noticed the kittens and smiled. 'Cute.'

She stared silently at him, wondering what he wanted.

'I… er… wondered how you were getting on,' he said.

Molly was perplexed. She had seen him several times earlier, had actually had her hands on his body twice, yet he had chosen to come to her room when he should have been tucked up in bed, to ask her something he could so easily have asked her a couple of hours ago.

'Fine, I think,' she replied cautiously.

'I'm asking because…' he paused, then smiled awkwardly. 'Because I'm concerned about you?' The last bit came out as a question.

'You are? Why?' Molly was aware she was coming

across as defensive but having him here in her room was doing odd things to her tummy. It fluttered and swooped, and she couldn't for the life of her work out why she was so affected by him now, when he'd been semi-naked lying on the physio table less than three hours ago.

'Because I brought you here and I kinda feel responsible for you.'

'Don't be. I'm a big girl. I can look after myself.'

'I know, it's just...' He stared at her helplessly.

'Just what?'

'You've been so distant, so aloof. I might have got it wrong, but I'd thought there might have been something between us, but now...' It came out in a rush, and Molly gasped. He'd felt it, too?

'I'm sorry,' he hurried to say, misinterpreting her shocked expression. 'I'll... um... go, shall I? I didn't mean... I didn't want... Oh, hell!'

'There was, there is,' Molly said, wincing as the words left her lips. She shouldn't be saying this, she really, really shouldn't be encouraging him, but he looked so lost and so deflated standing there, that she couldn't help herself.

'There is?' he asked, his eyes lighting up.

'Yes, there is,' Molly said firmly. 'But—' She held up a finger. 'We can't and we won't do anything about it. I like you and you like me, but that's as far as it goes.'

Alex flushed and his mouth dropped open. 'Do you think I knocked on your door wanting a *booty call*?' he asked slowly.

The thought hadn't crossed Molly's mind and that was certainly not what she'd meant when she'd said she wasn't going to take things any further. 'No!' she cried, but the damage was done.

Alex shook his head and backed up to the door, all of three steps away. His hand felt behind him for the handle. 'I would never disrespect you like that, and I'm hurt you think that about me.'

'I don't!' she said. 'I simply meant—'

But he was gone, out of the door, and she watched as it clicked shut behind him, the noise loud in the sudden silence.

What on earth had just happened?

Perplexed and unhappy, it was a long time before she got to sleep that night, and when she did her dreams were plagued by his hurt and disappointed expression.

CHAPTER 14

Avoiding Alex was physically impossible. Not that Molly really wanted to avoid him as such, but the time which they did actually spend together was tinged with an awkwardness that hadn't been there previously.

Polite was the term that came to mind whenever she thought about their relationship, and she thought about it often. Not that they had a relationship, aside from a working one, and that was exactly how it should be, she told herself, but it didn't stop her stomach from flipping over every time she caught sight of him unexpectedly, or her heart from constricting when she knew he would be at dinner, or in the team meeting, or appearing at her door every evening for treatment.

Once or twice she had been tempted to say something, but she'd held back. It was better this way. More professional. Less chance of her slipping up.

But that didn't stop it hurting and she continually thought back to that carefree afternoon on the Mont, when she had been certain he had been about to kiss her. Or maybe that had been nothing more than wishful thinking on her part, and she had read far too much into it all?

Yet… he *had* said he'd thought there was something between them, hadn't he?

Two days had passed since he'd knocked at her door. It was now the morning of Stage 5 and just when she'd thought she knew the routine, it all changed. Today was the individual time trial, when each rider was out there on his own competing against the clock. Of course, he was also competing against everyone else too, but seeing the riders all alone on the road made the race seem more real somehow. And a stage win for BeSpoke suddenly became much more achievable.

There were nineteen minutes and seventeen seconds between the race leader, Oscar del Ray in his yellow jersey, and Tim Anderson – an insurmountable task. If Molly hadn't joined the team with the knowledge that BeSpoke were total outsiders, then the penny would surely have dropped by now. Nineteen minutes didn't seem much of a gap when there was still over two weeks of racing to go, but by the Tour standards it was the equivalent of the Grand Canyon. And when she studied the GC rankings (oh, yes, she scrutinised them on a daily basis now) there were only thirty-three seconds between the yellow jersey and his nearest rival. In between del Ray and Tim, there were forty-nine higher-ranked riders.

Tim and BeSpoke were ecstatic to have done so well. Three out of the last four days had been won by those teams with sprinters, and the climbing teams (those teams whose riders specialised in powering up the sides of mountains) were way down in the rankings, BeSpoke included. But yesterday had been a hilly day and Tim had clawed back twelve minutes, which he was delighted about. Because he'd been on

Alex's wheel almost until they had crossed the line, Alex had also moved up the rankings.

Alex, though, didn't seem nearly as happy about it as the rest of the team, and Molly wondered if he was fretting about the pavé stage tomorrow. He'd not said anything further to her about the dreaded cobbles, therefore she'd not mentioned it either, but she did notice that he iced his wrist every night without being reminded and he got Mick to tape it up for him after she'd run through his treatment session. Technically, she should be the one taping it, but she was run ragged looking after the other seven riders, and she welcomed any help she could get. With four stages under their belts and the riders suffering exponentially, she was no longer able to massage each and every one of them after each race, so the swannies stepped in to do the routine stuff while she concentrated on the more complicated treatments. And every evening, after the riders had retired for the night, she and Henno settled down with a glass of something alcoholic and discussed the cyclists in detail.

Henno's face was the first one she saw when she came in for breakfast this morning, having spent the last hour or so stocking the fridge and the cupboards, as usual.

'Short and sharp today,' he said in his slightly accented English.

Molly nodded. With 37 kilometres of fast, flat roads, today was all about each man for himself. There would be slightly different issues on the injury-front too as all the riders raced hard and fast, and she prayed none of the team would come off, or worse, crash out. The Tour organisers had made up for the flatness of the terrain by the complexity of the course, having planned it to traverse through narrow streets, around hairpin bends, and to be confronted by vicious crosswinds, which could knock an unprepared rider sideways. Chuck-n-Greg had done their homework and had studied the course in detail, sharing their knowledge with the riders last night, and would probably discuss it again this morning on the way to the start. Heck, even Molly had become so familiar with the route that she felt she could walk it blindfold.

'Tim should be able to move up the rankings one or two places today,' Henno was saying as he helped himself to a croissant and a Danish from the buffet.

Molly was about to say something innocuous, when she saw Alex walk into the dining room and she flinched.

'Have you two fallen out?' Henno asked.

'No.' Molly grabbed some bread and jam, not really taking any notice of her food choice, and stalked over to a free table.

'You seem upset,' the doctor continued, following her.

'I'm not,' she insisted.

'Good. Make sure it stays that way.'

Molly forced some breakfast down with difficulty, smarting at Henno's words, keeping her attention firmly on her plate. She felt like she'd just been told off, and as soon as she could make her excuses, she left the dining room, almost in tears.

And bumped straight into the one person she seriously didn't want to see right now.

'Hey, are you OK?' Alex asked, his hands on the tops of her arms to steady her.

Molly nodded, furious with herself. He had been standing in reception and she had barrelled right into him.

'Look at me,' he insisted, letting go of her, only to lift her chin with warm, gentle fingers.

Molly looked, blinking back those treacherous tears.

'Has someone upset you?' Alex persisted, his eyes boring into hers, concern written all over his face.

'Yes.'

Alex waited for her to continue, saying 'Who?' when the silence stretched for too long. 'Here,' he said, leading her to one of the chairs overlooking a lawned area. Molly sank into it; Alex's nearness and obvious anxiety were doing inexplicable things to her state of mind.

'Who has upset you?' he continued. 'Is it Henno? I saw you with him at breakfast.'

Not wanting to be disloyal to the doctor, because he was only doing his job, after all, Molly said, finally. 'You.'

Alex recoiled, sitting back in his seat as if he had been shot. 'Me? What have I done?'

'Henno thinks we have fallen out and he is not happy about it.'

Alex shifted in his seat. 'We've not fallen out. It's just…'

'I accused you of making a booty call?'

The rider's lips twitched. 'You did.'

'When I said we couldn't take things any further, what I meant was…' Molly hesitated, unsure how to explain without laying bare her feelings for him and making a total prat of herself.

'I know what you meant,' he said softly. 'That's

why I've been so…'

It appeared that neither of them could finish a sentence this morning.

'Shall we start again?' Molly asked. 'Pretend the other night never happened?'

'If I remember rightly, nothing did actually happen,' Alex chuckled.

'And it's not going to,' she said. 'Everyone has made it totally clear that staff don't have relationships with riders, and that's how it should be.'

He drew in a long breath. 'I know, but I can't help wishing things were different.'

'You were the one who talked me into this, remember?' She took the sting out of her words with a small smile. 'And I'm glad you did. It's an experience I wouldn't have missed for the world.'

'And this is just the start of it,' he replied. 'There's the Vuelta in Spain next month. You'll love Spain,' he added.

If she managed to actually get to see any of it, she nearly said. He was trying his best, but he had misled her a bit, and she wasn't yet totally convinced that she wanted to carry on traipsing all over the world, especially since she'd never be able to relate to Alex in any other way than as a colleague. But if she returned home, she'd probably never see him again, what with him being in a different part of the world every few weeks, and she wasn't sure she liked that scenario, either.

How could anyone have any kind of a relationship under those circumstances? She was fully aware that riders had wives and girlfriends, but she'd bet her hat that none of them was on the staff. But then, Molly didn't have to be on the staff after the end of the

Tour if she didn't want to be, and she was thankful that she hadn't burned all her bridges back home.

Oh lord, she wished she knew what to do!

She was well and truly caught between a rock and a hard place. If she returned to England, there was little chance of having a relationship if she hardly ever saw him, but if she stayed on the team so she could see him every day, they wouldn't be able to have a relationship, anyway.

For now, though, he was off-limits and it would be better for both of them if they were simply friends. It wasn't as if she had any choice.

But Molly hadn't counted on the cobbles.

CHAPTER 15

Arras to Roubaix; 154 kilometres of racing, twenty-two of them on pavé as it was called in the cycling world; over fifteen separate sections of cobbles, ranging from a jarring 500 metres to a bone-breaking 2.4 kilometres, with tarmacked stretches in between.

Nothing, but nothing could have prepared Molly for the sheer drama of it. Drama she could do without.

The stage had started innocently enough, with the riders relatively fresh from their shortened race yesterday, although the individual time trial had been full-on and intense. Tim had done well and Alex even better, climbing up the rankings and leap-frogging over a couple of riders who had been above him, and gaining some valuable extra seconds. Not that it would make any difference, but Molly was delighted for him nevertheless, and even more so when she overheard some Westmore DBN staff saying how well he was doing for his first Tour de France.

They had been careful around each other yesterday evening, Molly especially, as she took extra pains not to treat him any differently from his team mates. It was bad enough that Alex realised she might have feelings for him without the rest of BeSpoke realising it too, although she knew Chuck, Mick, and possibly Henno, guessed. However, none of them had said anything further to her, and she suspected that as long as she carried on the way she was, no one would.

This morning she strapped up his wrist, winding tape round and round the joint between the thumb and forefinger, trying to provide as much support as possible, both of them silent. Alex, she could tell, was thinking about the day ahead, so she kept quiet. But she ached to kiss the apprehension from his face and tell him everything would be OK.

'Don't worry,' he said, breaking the silence, and Molly's head jerked up. 'It'll be fine. *I'll* be fine. The bigger riders do better on cobbles than the lighter ones.'

'They do?'

'The big guys generate greater force and more momentum than the smaller ones, so the smaller, lighter ones are at a disadvantage, as they get bounced around a bit more.' He flexed his wrist, possibly to check that he could still move it after all the tape (pink, to match the main colour of the team's jerseys – how cool was that?) she'd stuck on him. Maybe she had gone a bit overboard, she conceded, but Henno and Chuck had been adamant that Alex's wrist would need all the support it could get, and then some.

'It might be one of the reasons I was entered for the Tour,' he said, and smiled faintly. 'When riding on cobbles, it's all about the wattage.' He began to explain but Molly kind of zoned out, and let his words flow over and around her as she watched his lips move, and she wondered how they would feel on hers…

116

'It's like pedalling through bloody gravel,' he was saying. 'Every bounce, every slip and the bike loses momentum, and— You're not listening to me, are you?'

'I am,' she insisted, guiltily. In a way, she was listening, just not to what he was saying – she simply liked the sound of his voice.

'I still reckon I'll do well if I get to the end without incident,' he added, sounding remarkably like Eeyore. 'You wait, everyone will be crashing everywhere, and that's without the punctures and various bits falling off your bike.'

'Is it really that dangerous?' she asked, beginning to get worried.

'It can be. Accidents are common, but serious injury is rare because you're simply not going fast enough. I'll be fine,' he said again. 'In fact, Tim and I might stand a chance of gaining some seconds, maybe even a couple of minutes on the GC guys.'

'Tim's smaller than you – I thought you said the lighter riders came off worse over cobbles?'

'They do, but if he sticks close to me, he might be OK, though it tends to be every man for himself when it comes to the cobble sections.' He levered himself off the treatment table. 'I'd better get going. As much as I would prefer to stay here all day chatting to you, I've got a race to ride.'

'You don't mean that,' she laughed, but sobered immediately when she saw his expression.

'I think I do,' he said quietly, then was out of the door and down the stairs before Molly could think of a reply.

Darn it – but he wasn't making it easy for her to ignore him, was he?

She thought about those four little words as she swiftly packed her case and helped the swannies load everything into the vehicles, and when the bus left, she could have sworn she could see Alex's smile through the tinted windows. Impossible, of course.

Then they were on their way, Molly and Mick in their usual seats, eyes glued to the live feed from the on-site TV cameras.

'Crikey!' she exclaimed when one of the overhead shots zeroed in on the start. 'Are they taking the mickey, or what?'

She couldn't believe what she was seeing! The race was scheduled to start at the Citadelle d'Arras – a beautiful old monument surrounded by acres of parkland and with a huge square at its centre. The buildings were impressive enough on their own, but what caught Molly's attention was the fact that the whole area was cobbled. Talk about the irony – someone must have a wicked sense of humour, she thought.

One of the cameras focused in on the bunch of BeSpoke riders, and Molly caught a tantalising glimpse of Alex's face before the cameraman found something more interesting to aim his lens at, like del Ray, the wearer of the yellow jersey and the race leader.

Maybe, after today, that might change, Molly mused, as the peloton trundled over the cobbles to reach the road and the racing began in earnest.

Paying no attention to the motorway flashing past, she didn't take her eyes off the screen until after the first 50 or so kilometres. But when nothing much had happened, she began to relax. Not even the scenery was that exciting, apart from the occasional pretty village. If Molly had bought a package holiday on the basis of Alex's description of the fantastic places she would see and visit, then she'd be demanding her money back. The only thing she saw was the inside of a hotel (and they were all much of a muchness) and mile after mile of roads. She had to rely on the helicopter shots of the countryside to get even a glimpse of the France she'd been promised.

The race wove its way through the town of Arras and the surrounding urban areas, and then they were out in the country once more with open fields and stands of trees, farms and hamlets, and through more towns, until Molly was beginning to wonder if this pavé-cobbles business had been blown out of all proportion when the commentator cried that the first stretch was just ahead. Abruptly the race leaders swung left, leaving a nice tarmacked road behind them and riding onto what looked to Molly, like a tiny dirt track, and out of nowhere, the riders were bumping and bouncing over the first stretch.

Norris was saying, *There are a few corners to contend with and the Tour officials have erected blocks either side to prevent anyone from riding in on the edges. That's sneaky, Eamon, don't you think?'*

Eamon clearly did, and he added, *'I think the biggest challenge could well be the wind. This sector is quite exposed, and there seems to be a good breeze blowing across it. What with the narrowness of the track and the wind, we should see a strung-out peloton, and the danger here is that some of the guys will try to move up to the front of the race, so we should see a few crashes, too.'* Eamon sounded positively cheerful about the prospect, to Molly's disgust.

This might well make for better viewing, but all Molly could think about was Alex (or Tim, of course she was thinking about Tim and the other six, too) on the ground, with God-knows-what sort of injuries. She just hoped and prayed that Alex's wrist would hold out.

'Oh! There goes Cambert! And he's come down heavily and taken a few others with him. Is that Jan Bracher from Xeno Portal on the ground? It is. It's Bracher and from the way he's holding his arm, I'd say that's a broken collarbone for sure, so that will be the end of his hopes to win this year's Tour.'

Damien had slowed the car so much that they were practically crawling along, and after several drivers blasted their horns at them as they blew past, he pulled over, and all four of them leaned towards the screen, holding their collective breaths.

'There's Alex, with Tim in front. They've got Elias and Carlos with them too. I can't see the others,' Jakob said, 'but we'd have heard by now if they've crashed.'

Chuck-n-Greg were in constant contact via radio with both the other team car travelling with the peloton, and the riders themselves, but they could also radio in to any of the support staff if needed and a crash would be news indeed, affecting everyone from Henno and Molly, down the mechanics, who might have a poorly bike to fix by tomorrow.

Four pairs of eyes swivelled to the radio, but thankfully it remained silent.

When the race trundled back into civilisation and onto proper roads once more, Molly let out a breath she hadn't realised she'd been holding, and Damien pulled back into the flow of traffic.

There wasn't much respite for the riders, though, with the next section of cobbles coming up very quickly afterwards.

'Here we go again,' the TV squawked. *'This section is marginally narrower than the last one, and the higher embankment, together with the blocks, will make it feel tighter again.'*

'Oh, they're not going to be happy.' Eamon was delighted. *'Wind could play a factor, too, with wide-open fields as far as the eye can see on either side.'*

Once again, Damien pulled over and the four of them watched with their hearts in their mouths until all eight BeSpoke riders were accounted for on the other side of the cobbles.

'It's getting hotter,' Mick said, as plumes of dust billowed behind the last of the stragglers as they negotiated the cobbles. He pointed to the temperature display on the dashboard, which said 30 degrees Celsius.

Great, we might have heat exhaustion to contend with too, Molly thought and she was glad Henno was on hand, just in case.

The next sector of rough track was about a kilometre in length and wove its way through the countryside with some sharp turns, which caught a couple more riders out, as three more crashes brought several down and saw two poor souls retire from the race completely.

It was the next section that was the killer, Molly discovered; at 2.7 kilometres, it was the longest stretch on the stage. The riders were already tired and must be hurting and she wished she could catch sight of Alex's face to see what sort of state he was in, but the cameras were too busy focusing on the stage leaders and the overhead shots.

The commentators described the horrors of the uneven surface for the benefit of the viewers, but

Molly wished they'd shut up, because every word the pair of them uttered only served to worry her more.

'These cobbles are jagged, uneven, and rough. The road itself is higher in the middle, with sloping sides that will keep steering the riders into the blocks. Great for water run-off, but not so good for cyclists,' Norris told her.

Yeah, thanks for that, she thought back at him, then she heard him say the words she had been dreading and her heart stopped.

'Alex Duvall is down!'

CHAPTER 16

'Tim Anderson's right-hand man has crashed, and some others have gone down with him. Can we see what happened?' the commentator's voice rang out from the speakers.

Oh, my God! *Alex!* Molly watched in horror as the footage rewound to just before the accident and played again, this time in slow motion. A Kontrol Data rider had cycled too close to one of those stupid blocks, tried to overcompensate, and had touched wheels with Alex, whose bike juddered sideways on the uneven surface and catapulted him over the handle-bars.

He was on the ground in a tangle of wheels, arms and legs, and Molly was practically in tears.

'Anderson is okay. BeSpoke's team leader managed to avoid it and three of his team mates have rallied around him, but the question is, how much of a blow will it be to him to lose his second wheel?'

For far too brief a moment, the camera showed a close-up of Alex, and then it returned to the front of the race.

'Is he okay?' Mollie cried, frantic with worry, and Mick shushed her as the crackle of the radio filled the car, followed by Chuck's tinny, squawking voice.

'Alex is back on his bike. Repeat, Alex is on his bike. He has lost some skin, but he is fit to ride. Copy?'

'Copy,' Jakob replied, and there was a collective sigh of relief.

But not from Molly. 'What does Chuck mean, "lost some skin"? How badly hurt is he?'

'If he's riding, he's fine. Don't worry, darl, eh?'

Molly shot Mick an incredulous look. He clearly wasn't too bothered, but Molly certainly was. She had seen how much pain Alex could endure, and how well he could suppress it. For all she knew, he might have reinjured his wrist, but the silly man was too stubborn to admit it and would keep cycling until he collapsed.

Desperate to check him over and see for herself, she nibbled at her bottom lip with her teeth.

The remainder of the journey passed in a fog of worry, and Molly had never been so pleased to step out of a car in her life. If she had to spend any longer cooped up with those three, she thought she might scream. And the riders wouldn't be at the finish line for another couple of hours yet.

Restless and out of sorts, she grabbed a coffee and headed for the tour bus.

'I heard Alex came off,' Tony, the driver said. 'Tim's OK though.'

Molly bristled with indignation. All anyone ever thought about was Tim, she wanted to scream, but she took a deep breath instead. Part of her knew they were right to do so, and that Alex and the other six domestiques knew full well what they were signing up for when they… well, signed up. Theirs was the life of a rider whose job, for this particular tour anyway, was to give the team leader the best chance of winning the race. Maybe Alex would get a chance another time, maybe they all would, but for now they had a job to do. Everyone did, including her – but God help anyone who made her treat Tim first when it was Alex who had crashed, and she was determined to stick to her guns on that.

When BeSpoke and the rest of the riders wheeled wearily over the finish line, Molly waited anxiously for Mick to grab Alex and lead him to the turbos for the warm down. She watched as Alex gingerly dismounted and hobbled towards the turbos, getting on his machine with some difficulty. Although, if she was being honest, none of the other riders seemed to be in any better shape than he was. Scrutinising each one, Molly arrived at the conclusion that Alex was the only rider to have sustained any visible injury, and normally she would have examined him first, but Henno appeared at her shoulder.

'See to Tim, first,' he advised. 'As soon as Alex has finished on the turbo, I want to get him in the shower and dress his shoulder.' He let out a sigh. 'I knew it was going to be hard,' he said, 'but they all look… what is the English word? Wrecked?'

Molly had to agree that they did.

All the riders had what Molly could only describe as a shell-shocked expression, staring doggedly into the distance as they grimly pedalled the turbos. It was as though the rest of the world had ceased to exist for them, and they were cocooned in pain and exhaustion, red-eyed and sallow-skinned underneath the layers of sweat and dust.

Alex had dark circles of pain around his eyes and his jaw was clenched, his hands gripping the bars like claws. Molly thought it a wonder he was still upright, let alone peddling a turbo. Finally, Chuck declared the warm down over and there was a collective groan of relief.

Mick helped Tim clamber ungainly off his bike and, without thinking, she stepped forward to give Alex a hand.

He smiled at her gratefully, but she noticed the pain in his eyes and she quickly checked his injured shoulder. The jersey was a write-off, torn and shredded in several places, but it was the skin underneath that made Molly gasp. His shoulder was red, as if it had suffered a burn, with the top layer of skin rubbed off. If she looked closely, she could see blood seeping around tiny pieces of dirt and gravel which were embedded in his flesh. She also noticed some smaller abrasions on the side of his knee and his elbow.

No wonder he looked the way he did. He must be in so much pain.

'Let me take him,' Henno said, and she was forced to release Alex into more capable hands, so she returned to the bus and sat listening to the two showers sluicing the dirt, grime and sweat off BeSpoke's best riders, and feeling at a total loose end, her only contribution being to hand over some more electrolyte drinks to anyone who wanted one.

By the time Tim came for his massage, she had composed herself, although she still couldn't get her head around the level of pain these athletes were willing to endure for their sport. The BeSpoke's team leader's shoulders were badly knotted and the tension radiated down his back and into his neck. His arms and hands were even worse, his fingers unable to flex properly.

'My head knows I'm lying in the back of the bus,' he told her, when they were done. 'But my body feels like it's still on the bike. Those damned cobbles!'

Alex was, as she'd thought, in even worse shape. He staggered to the back of the bus, naked except for boxers and a large white dressing on his shoulder. The abrasions on his elbow and knee had been cleaned but were open to the air.

She had to help him onto the table, shaking her head at the state of him.

'Who will be second wheel now?' she asked, as she tried to work her way around the dressing, being very careful where she put her hands.

He barked out a strained laugh. 'That'll still be me.'

'But you're injured!'

Molly felt the shrug in his good shoulder. 'It's nothing. Thankfully, tomorrow is a hilly day and not a mountain stage, so I should be able to take it a bit easier.'

'You're still in the race,' she stated, her voice neutral. For some reason, she'd expected him to have been withdrawn. Several other Tour riders had crashed out over the course of the past five days, and today it was rumoured that a whole bunch more wouldn't be showing up at the starting line tomorrow. Even the commentator had assumed Alex was out.

Molly didn't know how she felt about the news that he was carrying on. Angry at his stubbornness and stupidity? Relieved that she'd get to spend a few more days with him because he wasn't being sent home? And that got her to wondering whether she had been so upset earlier because she thought he was about to return to England and not remain in France with the Tour.

Shoving the idea to one side, she concentrated on trying to free up some of the hideous knots in his back while, at the same time, avoiding hurting him any more than he was hurt already. When she had done what she could, she turned her attention to his wrist, seeing that the cobbles hadn't done it any favours at all.

He winced when she flexed and bent it, and his grip was almost non-existent, although to be fair, it was virtually the same with his right hand.

'It'll be like this for a couple of days,' he warned her, as she massaged the palm of his hands and pulled at his fingers.

In an attempt to lighten the mood, she joked, 'You're going to need someone to cut your chicken up for you tonight.'

He turned his head to look at her and asked softly, 'Are you offering?'

'If you want me to.' She paused, both of her hands wrapped around one of his, and stared back at him.

'Mick will do it,' he said with a sigh and a chuckle, 'but I'd much prefer you. You're prettier and you smell nicer.'

'Gee, thanks. You know how to give a girl a compliment,' Molly quipped back, relieved to hear he sounded more like his old self. Not that his old self had ever called her pretty, but she'd take whatever she could get, whether it was meant as a joke or not.

Both Molly and Henno were kept busy until well after dinner and the inevitable team meeting, but when she could finally fall into bed she was too wired to sleep. She was even too agitated to head for the hotel bar and a shot of something strong and mouth-numbing, because it wasn't her mouth that needed numbing – she would need more than one drink to numb her mind. Anyway, Henno had also gone to bed, she didn't fancy drinking on her own, and even if she did, the thought of getting up at silly o'clock and facing another long day while in the throes of a hangover didn't bear thinking about, so she decided to step outside instead.

Apparently, BeSpoke were housed for tonight in a hotel on the outskirts of a town called Troyes which was on the River Seine, and when she looked the location up using Google Maps, she was pleased to see that the hotel was only a short walk away from the town centre.

Knowing she would regret the impulse in the morning, but desperate to clear her head, she donned her trainers and grabbed her bag. Thinking it prudent to inform someone where she was going, she told the guy manning the reception desk that she was going for a stroll into town, then she headed for the revolving door and freedom.

'It's further than you think,' Alex said from behind, making her squeal with fright. He was sitting in one of the high-backed chairs in reception, a bottle of water on the table in front of him and an iPod in his hand. 'I also think you'll find he doesn't speak a word of English.'

'Oh? Never mind, I'll tell you, instead. I'm popping out for a walk.'

'It's late,' he pointed out.

'I know.' She peered at him. 'Shouldn't you be in bed?'

'Can't sleep. Shouldn't you be in bed?' he countered.

'I'm not the one daft enough to cycle over 200

kilometres tomorrow,' she flashed back at him.

'Touché. But I still can't sleep.'

Molly was instantly contrite. 'Is it your shoulder? Can I get you anything? Do you want me to fetch Henno?'

'Yes, no, and no. But I'll come with you for that walk, if you'll let me.'

Molly was horrified. 'You can't! Not in your state, and besides, you need all the rest you can get and I'll be shot.'

'Not if no one knows about it.'

'Surely Tim will notice if you're not in bed.'

He smiled, his eyes crinkling at the corners. 'Because of this,' he lifted his wounded shoulder a little, 'I get a room to myself. Chuck doesn't want to risk me disturbing any of the other riders. He expects me to have a restless night.'

'I bet he doesn't expect you to go traipsing around Troyes, though.'

'It'll help relax me,' he assured her, then hesitated. 'Um, that is, if you don't mind me coming with you?'

'I don't mind.' In fact, she welcomed it. Maybe walking around a strange town at close to midnight on her own wasn't the best idea she had ever had, but she needed to get out and look at something other than the back of a bus, the inside of a hotel, and a TV screen.

Alex knew what he was doing, she reasoned, and if a gentle stroll would help him sleep, then a gentle stroll was what he would have.

At first, Troyes seemed no different from any other town, but after about fifteen minutes the street became narrower and the buildings started to look quite old. It was difficult to tell in the dark, but many of them appeared to be medieval with their overhanging upper storeys and half-timbered frames.

Alex grimaced. 'They're everywhere,' he groaned, pointing to the ground, and when Molly glanced down at the road and saw what he was referring to, she stifled a giggle.

Cobbles.

He raised his face to the heavens and said, 'Someone up there seriously doesn't like me.'

'At least the pavement is paved and not cobbled.'

'Are you saying that I should be thankful for small mercies?' he asked playfully.

She smiled at him, thankful to see him in such good spirits, but then a wave of concern that he should be tucked up in bed and soundly asleep washed over her.

He seemed to sense her thoughts and took his phone out of his pocket. Molly assumed he was going to ring for a taxi, hoping that one of them still operated at this time of night (or morning as it now was) and that the person on the other end spoke English, but that wasn't what Alex had in mind.

'If we take a right here, then another, we will be heading back the way we came,' he said. 'See?' He held up his phone and Molly was surprised to see how far they had walked from the hotel.

'Apparently, there has been a settlement here since about 600BC,' he told her. 'And the Romans were here too.' He glanced around him. 'But most of the buildings date from the mid-fifteenth-century because the town had to be rebuilt when it was destroyed by a fire.'

Molly wished she could see it in daylight but, on the other hand, there was something quite romantic about wandering its narrow streets in the middle of the night, with hardly anyone else around.

The further they walked, the older the buildings seemed to become, until she could almost imagine that it really was five hundred years ago – if she ignored the bollards, the parked cars, and the streetlights. Still, she tried her best to see the town through the eyes of some long-ago woman, and she tried to imagine the kind of life she might have led.

Finally, they were back on the tree-lined main road leading to their hotel, and Molly felt a sense of loss. She knew they had to return sooner rather than later, because both of them desperately needed some rest (Alex more than her) but she was reluctant for the night to end.

'How are you feeling now?' she asked him.

'Fine,' he said, but she could tell by the swiftness of his response and the tone of his voice that he wasn't being truthful with her.

'I didn't realise it would be so hard,' she said, hesitating just as they were about to walk into the hotel.

Alex took a deep breath. 'It's my fault, I shouldn't have made the job sound better than it is, but I really wanted you to be my – *our* – physio. If you're not enjoying it, I fully understand. This life isn't for everyone and while you're on the road it can be damned hard work.'

'I wasn't talking about me,' she said, softly. 'I meant you, the riders.'

'We're used to it, it's what we do.'

Molly turned to face him. 'I see the state of you afterwards. How do you put yourself through that day after day?'

'Because I love it. It's what I've always wanted to do.'

Alex's voice was so full of passion that it stole Molly's breath. She'd never before met anyone so dedicated to their job, and at that moment she realised that it wasn't simply a job to him, it was a vocation. It was something he was compelled to do, and he loved cycling and racing with every cell of his body.

'I envy you,' she said softly. 'I wish there was something I felt as passionate about.'

He shifted from one foot to the other, and sighed, the noise loud in the quiet of the night. 'There is a downside. This can't last forever. I'm coming up for thirty – I don't know how many years I'll have left in me, competing at this level. One day, I'll have to stop racing.'

He sounded desolate and she wished she knew how to comfort him.

'I can't imagine a life without it,' he said. 'Or, I couldn't until...' He looked up, his eyes gleaming in the reflected light from the hotel's façade.

'Until what?' she asked, and he brought his attention back to her.

'Nothing. Let's go inside. I think I might be able to sleep now.'

'Can I get you anything? Water, juice?'

'No, but thank you for asking.'

'And thank you for accompanying me tonight.'

Suddenly, they had gone from easy, flowing conversation, to stilted awkwardness and Molly had no idea why.

'I could hardly let you go alone, could I?' Alex said wearily, swaying on his feet, and she realised just what their "little stroll" had cost him. He was totally and utterly exhausted, and it was all her fault.

'Here,' she said, jamming her shoulder underneath his armpit and half carrying him towards the lift. 'Which floor?'

'Second, I think,' he murmured, and Molly realised he was practically asleep on his feet.

'Room number?' she demanded, wondering if she would actually be able to get him to his room or if she would be forced to call for help. Most of his weight was on her, and he might be slim, but he was solid muscle.

He rooted sluggishly around in his pocket and came out with a key fob with his room number on it. Molly took it, and steered him towards the correct door.

As silently as she could, she unlocked it and manoeuvred him inside. Alex made straight for the bed and collapsed on top of it.

For a few moments Molly dithered, wondering if she should just leave him as he was, reluctant to disturb him, but she couldn't let him go to bed with his trainers on, could she? And once she had taken those off, she felt it was only right to ease him under the covers. She debated whether to remove his jeans, because he surely wouldn't be comfortable sleeping in them, but she lost her nerve.

So, with a last lingering look at his face, she tiptoed towards the door.

It was just as she was closing it gently behind her, she heard him whisper, 'I really enjoyed tonight.'

Yes, that was the problem, she thought, as the latch clicked shut – she had really enjoyed it, too.

CHAPTER 17

Hilly, that was the best way to describe the following three days of racing. Lots of little ups and downs, just like Molly's emotions, with long stretches of flat in between.

Expecting to be hauled in front of Chuck-n-Greg at any moment, she had spent the morning after the midnight excursion into Troyes fearful for her job and Alex and BeSpoke's chances, and not necessarily in that order.

Alex was a little withdrawn at breakfast the following morning and Henno reported after he'd changed his dressing that the rider hadn't slept particularly well, which was to be expected. When no mention was made of their little jaunt, after a while Molly began to relax. Their walk had gone undetected, but as much as she'd enjoyed it, she vowed not to do anything so rash again; she had a duty of care to the riders, and putting Alex in a position where he felt he had to accompany her for her own safety was unprofessional of her at the very least, and totally unfair to him.

Molly didn't actually get to speak with Alex until that evening, when she put him through a series of exercises designed to stretch and flex his still-knotted muscles.

'I see today went well,' she said as an opening gambit, figuring it was safer to talk about racing than anything else.

'Yep. Tim is right on form.'

'I was referring to you,' she said.

He did a one-shoulder shrug. 'I wasn't at my best.'

'You pulled him up that Category 2 climb,' she said, repeating what she had heard in the car earlier.

'He'd have gotten up there just as easily with any of the other guys,' Alex said modestly, but Molly had seen the effort it had cost him when one of the cameras on the back of a Tour motorbike had caught the grim and determined clench of his jaw as he pedalled in front of Tim.

'You both gained some time,' she pointed out.

He smiled, finally. 'We did.'

There was still a massive (by Tour standards) amount of time between the race leader and Tim (with Alex fairly closely behind Tim) but the gap had closed a little today, and both BeSpoke riders had climbed up the rankings a few notches, mainly due to the poor performance of del Ray who was still wearing the prestigious yellow jersey, and his nearest rival Mateo Rohjas who had a puncture, followed by some other mechanical problem. Added to that was the fact that two of the riders above Tim's position on the leader-board had pulled out after yesterday's cobble section, and Tim and Alex had found themselves in a better position this evening than they had when Stage 7 started that morning.

It was at the end of the session that Molly finally found the courage to apologise to Alex, as he was gingerly pulling a T-shirt over his head, the session finished.

'I'm sorry about last night,' she said, her voice little more than a whisper because she didn't want to risk anyone in the front of the bus overhearing her.

'I'm not,' he replied, his voice muffled. His head popped out of the neck and he grinned at her. 'It was fun.'

'You were bushed,' she said, borrowing one of Mick's phrases.

'Yeah, but I couldn't sleep, so it was better than sitting there listening to music.'

'Why were you in reception and not in your room?' she asked him, the thought only now occurring to her. He had a single room last night, so there hadn't been any risk of his restlessness keeping another rider awake.

Surprised to see a hint of pink creeping into his tanned cheeks, she waited for him to say something.

'I was hoping you'd have your usual pre-bed tipple,' he said by way of explanation.

'Oh, sorry, I didn't realise. Henno was tired and I didn't fancy drinking on my own. If you'd have mentioned it earlier I'm sure Henno would have stayed up, but I'm also pretty sure he wouldn't have let you have any alcohol,' she pointed out.

All the riders were on carefully controlled diets and there was a long list of what they could, and couldn't, eat and drink. Apparently, there was some champagne stashed somewhere, which was only to be brought out in the rare event of a stage win, and Molly purposely didn't mention the beer and other assorted goodies that the swannies and the mechanics had hidden in their luggage.

Alex's face turned a slightly deeper pink and he

stared at the floor. 'I knew Henno wouldn't be there,' he admitted. 'It was you I wanted to see.'

'Me?' The air seemed to have left Molly's lungs as she squeaked out the question.

'Yeah.'

'Why?' she managed, leaning back against one of the cupboards for support.

He lifted his head and looked at her. 'I think you know why.'

Oh, my. Did she? She hoped she did. 'We can't,' she breathed, shooting a quick glance at the partition dividing the back of the bus from the area where the rest of the riders were sitting.

'I know,' he replied. 'And it's not fair of me to say anything. I'm sorry.'

Molly wasn't. She was glad. More than glad – thrilled. But even if she ignored the position she was in at the moment as one of BeSpoke's support staff, Alex was a professional cyclist and hardly ever in the UK, and once again the argument that it would couldn't possibly work because they'd never see one another, floated into her head. So she shoved the idea of them ever having a relationship to the back of her mind.

'That's OK,' she replied, stiffly, wishing she could tell him how she really felt, but recognising the futility of it.

Avoiding his eyes, she let him leave without another word.

But as soon as the partition swished closed behind him, she sagged back, breathing hard. It was the right decision, she knew, but that didn't make it any easier. The cons outweighed the pros by about two to one. Not only was she support staff, but she hadn't yet made her mind up about whether she would carry on being employed as BeSpoke's physio or whether she would return to England and her former life at the end of the Tour.

Should she call it quits now, while she still had her heart more or less intact and no damage had been done on either side?

She could return to her home, her family, and her job, with lots of memories and a fantastic experience, and Alex could concentrate on his cycling. He'd soon forget her, his attention and passion caught by his next big race, and she'd... What? What would she do? Continue with her not-very-exciting life? She should get out more, she thought, then almost laughed out loud as she realised that was exactly what she was doing by accepting this job. And if her life at home was boring (although she hadn't really thought it was until she'd joined BeSpoke) then maybe she should consider making it a bit livelier by internet dating or something, because she clearly wasn't fulfilled by either her job back home or her social life.

Actually, come to think of it, when was the last time she had been on a date?

It was so long ago she couldn't remember; no wonder she had latched onto the first attractive man who had shown even a teeny-weeny bit of interest in her.

Molly Matthews, she said to herself sternly, you need to get a life.

CHAPTER 18

'When was the last time you rode a bike?' Alex asked her.

Molly had been looking forward to getting a few chores done – like giving her clothes a proper wash, especially her tunic. For once, the team would be staying in the same hotel for two nights running. It was located just outside a town called Brioude, in the middle of the Auvergne, as the Tour made its way down to the Pyrenees and the mountain stages. She had intended to borrow one of the team's washing machines. It was going to be the highlight of her day – that, and not having to pack her case for two days.

'Why do you ask?' she replied, her tone guarded.

'Because I think it's about time you got in the saddle again.'

'I don't think so. The last time I was on a bike I must have been about ten-years-old.'

'Then it's high time you got reacquainted.'

'Why?'

'It's a good way to see the sights.'

Molly put her hands on her hips and glowered at him. 'Haven't you got a training ride to go on, or something?'

'Been there, done that, got the T-shirt,' he replied, with a cheeky grin, pulling at his BeSpoke top.

Today was the first of two rest days, which were spread equally throughout the race, and Molly had intended to spend some of it doing exactly that – resting – as well as doing the washing, and having a relaxing half hour with a book. But she was shocked to see that the morning had already disappeared and it was now lunchtime.

Alex had cornered her just as she was about to enter the dining room, which was unexpected considering they'd had little contact over the past couple of days apart from the treatments after each stage.

'Alex,' she warned. 'I don't think it's a good idea.'

'It's true, you never forget how to ride a bike. Once you get on it, it'll all come back to you.'

'That's not what I meant.'

The teasing expression left his face. 'I know.'

'Well, then,' she retorted, expecting that to be an end to it.

She hadn't factored Alex into the equation though, because as soon as lunch was done, he was at her side again. 'We could always take Mick as a chaperone, if it'll make you feel better?'

She narrowed her eyes at him. 'Why do you want me to get on a bike?'

'I want to show you Brioude and I thought the best and quickest way would be by bike.'

'You don't have to make it up to me, you know,' she pointed out.

He shrugged and focused on a spot over her left shoulder. 'I know, but it seems a shame to be only a couple of miles outside one of the prettiest villages in the Auvergne and not see it.'

'Couldn't we take a car, or walk?'

'Can't find any car keys. I think Chuck has hidden them. And walking would take too long. We've only got a couple of hours.'

Molly played her trump card. 'I haven't got a bike, and I don't think any of the mechanics would be too pleased with me borrowing one of BeSpoke's.'

A slow smile spread across Alex's face. 'If I can find a couple of bog-standard bikes, would you come out for a ride to Brioude with me?'

'You've already found some, haven't you?'

'Yep.'

'Where?' she demanded.

'There's a hire place just up the road. I've taken the liberty of hiring us a couple.'

'You might have wasted your money.'

'Is that a yes?'

Molly honestly couldn't say why she agreed to such a silly idea, but twenty minutes later saw her wobbling uncertainly down the road behind a much more assured Alex. So far, she wasn't impressed, either by her performance on the bike or by what she was seeing of Brioude (when she risked looking around).

Gradually, after a few minutes, when she got the hang of it once more (Alex was right, she hadn't forgotten), she began to unclench her jaw and her shoulders relaxed a little. She was still gripping the handlebars as though her life depended on it, ready to grab for the brakes, but she found she was beginning to enjoy herself.

Thankfully, there were very few cars on the road, and the ones that passed her gave her a wide berth. So, with her confidence growing (and trying to ignore the pressure of her bottom on the unfamiliar saddle), she caught up with Alex and rode alongside him.

'You OK?' he asked and she nodded.

She had a feeling her behind would pay for it in the morning, but for now she was having fun, with the wind riffling through her hair and the sun on her face.

So far, Brioude hadn't looked much different from any other French village, but when they turned off into a little side street, Molly began to laugh.

Cobbles, lots of them. Oh dear, with all the shaking, she thought she might come off her bike.

'It's not funny,' Alex cried, laughing along with her and she bounced over the gnarly little pebbles.

Poor Alex and the rest of the team – she would definitely have more sympathy for them after this. Not that she hadn't had sympathy for them previously, but even a short stretch of leisurely trundling over the darned things was quite unpleasant, and she couldn't begin to imagine what they had gone through.

Admitting defeat, Molly got off her bike and pushed it. Alex circled her for a few paces, before he also dismounted.

'How are you enjoying it so far?' he asked her.

'Brioude? It's pretty.'

Not Brioude, although I agree, it is pretty. I was talking about the Tour.'

'It's beginning to grow on me,' she conceded.

He nodded once. 'Good. I was hoping it would.'

'Ooh, look, what a fantastic old church!' she exclaimed, in a blatant attempt to change the subject. What was she supposed to say? Especially since she'd not made her mind up whether to stay or go.

143

'Have you been avoiding me?' he asked, ignoring her feigned enthusiasm.

'A little,' she admitted, having seen very little of him yesterday and the day before. She was basing her avoidance of him on the premise that if she didn't have anything to do with him, she'd be able to push her treacherous feelings to the back of her mind.

It hadn't worked.

And today wasn't helping either. What had possessed her to agree to this little trip with him? Did she *like* torture?

'I understand,' he said, and she hated him for being so reasonable, especially when she, herself, didn't understand anything anymore.

They stuck to safer topics from then on, talking about the race (naturally), music, and films, as they dawdled around the charming old streets. The enticing smells of coffee and food from the pavement cafes wafted across her nose (food was another subject they tended to avoid) and although she dearly would have loved to suggest they stop for refreshments, she didn't.

When they'd had their fill of the pretty streets and occasional squares, they got on their bikes once more and slowly cycled back the way they came.

'Thanks, that was fun,' Molly said when they reached the hotel. It really had been, even though her backside was smarting a bit and her legs felt somewhat achy.

And being on a bike, experiencing a little part of Alex's world, made her feel closer to him. Which was dangerous, because being close to Alexander Duvall was the last thing she needed to be. Not if she was to survive the next two weeks with her heart intact.

CHAPTER 19

Saint-Étienne to Brioude, then Brioude to Saint-Flour were both hilly stages, carrying on from before the rest day. After that, there were two stages which were mostly flat.

Molly settled back into her routine after the rest day, trying once more to stay out of Alex's way – not easy when she had to lay her hands on him as part of her job, or during mealtimes, or meetings. She managed to keep any contact with him professional and Alex seemed to respect that, almost to the point that Molly began to wonder if she had imagined the fleeting closeness between them. Perhaps he had simply been friendly, and her attraction towards him and the unnatural, almost holiday feeling of being on the Tour had contributed to her fantasy that he felt the same way about her.

But when Mick asked her if everything was all right between her and Alex, Molly realised she might have taken her professionalism a bit too far.

They were on the way to Toulouse and the finish line. La Ville Rose, or "the pink city" as the town was known because of its buildings constructed out of terracotta bricks, was the fourth largest in France, and to Molly it felt strange to be in a city again after

145

spending so much time in rural France.

As Damien tried to find their hotel, Molly was fascinated by the city's wide, serene river and the multitude of narrow streets which were crisscrossed by wide boulevards. As with many of the towns and villages she had seen along the way, there was a wonderful old church at the heart of the city, and lots of cafes and restaurants.

Mick asked her again, this time a little more forcefully. 'What's up with you and Alex?'

'Nothing,' she replied after a too-long pause.

'It doesn't seem like it from where I'm sitting,' he replied. 'You've got a face like a slapped arse, and he's been moping around like a teenage girl. Have you had a lover's tiff?'

'Of course not!' Molly was appalled that Mick could think such a thing.

'Hmm.' He didn't sound convinced.

'It's not allowed,' she added primly.

'There's a lot of things what ain't allowed, but it don't stop them from happening.'

'I wouldn't do anything to jeopardise Alex's Tour de France,' she retorted. Her cheeks felt hot and she knew she was blushing.

'I know you wouldn't, darl.'

There was a "but" – she could hear it in his voice. He didn't say anything further though, and she didn't push him, preferring not to talk about it.

Molly had a concern of her own, and it flitted around her mind for the rest of the day and all through the next one – if Mick had noticed, then other people were bound to have noticed too...

CHAPTER 20

'There's no need to rush off today,' Mick said to Molly as the last of the riders climbed aboard the team bus and set off for the start of the race. He pulled out one of the race bibles, an information book which the Tour supplied to every team, and opened it to the Lourdes to Laruns stage. 'We're here. We need to be there in a few hours' time.' He drew a line with his finger from the start to the finish. 'This is the way the race will go.' He traced a route in the opposite direction, drawing a large loop. 'See? We can get to Laruns in an hour, so how do you fancy bunking off for a bit?'

'What did you have in mind?' she asked cautiously, and Mick treated her to one of his wide, happy grins.

'You can't come all the way to Lourdes without seeing something of the place,' he said. 'And I think we could do with all the prayers we can get.'

'Are we allowed?'

'Yeah,' he said expansively. Jakob and Damien said they'll grab a coffee or three and some cake, while we do the touristy bit.'

Molly could hardly contain her delight. She had read so much about Lourdes, and had been disappointed to find that the hotel was too far away

147

from the town centre for her to sneak out in the middle of the night and go exploring.

After loading her case into the truck which transported their luggage (along with goodness knows what else), Molly hurried to the car and strapped on her seatbelt.

'Someone is super eager today,' Jakob said and Molly smiled happily at him.

She felt like she was bunking off school; not that she had ever bunked off (OK, she had once, but hadn't found it all that much fun and had been bored witless), but this trip had an almost illicit feel to it.

Mick sat next to her as he usually did, with Damien driving and Jakob in the passenger seat. 'Right, listen up, fellas. I'm taking our Moll to see Bernadette Soubirous. You can come with us, or you can grab a coffee and a sanger. It's up to you.'

'Sanger?' Molly asked.

'Aussie for sandwich,' Mick explained to her, then said to the other swannies, 'Or, if you want to be all French, you can treat yourself to a crepe,' he added.

'Isn't she dead?' Damien asked.

'Who?' Mick leaned forward and scratched his head.

'Bernadette Soubirous.'

'Oh, her? Yup.' He dragged his phone out of his pocket and, after poking at the screen and frowning, he announced, 'She was buried in 1879, so I'd say she's deffo dead. TB got her.'

'Tuberculosis?' Molly said.

'That's the fella!'

Molly shot the swannie a sideways glance. There was something not quite right with Mick today. It might be her imagination, but he'd suddenly become

148

much more Australian than he normally was. She was accustomed to his accent, but today he seemed to have cranked it up a notch, and was throwing in slang too. And he'd never once called her Moll until today. Strange…

'Isn't she the girl who saw visions of the Virgin Mary?' Molly mused.

Mick consulted his phone again. 'It doesn't seem they can agree on who or what she saw,' he said after a pause to read whatever page he'd managed to load. 'It could be.'

'I didn't know you are religious,' Damien said. 'Wouldn't you prefer a… what did you call it? Singer?'

'Sanger. And no, I wouldn't. I told you, I'm taking Moll to see the sights.' He turned to her. 'We haven't got much time, so it's up to you – do you wanna see her birthplace or the grotto where she was supposed to have had her visions?'

'Actually, can we go to the Château Fort,' she asked, and laughed when Mick did a kind of double-take.

'Where?' he wanted to know.

'It's on the edge of town but apparently it has the most spectacular views over the city,' she told him.

'Er, I suppose.' Mick looked a little put out, and Molly instantly felt contrite. What if Mick really wanted to see the grotto or the Basilica and he was using her as an excuse?

'We don't have to go to the Château Fort,' she said. 'I honestly don't mind either the grotto or her birthplace.'

'Make up your mind,' Damien said. 'I need to know which way to go.'

'Turn left here, then left again,' Mick told him after

a swift consultation of his phone, and in the space of a couple of roads they were travelling down narrow one-way streets, the houses on either side sporting shutters on the windows and tiny Juliette balconies. As they went further into the town, the houses were replaced by little shops with apartments above, and every so often the delicious smells of coffee, or baking, or herbs and garlic drifted in through the open car windows.

Without warning, they came into an open area, with several cars parked in the middle and lined with trees.

'That way. Go down there,' Mick said, pointing, his arm nearly smacking Damien in the side of the head. Then once more they were plunging into an even tinier street, this one with room for only one car, and Molly held her breath, praying they wouldn't meet anything coming the other way.

'There!' Mick cried. 'Up ahead. Do you see it?'

Molly stared straight ahead, concentrating. At the end of the little street was what looked like a huge obelisk, a massive square wall of a tower, shining white in the midday sun, and above that, perched on an enormous slab of rock, was a turret, a conical one, with a round pointy roof, the sort Molly always imagined when she thought of fairy-tale castles. Radiating out from it was a stone-built wall, circumnavigating the top of the rocky outcrop.

Without warning, the little street opened up into a larger area, and Damien aimed for a parking space like an Exocet missile and slid into it.

When the car came to a swift halt, Mick pointed to a small café opposite the tower, which appeared even bigger now they were at its base. Damien and Jakob, after craning their necks to stare up at the tump of rock, headed hastily towards a table and coffee.

'Wave when you get to the top,' Jakob said. 'I will look out for you.'

'We'll be back in an hour,' Mick promised. He checked the time. 'The riders should be at the start by now and halfway through their warm up. The race kicks off in forty-five minutes, but there shouldn't be much action before the Col d'Aspin, so we should be OK for a while. Give us a bell, if anything happens that we should know about, yeah?'

'Okay,' one of them called, far too busy settling themselves in their seats to be concerned with Mick and Molly's adventure.

Molly chuckled to herself – Mick and Molly's adventure sounded like a children's story, and she felt as excited as a kid herself. This was more like it! If every day was like this, a couple of hours work followed by a spot of sightseeing, before going back to work, she'd be very happy indeed.

'What's the tower for?' she asked, 'and how do we get up there?' She pointed to the monument high above them perched on its pinnacle of almost sheer stone.

'We can walk up those steps over there,' Mick said. 'Or we can take the elevator. We've not got much time, so…?'

'The lift it is, then,' Molly declared, scampering off with Mick hot on her heels.

'Oh, wow!' she cried when she got to the top and saw the city spread out below, with the mountains all around.

But it wasn't just the view that captivated her, it was the age of the Château itself and the history it exuded. As they began to explore, they came across information boards dotted every so often on the path, which were helpfully displayed in English as well as a few other languages. Molly was fascinated to read that the fortress was over a thousand years old and had never been conquered. Looking at its location, she could see why! Charlemagne had given it a go (she'd heard of him from somewhere – wasn't he called the Father of Europe for uniting most of Western Europe in the Dark Ages?) but hadn't succeeded, and she read that a couple of others had tried since and had also failed.

But what she loved most about this incredible place (and she was so glad she'd opted to visit this and not the more touristy Basilica or grotto) was the totally unexpected miniature buildings which were set within the botanical gardens. And don't get her started on the museum. Although they were strapped for time, Molly did manage to persuade Mick to venture inside, and the displays depicting historical life in the fort itself, as well as the Pyrenees as a whole, was well worth it.

'We really have to go now,' Mick insisted. 'I'm sorry, darl, I'd love to stay longer myself, but we've got work to do.'

Molly let out a resigned sigh. 'I know. Don't think I'm not grateful for you bringing me here, because I am.' She stretched up to plant a kiss on his cheek. 'Thank you so much for doing this for me.'

'Oh, it wasn't me— Er…' Mick rubbed his cheek where her lips had touched his skin and shuffled awkwardly.

'Mick, what's going on?'

'Come on, darl, we've gotta go,' the swannie said,

and began walking away but stopped when he realised she wasn't following. 'Please, we've gotta make a move.'

She shook her head. 'Not until you tell me.'

'Aww, you can't do this to me. I promised.'

'Who did you promise?' Molly had her suspicions but she wanted to hear him say it.

'He'll have my guts for garters,'

'Who will?' She crossed her arms and glared at him.

'I'll tell you when we're in the car,' Mick wheedled.

'I'm not falling for that. You'll tell me now.'

Mick grimaced. 'If I tell you, will you promise not to let on?'

A smile curled around her lips as she said, 'I promise.'

'OK, it's Alex.'

'I knew it!'

'If you knew, why did you put me through all this?' He reached for her and grabbed her elbow, and Molly let him steer her downwards.

'I didn't actually *know*, but I guessed,' she admitted. 'I wanted you to say his name, so I could be sure.' That was why the Aussie had been even more Aussie than usual today, she realised. It had been nerves. 'What I want to know is, why?'

'Aww, don't ask me that.'

Molly stopped suddenly and dug her heels in, physically as well as metaphorically – she was going nowhere until she had the whole story.

'OK, OK! It's because he can't take you himself, and he feels a bit of a mongrel for making you think you'd get to see the sights. The only sights you've been seeing is Elias's scrawny legs, and I wouldn't wish that on my worst enemy.'

'Did Alex really say that?'

'About Elias's legs? Nah, that's all mine. Now will you get moving.'

Molly trotted to keep up with him, all thoughts of the fort driven out of her head by the revelation that Mick had just blurted out.

'I mean, did he really say he feels a bit of a mongrel?' She wasn't entirely certain she knew what Mick meant when he said "mongrel", but she thought she got the gist of it.

'He did. He feels he persuaded you to join BeSpoke under false pretences. And he feels right bad about it.'

Molly smiled softly. 'He needn't,' she said. 'I'm really glad I came.'

It was Mick's turn to stop. 'But? I'm hearing a *but*.'

'I'm not sure if this life is for me,' she admitted, reluctantly.

'It's not always as manic as this,' Mick said, as they started walking again. 'And you do get to see something of the country you're in. Sometimes. Especially if we're at one of the training camps. Majorca is lovely in December. You'll like it,' he added confidently.

'I'm sure I will.'

'There's that *but* again. Go on, spill. I've told you my secret, now it's your turn.'

Her secret was quite a bit bigger and more explosive than Mick's and she wasn't sure it would be prudent to tell him anything. Anyway, what could she say – I'm not sure I'm committed to this whole bike racing thing, oh, and by the way, I've fallen for one of the riders? Yeah, that would go down really well.

CHAPTER 21

As she stared out of the window, her mouth open in awe at the scenery unfolding in front of her eyes, Molly decided that the Pyrenees must be one of the most beautiful and breath-taking places on earth.

Driving out of Lourdes and taking a more direct route to Laruns than the riders, half of Molly's attention was on the car's TV screen and the other was on the hilly landscape outside, with its pretty almost Swiss-like hamlets and chalets. As the car ate up the miles, the valleys seemed to get deeper and the mountains seemed to get higher until, in the distance, she could see rocky, towering peaks of purple and grey. The road they were travelling on became narrower and the scenery more like the Alps than she had expected, and she found she couldn't tear herself away from the scenery.

'Here they go,' Jakob announced. He'd hardly taken his eyes off the TV monitor from the moment they'd set off from Lourdes. 'The Col d'Aspin.'

Although Molly hadn't been watching the race, she had been listening to the running commentary. The Col d'Aspin was a Category 1 climb, a 1500 metre ascent over 12 kilometres. It would be a challenge for

155

most of the riders, and Molly knew that the teams with the sprinters wouldn't fare so well on these taxing hills. The BeSpoke riders, however, were looking forward to it – all of them, Alex and Tim especially.

Molly thought they must all be slightly mad. Every now and again she would glance at the screen to see riders gasping for air as they fought gravity to drag themselves and their bikes up slopes she wouldn't even dream of walking up. The scenery though was stunning, although she had a feeling none of the cyclists was in any state to enjoy it.

'Tim's doing well,' Mick pointed out. 'He's still got five of the guys with him, Alex included.' He gave her a sly look when he said Alex's name, and Molly was careful not to react.

Apart from the three BeSpoke riders who had used up all their energy to lead the team so far and were now towards the back of the peloton, the rest of the guys were in a strung-out line, one behind the other, with Tim last but one. His team mates were not only there to give him moral support and encouragement, they also provided the drag to reduce his energy output and carried the extra food and water he would need to get him through the race. The other BeSpoke swannies were stationed at strategic positions further along the course to hand out water, energy bars, and gels to fuel the cyclists.

This mountain was only the first of three horrific climbs up to the tops of some of the Pyrenees' finest mountain passes during this stage, and it was the smallest, so BeSpoke were intending to conserve their energy for the next mountain – the Col du Tourmalet.

Last night, during the team meeting, Molly noticed

how they said the mountain's name with a kind of awe and reverence, and she learnt that this was a monster of a climb, capable of bringing the greatest of riders to an almost complete stop.

There had been major discussions regarding wattage and power output compared to energy input, and where any breakaways might happen, and whose team had the climber on the best form, and which rider was the best descender. Yeah, that really was a thing, Molly discovered. Apparently, a cyclist could be fantastic riding up those stupidly high mountain roads, and could reach the top before anyone else, but if he was a bit timid on the equally stupid and scarily dangerous downhills, then any time which he might have gained going up, would be lost when he came back down. Molly had been told repeatedly that the Tour de France was won or lost on the mountain stages, and today she thought she might see the truth of that for herself.

Not that BeSpoke were going to win the Tour, but they were in with a chance of winning one of the stages, and this was the one they had decided to go for.

Most of the time, the discussion over tactics passed her by; the only thing she was interested in was how the race could affect the riders physically and what she might expect to find after they had crossed the finish line. But she had soaked up enough race-speak to know that Chuck-n-Greg wanted Tim, Alex, Elias, and Carlos to break away from the main body of riders at the bottom of the Col du Tourmalet, in order to give Tim a fighting chance of being somewhere near the front when they came over the top of the pass. Alex would then lead him down the wickedly steep descent and onto the next and final mountain of the stage. From there on, Alex would have probably used up all his energy, and Tim would be on his own.

If Tim didn't get the stage win he was after, at least the cameras would be on him for some of the time and BeSpoke would be pleased with the advertising.

'Oh my God, look at all those people,' Molly said. 'Is that a guy in a *mankini*? And why is he wearing a purple wig? It is a wig, isn't it?' she asked doubtfully, as the camera followed the bloke along the road. He was trying to sprint alongside the race leader and yelling at him (Molly had no idea whether it was encourage the rider or to abuse him), his naked backside jiggling about like a jelly on a wobble-board. It was enough to put anyone off their dinner.

'I forgot, you've not really seen supporters like this have you?' Mick laughed. 'There's something about the mountain stages of every big race that brings out the nutjobs. If you think this is bad, just wait until you see the idiots who line the roads on the Col du Tourmalet.'

Molly was horrified and riveted at the same time. She was used to seeing supporters and spectators along the roadside, especially near the finish line, but this was something else.

Men, women, and children crowded the sides of the narrow, bendy roads. Many looked as though they might have been there for days – tents had been erected on any remotely flattish areas, campervans listed drunkenly as they balanced precariously on the edges of the roads, cars with picnic tables alongside were everywhere, and cyclists had propped their bikes up against any available rock or left them sprawled haphazardly on the grass.

Flags, many of which Molly didn't recognise, were waved in the riders' faces and people pushed and shoved to get as close as they could to the cyclists, barely leaving enough room for them to get through, despite the race cars and motorbikes ahead of the race leaders trying to clear a path through the yelling, screaming throng.

It was a wonder no one got hurt, especially as Molly guessed that many of the picnic baskets probably contained something considerably stronger than water or soda.

Her heart in her mouth, she watched as rider after rider slowed to little more than a crawl as the road steepened, and she admired both their tenacity and their control; tenacity for tackling a road like that in the first place, and control because not one of the cyclists got off and punched any of the more annoying spectators in the nose!

As well as mankini-man, there was a Scooby Doo, several really odd costumes which she could only assume were some kind of national dress, more wigs than you can shake a stick at, and lots of men who had taken their tops off and liked to run up the road alongside successive riders while wind-milling their T-shirts above their heads.

It was sheer, utter chaos, and Molly was terrified that one of the riders was going to come off his bike. But just when she was certain the worst was about to happen barriers appeared, hemming the excitable spectators behind them and giving the cyclists a clear run to the top of the mountain.

Then they were over the top of the pass and there was only a moment when the camera panned across the fantastic view, before the riders were hurtling at breakneck speeds down the steep, winding roads, and she had her heart in her mouth once more.

It went on for miles, the riders hunkering down over their handlebars to avoid as much wind resistance as possible, their bikes listing dangerously as they leaned into the corners, one knee stuck out at a right-angle for balance (how a rider didn't scrape it on the tarmac and lose half his skin, Molly simply didn't know) until eventually the road levelled out and she could breathe again.

Damien and Jakob high-fived each other, and Molly guessed that BeSpoke must have given a good account of themselves.

She risked tearing her gaze away from the screen and peered out of the window.

'We're now travelling on the same road the race will be on later,' Mick told her.

And for the first time Molly could nearly appreciate what Alex and the others had to contend with. She could imagine them pedalling up this steady incline, powering into this corner or that, and all the while she was eternally grateful that a car was doing the work for her and that she was able to sit back, relax, and enjoy the scenery which, she had to admit, was worth coming all this way for.

Another look at the screen showed the riders coming into an impossibly pretty picturesque village with a gorgeous little church adorned with hanging baskets, and people squashed up against the walls of the buildings because there were no pavements. She squealed with delight.

'Look! It's so pretty,' she cried.

'That hairpin bend will catch some poor bugger

out,' Mick said in response, referring to the way the road doubled back on itself in front of the church, and Molly rolled her eyes.

Trust him! Actually, she might have guessed that almost everyone else associated with the Tour would be thinking the same thing, and not appreciating the beauty of the place. Heathens, the lot of them.

Nevertheless, she held her breath until everyone had safely negotiated it and the race was back on a steady uphill drag towards the next mountain, the Col du Tourmalet.

A sudden shadow fell over the cyclists and they seemed to be travelling underneath some weird concrete structure, almost like a tunnel on one side and on the top, but the other side was open. And there was another one up ahead. But the really weird thing was that the constructions didn't go through anything. They were just there, crouching over the road.

'What are those things?' she asked.

'Something to do with avalanches,' Mick said. 'They are put up in places at most risk, so an avalanche will sweep over the road and across the top of it and give any motorists a fighting chance of staying alive until they're found.'

Crikey! The thought of so much snow was completely alien to her. They didn't get more than a couple of inches at a time in the Midlands. But even that small amount could bring everything to a standstill. She couldn't imagine these barren Alpine-type meadows blanketed in several feet of the white stuff. But when the race swept through the odd little town of Bagnères-de-Bigorre with its strange mixture of pretty chalets and concrete buildings which seemed more like prison-blocks than hotels and she saw the ski lifts, did she realise people came to this area to ski, and she thought how lucky they were.

The view out of her own window was wildly beautiful; mountains and valleys as far as the eye could see, and all of it a lush green and dotted with trees. But once again her attention kept straying back to the monitor and the drama unfolding on it, as riders jockeyed for position on the narrow roads, and the helicopter hovered over one of the ski lifts, giving viewers a birds-eye shot.

The riders hadn't yet reached the top of this dreaded Col and Molly didn't think the road appeared terribly steep, but the gradient was relentless and had been going on for miles. She could only imagine what it must be doing to the cyclists. Then one of the cameramen on the back of a motorbike swung his lens back down the road, and she understood just how steep it was. Dear God! How they managed to keep pedalling, she honestly didn't know. No wonder the name Col du Tourmalet was said in awe – the climb to the top of the pass was brutal indeed!

More ski lifts, more switchbacks, and they were still going up, and all along the route were spectators, shouting and waving their fists (Mick explained that they weren't being aggressive, but encouraging), running alongside the riders and waving their flags. And once more, Molly cringed and winced as people came too close, the crowds who were flocking the road only parting reluctantly at the very last second to let a cyclist through. Mayhem didn't even begin to describe it.

Without warning, walls rose up either side of the road and barriers appeared, hemming the spectators in and giving the riders some relief from the relentless support.

'Look, there's Elias,' Jakob said, as the camera panned across several people sporting a variety of team jackets and holding out musettes, the little cotton bags containing food and drinks for the riders. A designated cyclist from each team slowed enough to grab the bag and sling it over his shoulder, distributing the contents later, when he had the chance.

The helicopter zoomed in to the crest of the pass and focused on a giant silver statue of a cyclist perched on a wall, but then the stage leaders were past it and over the summit of the Col and hurtling headlong as the road fell away, the camera on the chopper following them down.

Molly felt sick, especially when she saw Alex about ten riders from the front and leading Tim at a ridiculous speed as he negotiated the bends with their terrifying drops. The rest of BeSpoke had been left behind, their energy used up to get Tim to the top of this climb, and it looked like most of the other teams were in the same position, with only a rider or two near the front of the race.

She bit her lip as Alex, closely followed by Tim, slowed marginally to sweep around a hairpin bend, the road practically doubling back on itself. If anyone were to come off now...

CHAPTER 22

P hew, thank God that was over. Molly's nerves were totally shredded by the time the road had levelled out somewhat for a while (a very short while) and began to rise again as the Tour made its winding way up to the last mountain pass of the day, the Col d'Aubisque, another massive climb, but not quite as high as the last one, rising a mere 1700 metres above sea level, compared to the Tourmalet's 2100, although the distance was almost the same.

Relaxing a little, Molly concentrated on the drive into Laruns, another typically pretty village nestled in a small valley and surrounded by wooded mountains. As expected, the streets were packed with tourists (who had come for the outdoor pursuits), spectators, Tour officials and team staff, and Damien had to force his way slowly through the crammed streets to get to the area set aside for the various team vehicles.

Molly loved the chocolate-box chalets with their window boxes and hanging baskets, and the marble fountain in the square, and the cafes with tables spilling out onto the pavement. There was even a sixteenth-century church, and further into the streets surrounding the square, Molly noticed the lack of pavements that seemed typical in many French villages, giving the whole place a charming, rustic feel.

There were shuttered windows everywhere and pretty arched doorways, and then the car was out of the tiny streets and onto a road with detached houses and large gardens, until finally they left the village behind and were surrounded by open fields with the mountains as a stunning backdrop.

Eventually, they arrived at the finish line and Damien spotted the BeSpoke bus and trucks and headed towards them.

'Where were you?' asked Kieron. 'We thought you had decided you'd had enough, and you'd gone home.'

Mick lifted his chin. 'Our Moll wanted to see a bit of Lourdes, so we did a quick detour.'

Molly opened her mouth to deny the false charge, then closed it again. Maybe it was for the best if everyone assumed the Lourdes sight-seeing trip was her idea and not Alex's, so she nodded and smiled and tried to look as innocent as possible. Until Mick nudged her with his elbow and she realised she was probably overdoing it.

She was on the bus, doing a check of the supplies (although she had replenished them only that morning) when Mick appeared in the doorway.

'I know I've asked you before, but are you sure there isn't something going on between you and Alex that I should know about?' he asked, his usual sunny smile absent.

Molly put down the tape she had been holding and turned to face the swannie. 'Not really.'

'But you wish there was?'

'And as I've said before, I wouldn't do anything about it. I know any relationship is frowned on between staff and riders and I know he doesn't need any distractions right now. You don't need to keep telling me.'

'Too damned right, he doesn't,' Mick agreed. 'But there's something I've got to get off my chest.' He paused, fiddling with the door handle, and Molly could see that he was nervous. It was catching – she was nervous too, now, and she had no idea why.

'I've known Alex for a few years. I've swannied for him on and off, since when he was a youngster, coming up through the ranks. I've never seen him like this.'

'Like what?' Molly licked her lips, her mouth suddenly dry.

'All loved up.'

'Excuse me?'

'You know, panting over a sheila.'

Molly stared at him.

'OK, not panting, but all lovey-dovey, like.'

Molly continued to stare. She wasn't sure what Mick was trying to tell her.

'I'm not saying this too good, am I? I don't mean he's lusting after your bod, though I'm sure he is, because who wouldn't? You're a good-looker and— Aw, bugger. I think he's in love,' he blurted.

Molly blinked. 'Who with?'

'You, ya drongo.'

'Me?' Molly sat down on the treatment table, her legs suddenly too weak to support her.

'Yeah, you. I'm only telling you this because I don't want to see him get hurt.'

What was she supposed to say to that? 'I don't, either,' she replied, finally.

'He doesn't need any distractions,' he repeated yet

again. 'Not when he's riding his heart out. He's in the best form he's ever been in and I don't want anything to scupper that.'

'Like me?'

He nodded.

'Should I resign?'

'God, no! Just... I don't know.'

'Carry on as I am?'

'Yeah, that might do it. Look, Moll, you're a lovely girl and if you feel half as much about him as he does about you, then you need to keep your distance. Until the Tour is over, at least. After that...?' He shrugged.

'There won't be an "after that",' she said. 'I'm probably going to go back home. No, not probably – I *am* going back to England. It's been fun, but, you know.' She shrugged.

'Bloody hard work?'

'Yeah.'

'It's not a holiday, is it?' He gave her a narrow look. 'Did you think it was going to be?'

'I packed a bikini,' she replied, by way of an explanation, and he burst out laughing.

'No wonder Alex is feeling so guilty,' he chortled, then instantly sobered. 'But it's not just guilt that he's feeling, is it?'

Molly didn't know what she was supposed to say to that, so she didn't say anything at all.

'Do you want to tell me how you feel about him?' he asked. 'I know you feel something, I can tell.'

'I'm not sure.' She gazed down at her hands, which were twisting in her lap. 'It might be love, or else it might just be the newness of all this.' She swept an arm in the air. 'Like a sort of holiday romance.'

'See how you feel when you get back home, eh?'

Mick suggested.

'It won't make any difference,' she said. 'He'll be somewhere abroad, training for the next big race, and I'll be in Worcester. It won't work.'

'Who says? Of course it can work. Tim's got a wife, so has Pietro. Elias is engaged and Carlos has been going out with his missus for yonks.'

Yonks? Molly shook her head, but she got the drift.

'Hell, even I'm hitched,' Mick announced.

Her head jerked up in surprise. 'You are?'

'Yeah, four years now.' Pride and love glowed on his face.

'What's her name?'

'Zara. She's a Kiwi, but she lives in Spain. That's where our home is.'

'I didn't know.'

'Why should you? When we're on a tour nothing else gets talked about other than the race.'

'So I noticed,' she said. 'When do you actually—'

'Mick! Turn the TV on.' Jakob dashed up the steps and into the coach, his face pale. 'Tim's crashed out. And it's not looking good!'

CHAPTER 23

Mick let out an oath and flicked the switch on the TV screen at the front of the bus.

'Oh dear, oh dear, oh dear, it's not looking too good for Tim Anderson,' the commentator was saying. Incongruously, the footage on the TV was of the first few riders careering down the road. *'I don't think Duvall is aware that his team leader has crashed out. Wait a minute, he's on his radio, and he's slowed up. His sports director must be telling him to keep going, because Duvall's head is back down. What do you think Eamon?'*

'Let's look at that awful crash again. Do we know how he is?'

Molly felt sick as the screen showed Alex with Tim behind him approaching a bend. To her, it didn't look any different to any of the other bends she'd watched the riders negotiate – a rocky wall on the one side, a drop on the other. Many of the roads didn't even have a barrier between the tarmac and the drop, but this one did.

She watched Alex swing towards the outside of the road, taking the straightest possible line, Tim following a couple of wheel lengths behind.

Then Tim seemed to slide. In slow motion, she watched his bike slip out from underneath him and the low wall getting closer and closer…

He slammed into it, momentum taking him up and over the barrier, then he was gone.

'Oh my God!' Molly let out a sob.

Mick grabbed for the radio. 'Chuck? Chuck? It's Mick.'

The radio crackled into life. 'We don't know, we don't know. The Tour doctor is at the scene. We can't get to him.'

'What's going on? What's happening?' Molly cried, tears trickling down her face. She didn't think she'd ever get the vision of Tim being flung over the wall, his body thrown God knows how far down the slope.

'Chuck and Greg must be stuck behind some riders, and can't get past them. Luckily the Tour doctor was closer,' Mick explained.

'But, how is he?' Molly wanted to know.

Mick, all trace of colour leached from his face, said, 'You know as much as we do, darl.'

'Ask him, ask Chuck,' she insisted.

'We need to keep the airway free. We'll know something when they know something.'

'Why hasn't Alex gone back to help him?' she wailed. 'He can't just carry on as if nothing has happened.'

'Look, Moll, by the time Alex knew Tim wasn't on his wheel, he could have been a kilometre or more down the road. Even if he wanted to, he couldn't turn around and cycle back up, not with other riders coming at him as fast as bloody bullets. He'd be a danger to himself and to them.'

'But he didn't even stop!'

'No, he didn't. Greg would have told him to keep going. That's the way it is.'

'What if Tim is...?' She couldn't bring herself to say the word.

'Don't even go there,' Mick warned, glaring at her. 'He'll be OK.'

It was an agonising wait for news, and none of them seemed to know what to do with themselves. Every so often another team member would pass by, with a sympathetic nod or a pat on the shoulder. Several members of the press, noticeable by their bright yellow lanyards, began to hover, and once again Molly was astonished at how easily the press and the public could mingle with the staff.

One by one the riders came in, and she waited anxiously for Alex. Mick dashed into the road the second Alex sailed over the finishing line, pushing bike and rider towards their truck with the turbos waiting alongside. Someone, probably a mechanic, had removed one of them, so there were only seven machines and not eight. The sight of them made her heart miss a beat.

She watched Alex undo his helmet and she let out a soft cry. His face was whiter than she had ever seen it, his pain emotional not physical this time, as he staggered slowly towards the turbo and clambered onto it, his head hanging.

Unable to take any more, Molly went back to the bus to wait for him. He'd be a while yet, she knew, what with being weighed, the drugs testing that was so much a part of the backstage stuff, the shower... and probably the press. Some idiot was bound to ask him how he was feeling.

After half an hour, Keiron came to find her.

'Well?' she demanded.

'Suspected broken pelvis, head injury, broken leg.

He's being taken to hospital in Toulouse. Henno has gone with him.'

Molly closed her eyes. Poor, poor Tim. When she opened them again it was to find Alex standing in front of her. The ashen despair had cleared from his face, leaving weariness and sorrow behind.

'Are you OK?' she asked.

He nodded, a little uncertainly, she thought.

'Let's have a look at you,' she said, and he obediently hopped on the treatment table. 'What happens now?' she asked after a few minutes, during which the only noise was the steady hum of her ultrasound equipment

She sensed rather than saw his shrug. 'We go to Montréjeau tomorrow. It's another rest day,' he said.

It made sense to move onto the next hotel, because they were already booked into it, and it would give Chuck-n-Greg time to sort out the logistics of how to get the riders and the rest of the staff home so far ahead of schedule.

Molly tried not to think too hard about how she felt about having the Tour cut short, but she couldn't help it. Although she had more or less made up her mind to return to her old life, she wasn't quite ready to give this one up yet. There was still another six days of racing left, including the last day in Paris, and she was disappointed to miss it.

What was really upsetting her though, was knowing she would be unlikely to see Alex again after tomorrow, and she felt such a cow for feeling like this when poor Tim was so badly injured. She hated herself for being so selfish; there were far more important things to think about than her bruised emotions.

'Thank you for today,' she murmured. She hadn't planned on letting on to Alex that she knew what he had done but considering tomorrow might be the last time she'd see him, she decided she might as well.

Session over, Alex sat up, his legs dangling over the edge of the table as he reached for his T-shirt. He turned his head to look at her. 'Did Mick tell you?'

'Not really,' she said, not wanting to drop Mick in it. 'I sort of guessed. He can't keep a secret for toffee.'

'I'm just sorry I couldn't take you to Lourdes myself. What did you think of the Basilica? I've never seen it.'

'Neither have I. I talked Mick into taking me to Chateau Fort instead.'

'There's a fort?'

'Yep. A great big one sitting on a rock in the middle of the town.' She hesitated. 'It kind of reminded me of Mont Saint Michel.'

'But with an ugly brash Aussie instead of a handsome sophisticated Brit showing you around,' he quipped with the weakest of smiles.

He stood, less than a foot away from her in the cramped space, caught her gaze and held it. 'I mean it. I wish I had been with you.'

Oh, what the hell! This might be the silliest thing she had ever done, considering she would most likely be tucked up in her own bed at home tomorrow night. 'So do I.'

Molly had no idea how it happened, but one second he had been over there and the next he was over here, and his arms were around her, and his lips were on hers, and—

She broke away and stepped back, colour rushing to her cheeks, her heart pounding and her body trembling.

'I'm sorry,' he said, and stepped towards the partition.

At some point during the last half hour, everyone else had boarded the bus and it was on the move, but only now did she notice the noise of the engine and the movement of the vehicle.

He stopped, one hand on the little handle and turned back to her. 'Actually, I'm not sorry at all. I've been wanting to do that since the day we met.'

Then he was gone, the door sliding shut behind him with a soft click.

'I've wanted you to do that, too,' she said to the empty air, realising it was the truth.

A lone tear gathered in the corner of one eye, spilt over, and trickled down her face. What had she done? And how on earth was she supposed to slot back into her old life after that kiss?

Oh dear, she'd really, really messed things up for herself, hadn't she?

CHAPTER 24

The hotel in Montréjeau wasn't in the village at all. It was on the outskirts and by the time the BeSpoke bus arrived, the swannies had already checked the whole team in and Molly saw that she had a double room to herself again when she went to freshen up, and by the time she was ready to look over the remainder of the riders, Greg had some news.

'Tim's got a lateral compression fracture to the pelvis, but the good news is that there's no internal bleeding and his doctors aren't considering operating on it at this stage. He's got a concussion but they're not too worried about it, and once he's got the all-clear on his head, they're going to operate and put a pin in his leg. He's going to be out of action for at least two months, but hopefully he'll be fit enough to join us in Majorca in November.'

'The training camp,' Mick hissed in her ear, seeing her blank expression as the impromptu meeting broke up.

'You don't honestly think he'll carry on cycling after this, do you?' she asked.

He laughed. 'Of course, why wouldn't he? Riders have suffered worse injuries than this and have raced again.'

'Molly, can I have a word?' Greg was motioning to her and she told Mick she'd catch him later.

'Tim's wife, Gina, is flying out later this evening.' He rubbed a hand across his face and she noticed how weary he looked. It had been a tough day all round. 'I'm going to pick her up from the airport and take her to the hospital to see Tim, then bring both her and Henno back. I've asked, but there aren't any spare rooms here, and I don't want her on her own in a strange hotel with no one she knows.'

'Of course, she can stay with me,' Molly said immediately, her heart going out to the poor woman.

'Someone is flying out from headquarters in the morning to help organise Tim's return to the UK, so it's just for tonight, until we can get her sorted with a hotel in Toulouse.'

'I can stay there with her, if you like. I don't have to go straight back home.'

Greg cocked his head. 'Excuse me? I don't understand. God, I'm so tired I could sleep for a week. In fact, that's what I intend to do when this damned race is over.'

'I can stay with Gina in Toulouse,' Molly repeated with a frown. 'For as long as she needs me.'

'Don't worry about Gina, she's a tough lady. Anyway, you're needed here – there's still five days of racing left. Have I told you what a sterling job you're doing? The guys really seem to like you, and speaking of liking you, Alex—'

'What do you mean, I'm needed here?' Molly interrupted. 'I thought we'd all be going home after Tim…' She ground to a halt. 'We're not leaving, are we?'

'Good lord, no! Whatever gave you that idea? The race goes on, Molly. BeSpoke has invested too much into the team to let a crash stop play.'

'But we've not got a team leader, and surely Tim wouldn't expect us to carry on as though nothing has happened?'

'That's exactly what he *does* expect. And as for the team leader…' He nodded to himself. 'I'll see you after dinner.'

Shocked, Molly went to set up her temporary treatment room. Having a spare bed in her bedroom was coming in doubly handy today, but she still couldn't believe that Team BeSpoke were carrying on as normal as if nothing had happened.

She had mentally prepared herself for going back to England sooner than she had anticipated and now she had to get her head around staying in France for the next week. And seeing Alex.

She stopped in the act of plugging the mobile ultrasound into the mains as she suddenly remembered what Greg had been saying before she'd interrupted him; something about Alex liking her? Oh God, what if Greg knew how she felt? Apart from it being a no-no, the embarrassment would be awful. And what if the team manager knew that Alex liked her too?

She managed to get through the next couple of hours merely by the fact that she was so busy. Not only did she have her own job to do, but she was trying to do some of Henno's as well; treating saddle sores was not something she ever wanted to do again, thank you very much, and she had never been so relieved as when Alex told her (pink-cheeked and without meeting her eye) that his "undercarriage was fine, thanks".

Two of the other team members weren't so fortunate, and neither was Molly, and by the time she had showered and changed for dinner her appetite was well and truly gone.

The atmosphere in the dining room was subdued. No one said much during the meal and Molly's attention kept straying to the rider's table, and she realised everyone appeared lost without their team leader there.

She still thought they should cut their losses and go home. What was the point of carrying on without Tim?

'Alex, you're team leader. Elias, you're second wheel,' Chuck announced an hour later at the team meeting. 'We've got a rest day tomorrow to get used to the idea,' he continued, 'and three more mountain days after that. Right, you lot,' he pointed to the mechanics, 'I expect you've got some tinkering to do.'

The mechanics trooped down the steps muttering about gear ratios and other stuff that went straight over Molly's head.

'Right then, tomorrow will be a training ride, just a thirty-kilometre job, to keep your legs loose. Alex, I want you to…'

Molly tuned Chuck out, the words floating around her like so much confetti at a wedding. All she could think about was Tim hitting that wall and sailing straight over it, his bike a broken mess on the road, his body even more broken and lying for far too long on the side of a mountain before he was taken to hospital. He must have been in so much pain, and Molly knew from experience that there would be so much more to come during his recovery.

What if it had been Alex? How would she feel if he was in hospital right now? Poor Gina. She must be in a right state and Molly vowed to stay awake until Tim's wife arrived. No doubt she would need all the support Molly could give her.

***

A soft knock on her bedroom door woke her at something-o'clock and Molly sat up blearily and rubbed her eyes, trying to get her bearings. She had deliberately left a side-lamp on, but it still took her a moment or two to remember where she was and why she was there.

The knock came again, and she scrambled out of bed, suddenly wide awake and feeling apprehensive. She heard a low murmur of voices in the corridor and opened the door to find Greg and Gina standing outside, Greg holding the obviously pregnant and exhausted young woman's case.

'Come in, you must be Gina, Tim's wife,' Molly babbled. 'How is Tim? I mean, I know he's not good, but—'

'He isn't,' the other girl interrupted with a weak smile as Molly stepped to the side to let her in, Greg following behind with her case.

Over Gina's shoulder, Molly saw Greg cutting his hand across his throat. Molly took the hint and changed the subject. 'Are you hungry? Can I get you anything?' She was pretty sure the hotel didn't do room service but she had a secret stash of crisps in her bag.

Gina shook her head. 'No, thank you, but a cup of tea would be nice.' She lowered herself onto the spare bed.

Greg placed her case at the foot of it and said, 'I'll let you get some rest. Molly will drive you to the hospital in the morning and Andrea Lesley from BeSpoke will meet you there.'

That was news to Molly. She'd only driven in France twice, and both times someone had been with her. The first time had been when she picked Elias up from the airport and Mick had accompanied her, and the second time had been when she and Alex had sneaked off to Mont Saint Michel.

She wasn't sure she wanted to repeat the driving experience, especially when she had no idea how to get to Toulouse. She wanted to suggest that this Andrea person come and collect Gina but she realised how silly that sounded.

She closed the door behind Greg and switched the little kettle on, at a loss for what to say.

Gina solved the problem by bursting into tears. Molly sat next to her on the bed and, awkwardly at first, put her arm around the other girl and held her while she wept.

Eventually, Gina pulled away and wiped her eyes. 'I'm sorry, I'm not normally like this,' she said. 'It's the hormones. I'm crying at the drop of a hat, and I think I scared Greg half to death.'

'You're bound to be upset, it's only natural,' Molly said. 'I'd be too if my husband had suffered such a bad accident. I don't know how you stand it,' she blurted, standing up to make the tea. 'How do you cope?'

Gina shrugged. 'You just do,' she said. 'It's part and parcel of cycling. Of course, accidents as bad as Tim's don't happen that often. Thank you,' she added as Molly handed her a cup.

Molly joined her, and took a cup over to her own bed, where she sat and sipped the hot liquid.

'How is Tim?' Despite Greg's advice not to talk about it, Molly felt it was only polite.

'Sleeping. Comfortable, which is doctor-speak to say that they've not got any immediate worries and the pain meds are working. They let me poke my head around the door for a minute. Henno says he's going to be OK. It'll take time, though.' She smiled radiantly, much to Molly's surprise, then explained. 'He'll be home for this one's arrival, which will be nice. Not that Tim will be quite as happy about it – he was hoping to ride in the Vuelta a España in August.'

Molly was shocked. Fancy not wanting to be there for the birth of your own child! Her feelings must have shown on her face, because Gina added, 'He would have flown home the minute I went into labour, of course, but I bet he was secretly hoping the baby wouldn't come until after the middle of September. Take my advice, if you decide to have kids, try and get pregnant in late January, early February, so you get an October baby.'

'October,' Molly repeated blankly.

'You know, the month when nothing at all happens in the cycling calendar? I'm surprised Alex hasn't told you about it. It's when all the weddings take place. You'd better start planning,' Gina said.

Molly's mouth dropped open. 'Planning?'

'For *your* wedding.' Gina paused and her eyes widened. 'Oh, sorry, I assumed from what Tim said...' She flapped a hand in the air. 'Just ignore me.'

'What did Tim say? I thought he was sleeping.'

'He was, but we do speak, you know. Just because

181

he's on tour doesn't mean to say we don't phone each other every night.'

'Yes, but what did he say?'

Gina sighed. 'He said he thought you and Alex might be an item.'

'Whatever gave him that idea?' Molly wanted to know.

'Alex, apparently,' was Gina's dry reply. She smiled at her, and Molly saw just how pretty the young woman was, now that some of the strain had gone from her face. 'I think it's lovely, the two of you.'

'There isn't a two of us,' Molly protested. But this was the second person in less than twenty-four hours who had hinted at the same thing. I ought to know if there was anything going on between me and Alex, Molly thought, and I'm pretty sure there isn't – aside from a mutual attraction. Besides, she couldn't let there be, because in a week's time she'd be tucked up in her own bed in Worcester, probably thousands of miles away from wherever Alex was.

'What's stopping you?' Gina asked.

'Shouldn't you be resting?' Molly countered.

'I'm too exhausted to sleep, if that makes any sense. A nice girly chat will help calm me down.'

'If the chat carries on in the direction it's going,' Molly said, 'it'll do nothing for my nerves.'

'I'm pregnant. You should humour me.'

'Are you really going to play the pregnancy card to get me to talk about my love life?'

'Ha! You admitted it! Your *love* life? Oh, I think we're going to get on famously,' Gina said.

Molly wasn't so sure, especially when Gina repeated, 'So, what's stopping you?'

Okay, maybe it was time to have a girly chat, and

explain why she couldn't possibly have a relationship with Alex. It would help get things straight in her own mind, for a start, because right now her emotions and her resolve were all over the place.

'You win,' Molly said, settling back on her pillows.

'I'll just change into my PJs, then you can tell me all about it,' Gina said, disappearing into the bathroom.

She looked even more pregnant when she emerged, and Molly smiled at the other woman's tummy. 'Do you know what it is, yet'

'Yes, it's a little boy. Tim is over the moon. He's already talking about taking him on bike rides when he's old enough. Mind you, he'd probably be the same if it was a girl. Do you ride?'

'Not really, not since I was a child.' She thought it best not to mention her recent excursion with Alex. 'I used to have a pink bike with a bell on it and a basket. It had a Barbie logo on it, too. I used to pretend it was a horse!' Molly chuckled at the memory.

She watched Gina clamber into bed. The other woman had dark circles around her eyes and her brow was creased with worry.

'I still don't know how you do it,' Molly said. 'I didn't really realise until today, yesterday I mean, just how dangerous a sport it is.'

'Yes, it can be dangerous, but it's his job and his passion. If I want to be with Tim, then I have to accept it. You're right, sometimes it isn't easy.' Gina blinked and Molly saw she was close to tears again. 'When I had that phone call from Greg yesterday, I thought… I don't know what I thought.'

I do, Molly said to herself. You thought you might lose him.

Gina was saying, 'It's part of who Tim is, and I love him, so I have to deal with it.'

'Do you follow the race live?' Molly wanted to know.

'Good lord, no! For one thing, I've got a job, and for another, I don't think I could. I do watch the highlights on TV in the evening, though. *After* I've spoken to Tim and know that he's all right. Is that what you're worried about? Alex getting injured?'

'I wasn't until Tim crashed,' Molly admitted.

'What is it then? The fact that you're on the staff?'

'A bit, but I intend to go home at the end of the Tour,' Molly told her. 'Don't get me wrong, it's been great fun but it's not the life for me.'

'It isn't for me, either. I'd hate to live out of a suitcase for weeks on end. But,' Gina held up a slender hand. 'If you're no longer going to be on the staff, what's holding you back? I know Alex thinks the world of you; Tim told me. Don't say I said, but Tim reckons he's never seen Alex like this. He's smitten.'

'We've only known each other a few weeks,' Molly protested.

'I'm not saying you should go to Vegas tomorrow and get married, but if you don't give the pair of you a chance, you'll never know, will you?'

'Ah, now that's part of the problem. How are we supposed to have any kind of relationship when he's never home?'

'It would be no different if you fell in love with someone in the army, or who works on an oil rig. If you want to make it work, you will. Do you love him?'

Molly stared at the other girl in shock. What a

184

question to ask! 'I don't know,' she admitted. 'I really like him, and he's good-looking and great to talk to. But as for love…?'

'Look, my suggestion is, just see how it goes. If it works out for the two of you, then great. And if it doesn't at least you'll know, and you won't be thinking "what if" or regretting that you didn't give it a chance. What have you got to lose?'

'My heart?'

'Maybe, but if it works out, then you'll have gained his, and believe me, that's a treasure indeed.'

CHAPTER 25

In the end, one of the drivers drove Molly and Gina to the hospital. As Molly walked Gina up to Tim's room, she marvelled at how the girl had rallied overnight. Gone was the strained expression and in its place was nothing but love.

Henno had been on the phone first thing and had spoken to Tim's doctor, who had informed him that they were going to stabilise his leg today and he could fly back to the UK tomorrow to get it pinned and put in a cast. Gina was ecstatic to have him home, and Molly was pleased for her.

'Thanks for putting me up last night and for taking my mind off things,' Gina said, leaning in for a hug. 'And don't forget what we talked about.'

'I won't.' Molly gave her a gentle squeeze, the baby bump in between them.

'I think you care for Alex more than you let on,' Gina said in her ear. She pulled away to look at Molly. 'And just because you've only known him for a few weeks, doesn't mean to say you aren't in love. I know, I can tell.'

And with that, Gina kissed her cheek, then was gone, hurrying towards the lifts and her husband, leaving Molly staring after her.

In love? Her? How ridiculous.

Wasn't it?

It didn't help her confused frame of mind that Alex was the first person she saw when the car drove into the hotel's carpark next.

'Have you been on your ride?' she asked, wondering if he was waiting to see her, and thinking that he might have pulled something, or that his wrist might be playing up.

'Yeah. It was good. Nice to just get out with the guys and not have to worry about racing.'

The day was another warm one, the sun already high in an azure sky. Conscious that she was wearing jeans, a strappy top, and sandals, Molly said, 'Give me a minute to get changed and I'll start the physio sessions.'

It was part of the rest day routine that the riders continued to have physio sessions and massages, as well as ice baths, so Molly wasn't expecting to finish for a couple of hours.

'That's what I wanted to speak to you about,' Alex said, walking into the hotel with her. 'When you're done, do you fancy going for a walk this afternoon?'

'You're supposed to have an afternoon nap; Chuck said during the briefing last night.'

'I know, but I can never sleep during the day, unlike Carlos who can sleep standing up. Besides, I've got too much on my mind. A stroll around the lake will do me good.'

'There's a lake?'

'Yes, a nice one, with lovely walks and swimming. Fancy a dip?'

'Um, I don't think so.'

'Why not? I know you've packed a bikini. It would

be a shame not to give it an airing.'

Molly was going to give Mick a piece of her mind the next time she saw him. Fancy telling Alex about her bikini!

'There's a little beach, with fields and trees behind, and it looks lovely,' he continued. 'If you're really good, I'll treat you to a coffee and a slice of cake in the café.'

Do you know what, Molly thought, it was about time she lived a little. Gina was right – she had to give this a chance, and if it didn't come to anything or if she had her heart broken, then so be it. There was no crystal ball to see into the future; all she had was now, and if she didn't make the most of it, she would only have herself to blame. Alex was making it perfectly clear that he wanted to spend time with her, so that's exactly what she would do.

'OK,' she said. 'It sounds like fun.'

Which was why she was wearing a bikini under her sundress and a pair of pumps on her feet, when she walked into reception to find Alex waiting for her, later that afternoon.

'You look nice and summery,' he said, smiling down at her.

He didn't look too bad himself. He was wearing a pair of normal shorts (not the cycling Lycra variety) and a plain black T-shirt without a BeSpoke logo in sight, and his hair curled damply from his recent shower. When she got close enough she smelled soap and Alex's own enticing scent, and she had a daft urge to nuzzle his neck and breathe him in.

Clearing her throat, she said, 'Shall we go?'

He led her out of the door and they walked along the road for a short distance in companionable silence, Molly revelling in the feel of the sun on her face and the light, welcome breeze on her heated skin. The temperature was in the high twenties but it felt a lot warmer to her, and she thought she might be blushing.

It was disconcerting having Alex so close, even though (and she recognised how silly she was being) she was usually much nearer to him, with her hands on his shoulders, back, or legs. This gentle stroll seemed far more personal, somehow, and she was acutely aware of the man by her side.

'Have you heard anything more about Tim?' she asked, as Alex indicated they should go through a small gate set into a thick hedge. 'Oh my, this is lovely!' she exclaimed as the lake suddenly hoved into view.

'He phoned me to wish me luck for tomorrow. Poor guy, he's gutted to have crashed out.'

What was it with these mad cyclists? she asked herself. They were more concerned about not being in the race than being quite badly injured. They were a bunch of loonies, the lot of them!

'How do you feel about being race leader now?' she wanted to know, thinking it was probably best for Alex not to dwell on what might so easily happen to him on a future stage.

He ruffled his fingers through his hair and sighed. 'I don't know, really; scared that I'll let the team down, excited to be given the opportunity, sad that it has come about through Tim's misfortune.' He shrugged.

'You'll be fine,' she said. 'I'm sure you'll more than fill Tim's boots.'

'I'm not so certain. He's going places, is Tim. I

doubt if he'll be with BeSpoke next year. Already the odd rumour or two is flying around about who he'll sign with. Another few tours under his wheels and he'll be a serious contender for one of the big races.'

'His wife seems nice,' Molly said, having no idea what else to say. It was highly likely (almost a given) that she wouldn't be with BeSpoke next year either, but right now probably wasn't the best time to mention it.

'Gina? She's lovely. I went to their wedding a couple of years ago in Antigua. Nice place. Not much in the way of cycling, though.'

'You're obsessed.'

'We all are. Haven't you been bitten by the bug yet?'

'Yes, kind of. It's not what I had been expecting,' she admitted.

'The sport or the job?'

'Both.'

A path meandered around the edge of the lake, the sun sparkling off the water and tickly grass brushing against her ankles. The air had that distinctive fresh water scent and added to the smell of cut grass and growing things. Molly felt a million miles away from the busyness and the pressure of the Tour. This was exactly what she needed right now, especially after having had so little sleep last night. As she walked, she became calmer and more relaxed, more at ease in her own skin, and she realised she hadn't felt like that for a long time. Not even when she'd been in the UK.

Strange. The thought occurred to her that being away from home in a totally new and somewhat challenging environment was actually doing her some good.

But she pushed the other thought to one side, the one that whispered she might be feeling like this because of the man she was with. Once again, she had to remind herself that this wasn't the time nor the place to be thinking romantic thoughts about Alex, no matter what Gina said last night. He needed to direct all his focus and attention towards Stage 16 of the Tour de France, and not on matters of the heart. If anything happened to Alex because she had distracted him in any way, she'd never forgive herself.

The path led them away from the water's edge slightly and through a clump of trees, and when they came out the other side it was to see the crescent of a small, pale, sandy beach dotted with couples and families. Beyond it, and to the right, was a bar where people were sitting at tables outside, shaded by colourful umbrellas.

'Is this where I get my promised coffee and cake?' Molly asked.

'It is, but I fancy a dip first.'

Molly eyed the water with trepidation. The day was certainly hot enough to warrant a paddle, and there were several people in the water, mostly children and their parents, with a few of the more intrepid ones having swum out to the rope which cordoned off the beach area from the rest of the lake.

A paddle she could cope with; it was the thought of stripping down to her incy-wincy, teeny-weeny bikini that had her coming out in a sudden attack of hives.

Alex had no such qualms. And why should he? She'd seen him with little more than boxer shorts on more times than she could count. This wouldn't be any different.

There was also the fact that he was honed and toned, and fitter than a butcher's dog. Unlike her. Molly had wobbly bits. Being around so many professional athletes these last couple of weeks had made her realise just how unfit she was. And pale, let's don't forget pale, she thought.

Alex had pulled his T-shirt over his head and was in the process of taking his shorts off. When he was done, he folded them neatly and placed them on the sand.

'We've not brought any towels,' she pointed out.

'That's okay, we don't need any. The sun will soon dry us off. Come on, what are you waiting for? Last one in buys the cake!' And with that, he was off, charging towards the water like a small child, all pumping arms and legs.

Reluctantly, Molly slipped the straps of her sundress down over her shoulders and wriggled out of it. She popped it on top of Alex's clothes and removed her pumps. It felt weird to be half-naked in front of him, although she wasn't exactly in front of him, because Alex was now up to his waist in the lake and was standing with his back to her.

He didn't turn around until he heard her squeal as the cold water reached her thighs, and by then she was too concerned about frostbite to fret over the image she presented.

Gradually, her heated body grew accustomed to the temperature difference and once she was in, it didn't seem too bad. She splashed water over her shoulders, wincing slightly, then gathered her courage and leaned forwards until she was immersed up to her neck and doing a kind of doggy paddle.

'Lovely, isn't it?' Alex said, swimming closer.

Neither of them was out of their depth yet, but they both paddled around, enjoying the sensation of weightlessness. 'Better than an ice bath,' he told her. 'Think of this as being for medicinal purposes. You can say it was part of my treatment plan, if anyone asks.'

'Do you think anyone will?'

Alex's expression turned slightly sheepish.

'You're not supposed to be here, are you?' Molly asked him.

'I'm an adult,' he retorted sulkily. 'If I want to go for a swim with a beautiful girl, then I'm perfectly entitled.'

She cocked her head to one side, the water lapping around her shoulders. 'That's not strictly true,' she pointed out, trying to ignore that he'd called her beautiful and the effect the compliment was having on her insides. She'd gone all fluttery.

'Not really, but we're here now, so what can Greg do about it?'

Molly had no idea, but she guessed she probably wouldn't like it, whatever it might be.

'Look, Molly.' Alex swam closer until they were almost touching. 'I need this. All of it – not having to think about cycling or the Tour for an hour or so, not having the rest of the team around; I mean, I love them all to bits, but enough is enough. We've been living in each other's pockets for days now, and I can do with a break from them. Believe me, they feel the same way, too.'

He stopped swimming and stood up, the water at chest height, and right at her eye-level. She couldn't help looking at his smooth skin, the tanned pattern of it left by his jersey and gained from hours in the saddle. She couldn't stop tracing the contours of his muscles with her eyes, or staring at the width of his shoulders, or the way his chest rippled as his arms moved lazily through the water.

'I also needed a couple of hours of normality,' he continued. 'And being with you, right here, right now, feels very normal indeed. More than normal.'

Molly thought it best to let her feet drift to the bottom too, so she could stand up and not keep drooling over his chest. Looking him in the face would be far better for her equilibrium.

It was, but not in the way she thought.

He was close, too close. She could feel the warmth radiating off his skin. Or was she imagining it?

She raised her chin and their eyes met.

Molly thought she was going to drown, but it wasn't because of the water. His eyes had deepened from their usual green-flecked hazel to an almost velvety brown and he was gazing at her with such intensity it took her breath away. Their depths drew her in, and without realising it, she took a step towards him, then another.

Then, he was pulling her to him and suddenly she was in his arms, tight against that wonderful chest, and his head bent towards her just as she lifted hers.

The inevitability of the kiss, the rightness of his lips on hers, made her feel faint. His lips tasted sweet and slightly minty, his breath was warm on her cheek. Eyes closed, she melted into him, the water dancing across her shoulders, the sun hot on her upturned face.

One of his hands came up to bury itself in her hair, his other was wrapped around her, pinning her to him.

The world faded.

No one else existed except him, nothing else mattered but his mouth on hers, and for several long, blissful moments time stood still.

When the wonderful kiss finally ended, his lips fluttering against hers before leaving her bereft, she became aware of his quickened breathing and the pounding of his heart. Her own breathing was not much better, and her heartbeat drummed in her ears. She was surprised to discover she was trembling, but she was fairly sure it had nothing to do with the coolness of the water.

Caught in his gaze and unable to look away, she stared into his eyes.

'Can I do that again?' he asked and she nodded, not trusting herself to speak.

It was even better the second time. Never had she been kissed so thoroughly or so soundly, or with so much emotion, and when they eventually drew apart she wanted to pull him back to her, not wanting it to ever end.

'You're incredible,' he said, and he tucked a wayward strand of hair behind her ear, his fingers stroking her cheek.

She shivered, and he was immediately contrite.

'I'm sorry, I—'

'There's nothing to be sorry for.' She was quick to reassure him.

'Are you sure?'

'I've never been more certain of anything in my life.'

His smile was slow, his gorgeous mouth turning upward and his lips parted. Oh dear – she really wanted to kiss him again, but Alex had other ideas.

He looked towards the beach and said, 'We need to get back.'

She cleared her throat, disappointment flooding through her.

'I'd like to do this again,' he told her, taking hold of her hand as they waded slowly ashore.

Molly wanted to do it again too, but she'd settle for just the kissing. The beautiful lake had simply been an added bonus.

'There aren't any more rest days,' she pointed out.

'There will be some downtime after the Tour ends. I'm entered for the Vuelta a España, but that's not until the end of August. There is a bit of a problem, though,' he added.

'Yes, I know – staff and riders aren't supposed to have relationships.'

She wrung some of the excess water out of her hair as they stepped onto the hot sand and headed for the spot where they'd left their clothes.

'It's not the done thing,' he replied worriedly. 'Greg isn't going to like it and I suspect he might make it a little awkward.'

Should she tell Alex that she didn't intend staying with BeSpoke after the Tour, or was now not the best time? Not wanting to spoil this magical afternoon or to divert his mind away from tomorrow's stage, she decided not to say anything.

They walked slowly back along the shoreline, hand-in-hand, and it was only when they went through the little gate and onto the road leading to the hotel, did he let go of her, sending her an apologetic look.

And by the time they sauntered into reception and were once again immersed in the organised chaos that was the Tour de France, Molly noticed how Alex seemed to withdraw from her, his focus once more on tomorrow's stage and the job he needed to do.

She just hoped she could be as professional as he was being, and not let her feelings interfere with how she did her own job, because at the moment all she wanted to do was kiss him until they were both dizzy.

CHAPTER 26

Molly couldn't bear to watch, keeping her attention firmly on the hills rolling by outside and purposely ignoring the ones on the TV screen inside the car. She also jammed her headphones in her ears, not wanting to listen either.

'Alex will be fine,' Mick said to her when he realised what she was doing. 'The first 20 kilometres are all uphill, so there's no need to worry.'

'It's not the ups that bother me. It's the downs,' she retorted.

Uphill right from the start, Stage 16 began with a bang – a 1700 metre monster of a high mountain pass in the Pyrenees, called Port de Balès. "Another Col du Tourmalet", Chuck had called it yesterday evening during the team meeting.

'It'll separate the men from the boys right from the start,' he had chuckled gleefully. 'Everyone might be well-rested but the sprinters will suffer from the get-go and the peloton will be strung out like a bloody piece of string. It'll probably regroup on the descent but if some lucky bugger can get in the breakaway, he mightn't be roped back into the main group for miles. Alex!'

Alex jumped. 'Huh?'

'Are you listening?'

'I sure am; breakaway, not getting caught for miles. See?'

Chuck had narrowed his eyes at the new team leader, and Molly remembered feeling a horrid trickle of apprehension travel down her spine. Did Chuck know something? Had the sports director guessed what she and Alex had been up to that afternoon?

'You need to be part of that breakaway, Alex. Alex! Have you got something better to do tomorrow, mate?'

'Of course not!'

'Then pay attention.'

Oh dear, this was all her fault, Molly had thought. She'd never seen Alex so distracted or Chuck so cross.

When they had returned from their afternoon adventure, she could have sworn Alex was in the zone once more with little else but cycling and tomorrow's race on his mind, but last night he seemed totally out of it, and shortly after the meeting ended everyone went to bed.

She sincerely hoped that Alex and the remaining riders had slept better than she had, because she'd tossed and turned all night, thinking that what goes up must come down, and Chuck had been quite explicit when he'd talked the team through how fast and tricky the descent off Port de Balès would be. And that wasn't all – there was another mountain after that; not so high admittedly, but then neither had the Col d'Aubisque been compared to the Col du Tourmalet but it hadn't prevented Tim's awful crash, had it?

And that was precisely why she was stubbornly

refusing to watch the live commentary on TV this morning and had earbuds stuffed in her ears so she couldn't hear it either. She really didn't need to see Alex come off his bike in gloriously repeated slow motion. Being told about it would be bad enough.

Mick nudged her elbow, and when she looked up, he pointed to her headphones. Reluctantly, she took them out.

'What?' she demanded crossly.

'Alex and Elias are out in front. I thought you might like to know,' he said.

She both did and she didn't. Ignorance might be bliss, but the mental images swirling through her head were almost as bad. Now that she knew he was going hell-for-leather up some ridiculously steep incline, she simply had to watch, so she gave in with poor grace, put her music away and let the commentators' voices wash over her.

This pair was almost like old friends, their frequently inane banter and strange facts about the towns and villages the race passed through (often there were long stretches during a stage where nothing much happened and they had to fill the airwaves with something), had provided a backdrop to the whole race. Molly wondered if she would still hear them chatting away in her head long after she'd returned from France, her own uniquely personal version of hearing voices.

Alex and Elias were at the head of the race with three other riders, the rest of the peloton several seconds behind (which was a significant amount in cycling terms, and races could be won or lost on mere seconds alone), with the distance between them and the peloton steadily growing.

Norris was discussing their chances with Eamon and had come to the conclusion that this small leading group would be easily caught nearer the top. None of the riders in the breakaway was GC contenders (in other words, unlikely to come anywhere near the winner's podium) and the riders who were top of the leader-board were content to let this group blow off some steam and have their five minutes in front of the cameras, not considering them a threat to their own positions.

'Chuck-n-Greg will be pleased,' Molly stated. 'BeSpoke and the other teams' sponsors are getting their monies' worth.'

With all the teams having their various sponsors' names emblazoned over the riders' jerseys and shorts, and the commentators mentioning the teams at every opportunity, the companies behind each of the breakaway teams were getting some serious TV coverage. Alex and BeSpoke might not stand a cat in hell's chance of winning the stage, but for the moment they were out in front for all to see and that was good for securing future sponsorship for the team.

I'll watch until they crest the top of the mountain pass, she told herself. She could cope with viewing the uphill part, although she puffed and panted along with Alex with each downward turn of his pedal. She could tell he wasn't finding either the pace or the gradient easy, and she realised that he'd suffer from this bold move later on in the race. The riders in the peloton who hadn't gone all out to get to, and stay at, the front would be better rested; the stage had only just started and Alex and the other four in the breakaway group were already digging deep into their reserves of energy to maintain their precarious lead.

Alex would be in bits later, Molly knew, and she made a mental note to ask Mick to get as much ice as he could lay his hands on. Repeated immersion in freezing water would help Alex's legs recover faster and she was determined he'd have at least three cold water treatments this evening, no matter how much he complained.

To everyone's surprise, both Alex and Elias were still at the front of the race when the little group, which now only contained three riders, (the other two, spent and exhausted, having re-joined the peloton) reached the top of the incline and began to descend.

'Don't worry, Moll, Alex is bloody good on the downhill. He'll be fine.'

Molly prayed Mick was right, but she closed her eyes anyway, unable to bring herself to look. Just in case.

Letting Norris and Eamon's voices flow over her, she listened as the race unfolded, and tried to ignore the images of steep drop-offs and twisty, winding roads that they conjured up. And still Alex stayed ahead of the rest of the riders and was gaining time with every metre he travelled.

Molly understood that the situation couldn't last, because as soon as the rest of the riders crested the hill they would probably catch him. But for now, he was the stage leader and was doing his bit for BeSpoke. Elias had been left behind a little while ago, not such a confident rider on the descents as Alex, although Molly did wonder if Alex's confidence mightn't be better described as recklessness.

Unable to look away, Molly's eyes were glued to

the screen as she watched him crouch low over his bike, trying to offer as little wind resistance as possible as he plummeted down the twisting, narrow roads at speeds in excess of 110 kilometres an hour. That was a terrifying sixty miles an hour she translated and, as Norris was keen to tell her, Alex was occasionally hitting a top speed of sixty-five. She bit back a hysterical giggle when she heard that little nugget of information – as if five miles an hour would make any difference right now if he were to crash.

When the gradient finally levelled out and turned hilly instead of mountainous, Molly finally began to breathe easier.

At least for the moment anyway, because there was still another sodding great big tump to get up and over before she could relax a little and try to enjoy the scenery. One day, she promised, she was going to come back to this spectacular country and see it properly. And she prayed there wouldn't be a bicycle in sight when she did so.

To everyone's astonishment, Alex was still in the lead. Norris and Eamon had expected him to have been sucked back into the peloton at some point between one mountain and the next, but as he drew nearer to the next mountain, Col de Portet d'Aspet, his lead was an impressive, if quite unbelievable, twenty-three minutes over the rest of the riders in this stage.

He didn't look as though he intended to be reined back into the group anytime soon, and when he hit the slopes of the Col de Portet d'Aspet and began to ascend once more, he didn't look as though he was going to slow down, either.

Mick, Damien, and Jakob were going slightly crazy,

the tension in the car as real as a fifth person.

'I know Chuck told Alex to get in front and stay there for a bit, but I don't think he expected him to do this! Strewth, the guy's got some balls,' Mick said, his voice filled with admiration.

'Stamina,' Jakob said. 'And he's super-determined.'

'My only hope is that he finishes in time,' Mick added, his face creased with worry.

'Why wouldn't he?' Molly wanted to know.

Mick heaved a sigh. 'He's giving it everything he's got right now,' he explained. 'There's no way he can keep this up for much longer.'

'But he's twenty-three minutes ahead of the next fastest rider,' she said.

'He won't be for much longer. Once he starts to feel the bite of this Col he'll have to slow down.'

Molly still didn't understand. 'Surely the rest of them will slow down too, when they reach it,' she pointed out.

'Yeah, they will, darl, but they'll be a darned sight fresher than our guy. He's pushed himself to his limit to get to where he is now. I'll be surprised if he's got anything left in the tank at all. Once he gets swept up by the rest of them, he'll probably be spat out of the back of the peloton and will struggle to keep up. If he doesn't finish within the time limit, he'll be disqualified.'

'Oh, I see.'

'To put it bluntly, Mol, he'll be knackered. It'll be as much as he can do to stay on his bike.'

Suddenly, Molly had gone from praying Alex wouldn't crash out of the race, to praying that he'd actually make it to the end of the stage.

She didn't think her nerves would take any more!

CHAPTER 27

'nd there's the monument to Fabio Casartelli, the Italian cyclist and Olympic gold medal winner, who tragically lost his life here in 1995,' Norris said.

Molly's eyes widened as the camera zoomed in on a gleaming white monument.

'That's right, Norris, the Société du Tour de France and Team Motorola placed the monument at the site where he crashed. You can't tell from this angle, but it's actually a sundial arranged to highlight three dates — the date of his birth, the date of his death, and the day he won his Olympic gold medal. His bike is in the chapel at the Madonna del Ghisallo, which is a church and museum to cyclists near his home.'

'Those were the days when riders didn't wear helmets—'

Molly tuned out the voices from the TV, staring in horror at the monument where, more than three decades on, flowers were still placed at its base to honour the cyclist. Dear God, but this sport was a damned dangerous one.

And Alex was almost at the top of the pass.

He hadn't been caught yet, although his lead had dropped from twenty-three minutes to just under fourteen.

That was all about to change.

'My bladder can't take this much excitement,' Mick said. 'Pull over at the next café you see, Damien, and I'll get us some coffees at the same time.'

They were just coming into a village and Damien obligingly turned off the main road and headed down a side street.

Molly wrinkled her nose; she would be surprised indeed if they found a decent café in this place. Although she had become used to shuttered windows and grills across doors, instead of looking French, rural and quaint, the peeling paint and the rundown buildings here gave the village an air of neglect. The whole place appeared grim and grubby – until the car emerged into a kind of square with the obligatory church in the centre and she gasped in astonishment.

She'd gone back in time! All the buildings were positively medieval-looking, with wooden buttresses holding up the upper storeys of many buildings and half-timbered houses, shops, cafes, and restaurants were snuggled underneath. It was too charming for words, and she gazed around in wide-eyed astonishment. This was yet another place she needed to add to her rapidly growing list of places she intended to revisit.

Damien switched off the engine and Mick made a dash for the nearest café. Not wanting to waste an opportunity to visit the loo, Molly leapt out of the car after him and followed him inside.

By the time she came back out, Mick was paying for four coffees and stuffing packets of sugar into his jeans pocket.

'Here, take these, will you?' He handed her two of the takeaway cups and she inhaled the delicious aroma, trying not to worry about Alex. He'd be halfway down the mountain by now...

Her mouth was abruptly dry with fear and she closed her eyes briefly, feeling sick.

'Mick! Molly! Get in the car. We need to go now,' Jakob shouted at them and Molly's eyes flew open.

Please, no, not Alex. Don't let anything have happened to Alex!

She raced to the car and yanked the door open, almost falling inside. 'What? Is it Alex?'

'Shh, Damien is talking to Greg,' Jakob said.

'We're just passing Mirepoix,' Damien was saying, and wincing at the slight distortion of the truth, because they weren't passing, they were parked right in it. 'Why?'

'Get to Pamiers,' Greg crackled over the radio. 'One of you needs to be there with a feed bag. There's a bridge over the river, yeah? Position someone just before Alex gets to it. I want someone else at Belpech, one of you at Fanjeaux and the last one at Arzens. Please tell me you've got a full stock of gels and bars?'

'Of course we have,' Damien said, a huge grin splitting his face.

Molly hissed, 'What's going on?'

Mick was shaking his head slowly, his mouth open. 'I don't believe it. I bloody well don't believe it!'

'*What?*' she shouted.

'He's only going for the stage win,' Mick said to her. He was also grinning from ear to ear.

'Who is?' Molly grabbed hold of her seatbelt as Damien sped off up the road.

'Alex, of course,' Mick replied, still shaking his head.

'I thought you said—'

'Never mind what I said – Alex is going for the stage win; the wonderful, daft, stubborn, stupid bugger.'

He was doing what? Wow. Molly didn't believe it either, but what a feather in his cap if he did win it. 'What are his chances?'

'Slim, to non-existent,' Mick replied, cheerfully.

'So why is he—'

'Because he can. If he doesn't give it a go, he'll never know, will he? To be honest, I think it's a miracle that he's stayed in front this long. He's done over 100 kilometres already. It's gotta be a record. No one in their right mind makes a break for it right at the start of a stage and expects to win it.'

Slowly a wide smile spread across Molly's face. 'It seems like Alex does.'

'I dunno what's got into him, but I'm bloody glad it has,' Mick said. 'Right, you'd better be dropped off first, then one of the team cars can pick you up on the way past. Damien will have to be last, and he can swing by and grab the rest of us once the race has gone past. You'll need to be there for when Alex crosses the line,' Mick added, looking meaningfully at Molly. 'He'll be in bits.'

There was something Molly didn't understand. 'Why am I being dropped off, and what am I supposed to do when I get there?'

'Oh, shit.' Jakob glanced behind and caught Mick's eye. 'She has never done this before, has she?'

'Would someone please tell me what is going on?' Molly cried.

'You know you see team staff standing at the side of the road, handing out water bottles and those little cotton bags?' Mick said.

'Yes…'

'Well, that's what you're going to have to do. There's only so much Alex can carry and without a domestique to hand him food and water, he's going to run out of fuel pretty damned quick. The team cars are too far back to help, so it's down to us.'

'We will be there in ten minutes,' Damien informed them, checking the Satnav. He picked up the radio and spoke into it. 'ETA Pamiers ten minutes. Where is Alex?'

'Twenty-five minutes to Pamiers.'

'Copy. Molly is manning the first feed station.'

There was a brief pause, then, 'Tell Molly she has to get this right. The stage win depends on it.'

Oh, so no pressure then, Molly felt like saying, her stomach knotting.

'OK, as soon as the car stops,' Mick told her, 'I'll get you a musette from the boot and show you how to hold it out so that Alex has the best chance of grabbing it when he comes past.'

Musettes were small cotton tote-bags filled with a couple of drinks, rice cakes, energy bars, and sugar-rich gels. She'd watched the swannies prepare them on many an occasion, but never in her wildest dreams had she anticipated standing on the side of the road and handing one out. What if she didn't present it properly and Alex missed his chance of grabbing it?

Oh, God, she wasn't ready for this.

'Turn left here,' Jakob instructed, 'then right. That should bring us in from the side. Molly, you will have to get out on this side of the bridge and cross over it. Don't go too near to the bend or Alex won't see you in time as he comes around it. I'm sorry we can't get you any closer, but the police will have blocked off the road by now.'

Molly leaned down and picked her bag up from the footwell, one hand on the buckle of her seatbelt.

'OK, just up here… and – go!' Jakob yelled.

The car screeched to a halt and Mick leapt out, quickly followed by a very nervous Molly. He yanked open the boot and pulled a musette out of a box.

'Stand like this.' He stood to one side, his arm at a right-angle to his body. 'And hold the musette like this.'

Molly nodded; she could do this. She *could*.

'He's on his own, so he can afford to slow down for a second or two. Just try to stand where he can see you clearly, and if you can avoid being too close to any spectators, that would be even better.' He handed her the musette. 'Go,' he urged, giving her a little push.

She began walking away and heard the car door slam, then the sound of the engine revving as it turned around and roared away.

Molly gave the policeman and his motorcycle a worried glance as she trotted past. Jakob was right, police were preventing cars from travelling across the bridge in anticipation of the race shortly coming through.

Half expecting to be stopped and told she couldn't go any further, Molly sidled past the officer and scurried along the pedestrian walkway. She was only half-way across when the first wave of advance vehicles trundled by. Police motorbikes, tour motorbikes, and official tour cars all swept across the bridge. Up ahead, the road curved to the right, but in between the bend in the road and the bridge she had just scuttled over, was a straight bit of road.

Thankfully, there were only two spectators, a couple of elderly gentlemen, standing outside a short row of buildings, so there should be no chance of Alex not seeing her, but just to make certain, she positioned herself in the middle of the road and waited.

Every so often she stepped back when a motorbike came into view, thinking how surreal this whole thing was, and hoping that one of the team cars in the middle of the race would actually remember to pick her up. She seriously didn't fancy being stranded in the middle of France for the rest of the day.

The tooting of several horns brought her attention back to the bend in the road. Three motorbikes sailed past, then— Oh my God, there he was, and she couldn't believe how fast Alex was travelling. There was no way he was going to be able to grab the bag as he hurtled past.

Gritting her teeth, Molly stepped further into the road, her arm held rigidly out to the side and watched Alex bear down on her.

She couldn't see his eyes, only the lower part of his face, but the smile that spread across it when he saw her made her heart melt.

Closer, closer, and—

'This is for you, Molly,' he shouted as she felt him snag the musette, and she let go and whirled around as he sped off over the bridge and to victory.

CHAPTER 28

Watching Alex step onto the podium to accept the acclaim of winning Stage 16 of this year's Tour de France was one of the most memorable experiences of Molly's life to date. The pride she felt was immense, and when he raised his arms, a bouquet in one hand and a glass trophy in the other, she screamed and cheered until she was hoarse.

Unable to get anywhere near him because of the feeding frenzy of more media people than she had ever seen in one place before, Molly contented herself with catching glimpses of him from afar as he was ushered from bike, to turbo, to podium, and then to several impromptu interviews.

Earlier, she had sat speechless and overawed in the back of Chuck's team car, squashed between Henno and a mechanic, and had watched the race take place all around her, dividing her attention between the team radio, the TV, and chatter in the car.

It seemed everyone was stunned. Shocked, amazed, incredulous, disbelieving were other words which seemed to work equally well in describing how the team felt. It hadn't sunk in yet and everyone involved with Team BeSpoke wore slightly glazed expressions and, Molly suspected, so did she. Although, it wasn't so much shock that Alex had actually won a stage that dumbfounded her, rather it was what he had said when he'd sailed past her on that hot and dusty road a few hours ago. She'd spent the time between then and now mulling over what he meant, and she had yet to reach a conclusion. The only way she'd know for certain would be to ask him.

While she waited for him to return to the bus, she watched TV and listened to the commentators, who were equally as shocked, stunned, incredulous and so on, as everyone else.

'What a ride. This man is seriously coming into his own. 230 kilometres of cycling and most of it spent at the head of the race. Phenomenal.'

Ooh, there was a word she hadn't thought of. And for the little she knew about cycling and the Tour de France, Alex's achievement was truly phenomenal.

'He'll pay for it this evening,' Eamon joked. 'It'll be interesting to see what state he's in tomorrow, but however bad he is, it doesn't matter. He's done his bit for this tour, and he's shown us what he's capable of. It'll be interesting to see if he stays with BeSpoke next season or moves on.'

'I suppose it depends on what BeSpoke decide to do when it comes to Tim Anderson. You can't have two team leaders in the same race, and Duvall has shown he's a serious contender. After this stint at first wheel, he might not be happy going back to being a domestique. What do you think, Eamon?'

'He's certainly shown he's got guts, talent, and determination today, but can he keep it up? And I'm also thinking that if he had been a bit better placed in the rankings, then the GC riders would never have let him go.'

'So, you're saying he only won today because no one saw him as a threat?'

'Perhaps, although you can't take away an outstanding ride.'

'Do you think this was planned all along?'

'I doubt it. Duvall probably had instructions to get his jersey in front of the cameras for a while, and he just went with it.'

'More luck than judgement, you're saying?'

'Maybe. Let's see if he's got anything left in the tank for tomorrow, because the Tour is facing another mountain stage.'

'Well, there you have it – Alexander Duvall has won the 16th stage by an incredible nineteen minutes and thirty-seven seconds.'

Molly reached up and jabbed the off button aggressively. How dare those pair disparage Alex's win. They had almost implied that the GC riders had "allowed" him to win. The fact that they hadn't seen his potential had nothing to do with it. Anyway, he was one of the General Classification guys now, wasn't he? Whether the rest of them liked it or not. He might have won the stage by over nineteen minutess, but he had also moved up the leader-board and was now lying ninth overall. There were only eleven minutes between Oscar del Ray, who wore the yellow jersey of the race leader, and Alex. Eleven minutes.

It didn't sound a lot but it was; even Molly knew Alex couldn't repeat today's performance, and there were only four more stages to go before the ceremonial final stage into Paris, which didn't really count, she'd been told. There was no hope of him clawing back so much time, but she still resented those daft commentators for their lack of faith. Molly stalked down the aisle and back to her lair, bristling with indignation.

'Hi.'

She turned to see Alex behind her, a bouquet of yellow roses in his hand.

'These are for you,' he said, holding them out to her. 'Sorry they're second hand, but it was the best I could do under the circumstances.'

She took the winner's bouquet and buried her face in the petals, breathing in their delicious scent. 'Thank you, but are you sure?'

'I meant it when I said it was for you. I wanted this to be a Tour de France you would remember for all the right reasons, and not for the wrong ones.'

'Have you heard from Tim?'

'He phoned Greg. He's delighted for me, for the team. Gutted that it wasn't him.' He took his jersey off and Molly's eyes were drawn to his chest. He'd lost a little weight over the past couple of weeks, but he still looked gorgeous.

She noticed his movements were slower than usual after a race. He was clearly exhausted, with shadows under his eyes, his skin pale beneath the tan.

'Water,' she said firmly.

'Yeah, you'd better find something to put them in, otherwise the flowers will die.'

'I meant you.'

'Give me a minute. I can't face a shower just yet.'

Molly laughed. 'I meant, you need to drink some water. If you're not careful, you'll get dehydrated.' She knew both Chuck and Henno would be monitoring his fluid intake closely, but neither of them was here right now and she was, so she opened the fridge, took out a cold bottle of water and handed it to him.

'That was tough,' he said, between gulps of the cool liquid.

'I think that's an understatement,' she said. 'You look done in.'

'I am.' He smiled weakly. 'And I get to do it all again tomorrow. Yay.'

Molly studied him, seeing total and utter weariness in his face and his body. 'Go have a shower, then I'll see what I can do about working those kinks out. Is there anywhere in particular that is troubling you?'

His smile was small, but at least it was a smile. 'Mont Ventoux,' he said, before stepping into the shower and closing the door.

She listened to the sounds of water running for a few moments, a thought playing at the edge of her mind, just out of reach; then she became distracted by the others returning to the bus, loud voices and laughter filling the air. Everyone was on a high, except Alex, who should have been the highest of them all.

Something was seriously bothering him, and she didn't think it was the thought of getting back in the saddle tomorrow either.

'Any idea what's up with Alex?' she murmured in Mick's ear as he boarded the bus to collect Alex's kit. 'He mentioned Mont Ventoux, just now. That's the big mountain tomorrow, isn't it?'

'Yeah, but I'm not sure it's my place to say anything.'

'Mick,' she warned. 'This is me you're talking to.'

He gestured towards the compartment at the rear where Molly's physio table was housed, and she walked inside with the soigneur following. He slid the partition shut behind him.

'Well?' Molly folded her arms, trying to keep her concern in check.

'I've heard a little whisper that our boy is going to

do it again tomorrow,' Mick said in a low voice.

Her eyes widened. 'You mean…?'

'Yup.'

'How far out?'

He drew in a deep breath. '100 kilometres or so.'

'How long is the stage?'

'178 kilometres.'

'He mentioned Mont Ventoux. It's near the finish, isn't it?' she said, recalling various team meetings.

'It is the finish. 1800 metres of climbing, with a race to the summit.'

'Oh, my God.'

'Exactly! He's planning on going way before that, though; there's a Category 3 climb before they reach Mont Ventoux. He's planning a breakaway then.'

Molly shook her head. 'What if a group of riders are already out in front?'

'He probably hopes there is. It'll give him something to aim for.'

'And you know all this… how?'

Mick looked sheepish. 'I overheard him discussing it with Greg. No one is supposed to know, only the riders, Greg, and Chuck. I can see why they want to keep it hush-hush. To all intents and purposes, Alex is done. No one will expect him to make a run for it again tomorrow.'

'Actually, Mick, he *is* done. I'm not sure he's got anything left.'

Mick regarded her solemnly. 'That's where you come in.'

'Me?'

'He rode this stage for you. He needs to ride the next one for you, too, and the one after that.'

Molly gawped at him, suddenly angry. 'You're as

bad as those commentators,' she hissed. 'They think he only won today because the big boys let him.'

'You're wrong. He won because of you. *For* you.'

'Oh hell.' All the fight went out of her as she recognised the truth of Mick's words. 'He said as much to me.'

'Alex is passionate about his cycling and he wants to win as much as the next rider. But he needs that added something that only you appear to be able to give him. Races like the Tour de France are as much mental as they are physical. He's going to be hurting more than he has ever hurt in his life tomorrow. You need to be in his head to take his mind off the pain.' Abruptly Mick stopped talking and looked around. 'Where is he, anyway?'

'In the shower.'

'All this time?'

Now that she came to think of it, Alex *had* been in there a while.

She sidled around Mick and slid the partition door open. She could hear the shower still running. 'You'd better check on him,' she suggested to the swannie, not wanting to invade Alex's privacy.

Mick tapped on the shower door. 'Are you all right in there, mate?'

No answer.

'Alex?'

'Still no answer. Mick threw her a worried look and Molly nodded.

Mick opened the door. His mouth dropped open. Then he began to chuckle. 'Look,' he said to her.

Against her better judgement, but unable to resist, Molly looked.

Alex was scrunched up in the bottom of the tiny

shower cubicle, his head resting on his knees, fast asleep.

CHAPTER 29

Molly hadn't meant to kiss Alex, but she simply couldn't help herself. He'd been coming out of his hotel room just as she was about to return to hers, having forgotten her phone on the way down to breakfast the following morning.

They had met in the corridor. His hair was damp from the shower (she hoped he hadn't fallen asleep in that one, too) and the weariness had disappeared from his face. He looked bright and alert and quite delectable. So she kissed him.

'Mmm,' he said, when she finally let go. 'Good morning to you, too. What was that for?'

She shrugged. 'To keep you going today.'

Alex laughed 'Did Mick put you up to it?'

Molly was indignant. 'No. This is all my own work.'

'Come here.' He pulled her close once more and wrapped his arms around her. 'Kiss me again. Please?'

She did, and she thoroughly enjoyed every second. From the look in his eye when she finally stepped out of his embrace, he had enjoyed it just as much.

'I'm glad you agreed to come on this tour, Miss Matthews,' he said. 'Even though it's not quite what you expected.'

'Admit it, you sold me a pup.'

He raised his chin and looked loftily down at her. 'I might have embellished the truth a little.'

'A lot!' she protested. 'I'd have seen just as much of France if I'd stayed at home and watched the Tour on TV.'

'You saw Mont Saint Michel,' he said. 'You seemed to enjoy it. And Lourdes.'

'And I've seen lots of rolling fields, and pretty villages, and mountains. Mostly out of the window of the car,' she added.

He sobered. 'I know, and I'm sorry.'

'Don't be,' she replied. 'I'm not.'

'Alex! There you are,' Chuck said. 'I thought you'd gone back to sleep or something.' He gave Molly a look out of the corner of his eye when he said "or something" and she winced. Mick knew how she and Alex felt about each other, but she was pretty certain Chuck didn't, because he'd probably send her packing if he realised she was on kissing terms with one of the riders.

She and Alex studiously avoided each other's eye during the race preparation and she hadn't realised how much of a strain that keeping their blossoming relationship under wraps was causing, until when the riders were safely on the bus and making their way to the start at Montpellier, Molly rolled her shoulders to try to ease the tension in them and let out a long, slow breath.

'Good luck,' she whispered to the retreating bus, then helped the others pack everything up.

Driving straight out of Montpellier towards Nîmes, Molly was relieved to see that the terrain was much flatter than it had been recently, but her relief was short-lived when Damien turned the commentary on.

As anticipated, Norris and Eamon were discussing yesterday's remarkable stage win by Alexander Duvall, and speculating about how tired he was feeling today. When one of the cameras at the start of the race zoomed in on Alex doing the official signing-in thing before the start of the stage and she saw how he looked, she gasped.

What had happened to the buoyant man of earlier? This one looked as though he needed to sleep for a week. It wasn't so much his face, it was his body language.

'It's for show,' Mick whispered, seeing her distress. 'Remember what I told you last night? The plan is that he's going to try for a breakaway early on, but this time the GC riders won't let him get far. They'll keep reining him back in until it looks like he's given everything he's got, and then he's going to stay tucked into the peloton until they're about 50 kilometres out and they reach the first climb. It's only a little one, a Category 3, but by this time, they should just let him go.'

'Because they'll be expecting to reel him back in again?'

'Exactly!'

'And they won't be able to?'

'Let's just pray he's got the power in his legs. Norris and Eamon might be right – he might not have anything left to give.'

'But you think he does?'

Mick nodded. 'I think our Alex has got plenty more to give, but a lot can go wrong; an early break by any of the contenders who manage to stay clear of the rest, for example. And this is home turf for del Ray and Team Espanda, and he knows this mountain better than he knows his wife's moods. Kontrol Data want a piece of it too and with their team all being good climbers, Alex is going to have his work cut out. The only thing in his favour will be the element of surprise – they won't be expecting him to go for it again.'

'Will we be needed to hand out any musettes?' she wanted to know.

'Nah, Chuck's got it all in hand. There'll be a feeding station at the top of the Col des Trois Termes. He'll get his last musette there.'

Molly watched the race unfold exactly as Mick had predicted. Today the overall race leaders were rather more jumpy, and every time anyone tried to get ahead they were caught within minutes and sucked back into the body of the peloton. It made for quite a fast race over the first few kilometres, as all the teams jostled for position. Alex spent most of it near the front and to one side, trying to stay out of trouble (the worst crashes often happened in the main body of the peloton) and to be in the best position to make a run for it when the time was right.

'See this stretch of road?' Mick said, meaning the one their car was currently driving down, as they followed a similar route that the riders would be on in a couple of hours' time. 'It doesn't look much, but it's a steady six-kilometre gradient. When he reaches this point, Alex intends to pull away. Elias will be going with him and anyone else in the team who still has the legs for it.'

'Will the other teams let him go?'

Mick frowned. 'Let's hope so, or he's stuffed.'

The village where it all began was called Gordes and Molly thought how pretty it was with its little stone houses and dry-stone walls, but she guessed that Alex wasn't taking any notice of the scenery as he rode through it, Elias leading. She nodded to herself as the rest of the riders hunkered down and put their shoulders (or should she say, legs) into the incline and let Alex go.

He powered up the slope, gaining fifteen seconds on the rest of them and by the time he reached the top and was over the other side, he sailed down the gentle downward slope and barrelled into the next small hill.

'What is going on?' Damien wanted to know. 'Is Alex going for another stage win?'

'It looks like it, doesn't it?' Mick replied casually and Molly smiled to herself. He wasn't going to let on to the other swannies that he knew, not even at this late stage in the race, and she was glad he was able to keep a secret because she was certain he was fully aware of her relationship with Alex.

'Do you think he can do it?' Jakob wanted to know.

'He's looking strong,' Mick said. 'So, maybe. I hope so.'

'I'm surprised the big boys haven't rode him down by now,' Damien broke in.

'I'm not,' Jakob said, adding two words that would make or break the race and Alex. 'Mont Ventoux.'

As they drove through some more pretty hamlets and villages, Molly was hard-pressed to see what all the fuss was about. The terrain wasn't particularly arduous (as much as she could tell from the comfort

224

of the car). Alex, many miles behind them, was managing to keep his lead, although he wasn't able to increase it.

By the time she drove through a sweet little town called Mazan, Molly was beginning to wonder if Mont Ventoux was a figment of everyone's imagination, a mythical being like a unicorn. And even when they were through that town and had driven through the next few villages and the road began to rise, Molly was still feeling a little let down. She had expected drama and massive mountains, but what she was seeing were quaint, sleepy villages and pretty countryside.

Farmland became forested slopes, which in turn gradually thinned out, the deciduous trees giving way to conifers and pines as the car climbed higher. Reaching a place called Chalet Reynard, Jakob informed them that he'd gone skiing here once and that the restaurant on the side of the road served wonderful pastries.

'Or was it that I was super-hungry, and any food would have tasted like heaven?' he wondered, as Damien brought the car to a halt.

The place was surprisingly busy, with various Tour vehicles parked up alongside team buses and vans, with more vehicles arriving as she watched.

'Is this the finish?' she wanted to know. Somehow she'd been expecting something more dramatic. This was impressive, but it certainly didn't warrant any hushed tones or awe. Or was she missing something?

They all got out and Molly arched her back, easing out the kinks. The air was considerably fresher up here than it had been when they set off from Montpellier earlier, and she wished she'd brought a fleece.

'Mick, do you want to take her up to the top? We can manage without you. Just make sure you get back to the bus before the riders get here, or Chuck won't be happy.' Damien handed Mick the car keys.

'You heard the man. Get in,' Mick told her.

She got in. 'I don't understand,' she said. 'If this isn't the finish, then why are the buses here?'

'You'll see why when we get to the top. There's not enough room for all the Tour vehicles to park up there, so they have to wait down here. The poor bloody riders have to race up the damned thing, then turn around and cycle back down. Imagine if you're one of the last in and you see loads of other riders coming back down the mountain as you're going up. It must be heart-breaking.'

Molly prayed that Alex wouldn't find himself in that very position, and she checked the TV screen. 'He's still in front,' she said, watching him speed along roads she'd not long travelled over herself. It made her feel closer to him, somehow.

The landscape grew more barren the higher they went; rocky and dry, and Molly found it hard to believe that skiing took place on its almost bald slopes.

She hadn't been prepared for the sheer volume of people up here either; cars, campervans, and bicycles were parked haphazardly along the sides of the road, both sides if the terrain allowed, and the spectators were clearly here for the duration, many of them having set up folding tables and chairs. Some of them were already very enthusiastic, waving frantically at the BeSpoke car as it wound its way to the top, and Molly suspected their exuberance might be down to alcohol.

The last half a kilometre had the usual barriers along it, holding the crowd back, and when the car drove across the finish line Molly was in a mild state of shock.

'Alex has to cope with all that?' she asked, pointing back at the crowds. 'As well as the mountain?'

'Yep. It's brutal. Right, we can't hang about, we've got to get back to Chalet Reynard and the bus before they block the road off. We're cutting it fine as it is.'

Going down was no easier than going up, harder in fact, as they had to negotiate not only the people on the road, but advance traffic coming up, and a couple of times Molly closed her eyes and prayed as Mick eased around an oncoming car or van while trying not to knock a pedestrian over or drive their car over the edge of the road.

By the time they re-joined the rest of the BeSpoke staff, Molly was a bag of nerves as she focused on the TV.

'For the second day in a row, we're seeing some remarkable riding from BeSpoke's Alex Duvall. Can he keep this up, Eamon?'

How would Eamon know, Molly wanted to say. Alex was the only person who knew the answer to that, and even if he did keep up the blistering pace he was setting, del Ray, who currently wore the yellow jersey of the overall race leader, or Mateo Rohjas, who was close behind him in terms of time, might well try to ride him down.

It would actually be a wise thing for them to do, she realised, because at the moment Alex had gained another six minutes. He had become a serious contender and everyone knew it. If he could keep it up…

He didn't see her as he came around the bend at Chalet Reynard. How could he? There were too many people for him to pick one of them out of the yelling mass. But she saw him. His mouth was open, his jersey half unzipped, and water dripped off his head as he emptied a water bottle over himself in an effort to cool down. He was pedalling strongly though, and his face gave nothing away.

As soon as he'd turned into the bend and was lost from sight around the corner of the mountain, she rushed to the nearest TV to watch his progress, her palms damp, her mouth dry, and her heart thudding.

Whenever the spectators came too close, she wanted to yell at them, and the shot from the camera on the motorbike just behind Alex showed a sea of people slowly parting to let him through, waving fists in his face, screaming in his ear, and trying to pat him on the back.

She didn't know how he could stand it.

'Let him through,' she muttered. 'Just let him through.'

Then the camera showed a close-up of de Ray's tortured expression and Molly began to hope. He was several minutes behind Alex and the distance between them was growing by the second. The race leader was done. Finished.

By the end of today, another rider might have the coveted yellow jersey on his back.

The question was – who?

CHAPTER 30

It hadn't been Alex, although he had won the stage. Lying in third place as the race faced Stage 18 and another giant of a mountain, there were only seventeen seconds between del Ray, who was still the race leader, and Alex. Seventeen long, impossible seconds.

Impossible, because trying the same trick for a third time was never going to work. The rest of the riders, the GC contenders and the ones with everything to lose if they allowed Alex to gain any more time, stuck to him like glue. But it wasn't Alex or any of the other top five riders who came first on Stage 18 and the iconic Alpe d'Huez; it was someone much further down the Tour's rankings who was only just returning to full fitness after an accident.

Overall, Alex lay in third position, and unless something remarkable happened, it looked like he would probably stay there.

Not that Alex or any of the rest of Team BeSpoke were complaining – a place on the podium was more than anyone had dreamt of at the start of the Tour, and what he needed to do now was to hold onto it, but that was easier said than done.

'Do you know what I really want?' he said to her

later that evening.

Molly shook her head.

'A large, juicy steak with proper chips. Not fries, but real home-made chips. And without a hint of salad in sight.'

They were sitting on a hotel terrace somewhere in Megève. The view of the Alps was fantastic, but neither Molly nor Alex really noticed it. Molly was too busy studying Alex, and Alex was too busy thinking about food. Not that Molly could blame him – the poor guy had been living on chicken, fish, rice, salad and vegetables for weeks.

'And cake,' he added, dreamily. 'Chocolate, with a dollop of cream.

'Just a couple more days and you can eat whatever you want,' she said.

'Promise?' From his slow, sexy smile she guessed he was talking about more than food.

Molly hesitated. How could she promise him anything? She was about to return to life in good old England next week. He was about to come third in the Tour de France (fingers crossed) and his career as a professional cyclist was about to reach giddy new heights. In a couple of weeks he would be off again, training for yet another race. What time would they actually have to see each other? Unless, he was assuming she was going to continue to be a physio on the BeSpoke team?

She really should tell him that she was seriously considering going back to her old life, but she didn't want to spoil what little time they had left. The whole experience was surreal and since she'd joined BeSpoke she had felt as though nothing existed except the riders and the Tour. The outside world was forgotten; it wasn't important – their days were dictated by the race; preparing for the next stage, racing the stage, recovering from it. Then the cycle would start all over again. And Molly was so caught up in it, that she couldn't really think of anything beyond Paris.

Alex probably felt the same way, but for different reasons. Paris, for him, meant the chance of third place in the Tour de France.

Either way, Paris was a pivotal point for both of them.

Molly found she wasn't looking forward to it all that much.

The thought of going home was both lovely and awful at the same time. Lovely because she missed being in the same place every night (living out of a suitcase had quickly become tedious), missed her family, her friends, and her colleagues (even Finley). She was looking forward to watching normal stuff on TV (although she may well tune in to watch the cycling now and again). She missed simple things like beans on toast, and Marmite crisps, and proper full-fat milk (the French stuff simply didn't taste the same). But most of all, she missed having time to herself, to read or listen to music.

The awful list of going home had only the one thing in it – Alex. The thought of not seeing him again made her want to weep. She honestly didn't know how she was going to bear it.

But for now, it had to be business as usual, for Alex's sake – she didn't want anything to jeopardise the Tour for him.

'It's time for bed,' she said. 'You'd best make a move before Chuck or Greg comes looking for you.'

He heaved a sigh. 'I know, but I'm enjoying it out here with you, and a few more minutes won't hurt.'

'Yes, they will.' Henno's voice was loud in the relative quiet of the mid-summer evening and the peace of the little terrace was immediately shattered. 'You need to rest. Listen to your doctor, Alex, and get some sleep. The rest of the team retired over an hour ago.'

Alex sighed again, stood, and gave her a rueful smile. 'See you in the morning,' he said, then put a finger under her chin, tilting her head up.

Before she'd realised what he was doing, he'd leant forward and his lips brushed hers. 'Sleep well, mon amour. Bonne nuit.'

Staggered at what he had just done, Molly sat, stunned. Her eyes flitted from Alex's retreating back to Henno's pursed lips, and she grimaced.

Henno waited until Alex was out of earshot before he spoke. 'Molly, I am surprised at you. You know the rules. It is simply not acceptable to fraternise with the riders. You understand that I have no choice but to report this to Greg?'

Molly nodded, mutely, a sinking feeling in her stomach. She really hoped Alex wasn't going to get into trouble for this. Telling her off was one thing, but Alex didn't need any added pressure. He was under enough already.

Henno returned her nod with a curt one of his own, and she watched him stalk away.

Wondering if she should wait here, or if Greg would even speak to her tonight or leave it until the morning, Molly paced about the terrace for a good ten minutes before deciding that if Greg wanted her, he knew where her room was. She might be too on-edge to sleep, but at least she could try to distract herself by reading or something.

In the end, she phoned her mum.

'Hi, it's me. Sorry to call so late.'

'What's wrong?' was her mother's immediate response.

'Nothing. Just feeling a bit homesick.'

'Your man is doing ever so well,' her mother said. 'We've been watching the highlights every night on Eurosport. Your father wants to know if he's going to win, because if he is, he'll put a bet on.'

'Dad doesn't bet.'

'He will on this. If it's a sure thing.'

'Nothing is a sure thing,' Molly replied.

'You sound a bit down. Are you sure nothing's wrong?'

'I'm sure. Mum…?'

'Yes, love?'

'I'm coming back on Monday.'

'OK. It'll be lovely to see you. I've checked your house and everything is fine. How long will you be home for, or don't you know?'

'For good. I'm going back to work for Finley. Thanks for making me see sense. If it hadn't been for you and Dad, I wouldn't have thought about asking Finley to keep my job open.'

'Oh, love, aren't you enjoying it then? The last time we spoke you sounded as though you were having a great time.'

'I was. I am. It's just…'

'That kind of life isn't for you?' her mother finished, gently.

'No. When you're on a tour there's no time for anything; it's full-on from the minute you get up to

233

the minute you go to bed.'

There was a pause, and Molly wondered if they'd been cut off. 'Hello?'

'I'm still here. That doesn't sound like you, Molly. You've never been afraid of a bit of hard work. I think there's more to this than you're letting on.'

There was no pulling the wool over her mum's eyes, was there, Molly thought. 'There is,' she admitted. 'But I don't want to talk about him.'

'Him?' Her mother pounced on the word. 'There's a man involved?'

'Yes. It's complicated.'

'Love often is,' came her mother's wry response.

'Who said anything about love?'

'You didn't have to. I can hear it in your voice.'

Really? Molly hadn't realised she was that transparent. 'I don't know what it is, Mum.'

Another pause, then her mother said, 'Before you do anything drastic, don't you think you'd better find out?'

And Molly had to agree with her.

CHAPTER 31

Molly was on tenterhooks all morning, waiting for Chuck or Greg to say something. She'd caught Henno's eye at breakfast but he'd merely smiled politely at her, giving nothing away. She wasn't even certain the doctor had actually spoken to either of them yet and the suspense unnerved her. She was beginning to feel like a pupil waiting outside the headteacher's office.

When nothing had happened by the time the team bus drove away, headed for the start of Stage 19, she didn't know whether to breathe a sigh of relief or whether to stamp her foot in frustration. Of course she understood that there were far more important things going on than admonishing a staff member for becoming a little too familiar with a rider. Especially when that rider had a chance of a podium position in the most prestigious and famous cycling race in the world. When she looked at it like that, she was small fry indeed.

Molly had heard it said (mostly by those pesky commentators who she had a love-hate relationship with), that no one wins the Tour de France in Stage 19. She'd also heard them say that this year all bets were off, that seventeen seconds wasn't insurmountable, and anything could happen. They also didn't think either Mateo Rohjas, who was currently second on the leader-board, or Alex, had any more rabbits to pull out of their respective hats. Molly was inclined to agree with them, but she knew how driven Alex was. If anyone could do it, he could.

Today was the team time trial – a brief but incredibly fast race where each team set off as a group, and the teams were spaced at ten-minute intervals. The course might be a short one and each team would be done and dusted in a matter of minutes, but there would be a lot of hanging around before all the teams were through and the results were known.

For once, most of BeSpoke staff were at the finish, except for the mechanics who were in Megève joyfully fiddling with and tweaking the specialist bikes.

Sallanches, where the race finished, wasn't as quaint or as picturesque as many of the towns and villages she had passed through recently, but it did have a charm of its own, and it was filled with people waiting for the spectacle to come. The French really did love their cycling, Molly thought, as someone tried to give her a yellow balloon to wave as she hurried towards the town centre on foot. Alex and the team weren't due to set off for a while yet, so Molly used the opportunity to explore – anything to take her mind off her impending reprimand.

Considering Sallanches was surrounded by high mountains and was so close to the famous Mont Blanc, it was surprisingly open and spacious, and once she had managed to escape from the madness that was the finish line, she revelled in the relative peace and quiet. She also revelled in being alone.

Apart from when she was in her hotel room, Molly was hardly ever alone. None of them was, and she was beginning to feel a little claustrophobic. A wander for an hour in the unfamiliar streets of a foreign town would do her the world of good. It might also help to put things in perspective. Even a short time away from the Tour and all it entailed would be welcome.

Feeling naughty, she spied a pretty café with seating outside and bagged a table. Of course, the menu was in French, but she still recalled a few words she learnt in school and she certainly recognised "pain" and "fromage" – bread and cheese. That would do nicely! After stumbling over her order, the waiter smiled and Molly leaned back in her chair and closed her eyes, her face lifted to the sun. Now, if every Tour de France day was like this, she might be tempted to stay on.

Or would she?

Thinking back to her mother's advice last night, she examined her feelings.

She clearly liked Alex. A lot. Not only was he kind and funny and a lovely kisser, he was extremely attractive and fun to be with.

But did she love him?

She tried to imagine slotting back into her old life in Worcester and she had to admit, it did have a certain attraction; it was comfortable and familiar and she felt at ease there.

But, and this was a very big but – could she walk away from Alex? Possibly never see him again?

She wasn't sure that she could, and the thought filled her with a sadness so profound, her heart ached from it.

Darn it! She didn't have any choice, did she? If she

wanted to be a part of Alex's life, she'd have to stay with BeSpoke. The alternative simply didn't bear thinking about.

By the time her food arrived, Molly had made a tentative peace with herself; she would stay on as BeSpoke's physiotherapist and see what the future held. Alex was working on that assumption anyway, and he seemed quite happy for their relationship to develop. But there was one little problem – the rule that staff and riders do not mingle. Ever.

How, exactly, was she supposed to get around that?

She polished off her meal with gusto, following it with a cheeky glass of flavoursome red wine. Savouring every mouthful (it felt like months since any alcohol had passed her lips) she drank it slowly, and when she finished and paid, she wandered back to the finish line to watch BeSpoke come across it.

'Who do we have to worry about?' she asked, strolling up to Mick. He was sitting on a folding chair in front of one of the enormous screens, with a can of soda in his hand. When he saw her, he made to get up and offer her his seat, but she waved him back down.

'Team Braconti-Alba is leading,' he told her, 'but Espanda hasn't gone yet. Kontrol Data didn't do that well. Three of their guys were making great time, but the fourth held them back.'

Mateo Rohjas was second on the leader board yesterday. Today, that was all about to change as his team's less-than-stellar performance indicated. Molly just hoped that BeSpoke could hold it together and that four out of the eight made good time. Even though all eight team members (seven in BeSpoke's case) would start the stage, only the first four riders over the finish line would count towards the time. The fourth man's time would be applied to each of his team mates, so it was imperative that each team worked together, and once again the race wasn't about just about who was the fastest, but about tactics.

There was a lot more to this cycling stuff than just getting on a bike and peddling for all you were worth, Molly had come to realise. As well as the toll it took on the body (which she was fascinated by as part of her job) there was a large degree of mental toughness too, as each team psyched the other out. It made for surprisingly interesting viewing.

'Here they go,' Mick said as BeSpoke lined up.

'They've got twenty-three minutes and nineteen-seconds to beat,' Damien said, coming up behind them. 'I hope Carlos holds his nerve.'

Molly knew that, apart from the first kilometre, most of the stage was downhill, levelling out somewhat towards the finish line. Having to cycle against the clock and not jostle for space and position with the other riders on the road made for some dangerous risk-taking. This stage was all about technique and nerve, and who could hold theirs for the longest when skimming around the corners, before a final furious dash for the finish line.

BeSpoke came in at twenty-four minutes and three seconds.

For a long, tense time, there was silence in the BeSpoke ranks as they waited for the rest of the teams to finish their time trials. Eventually, Chuck appeared with a massive grin splintering his face.

'He's only gone and moved up from third to second!' he yelled, and the whole team let out a cheer.

Molly was crying and squealing, and jumping up and down, holding hands with Mick and Damien. She was so proud of Alex, and of the team as a whole, because one thing she had learnt since joining BeSpoke was that the Tour was a team event. It had been hard to get her head around the fact that in most other sports where there was a single winner, it was usually every man for himself. But cycling was different – the team chose the rider who they thought had the best chance and everyone got behind him. She'd never before felt part of something so big, so monumental; it was humbling and uplifting at the same time.

'Molly, can I have a word?'

Molly looked over her shoulder to see Chuck standing behind her. His previous delighted expression had been replaced by something more sombre, and she knew she was due for a reprimand.

Mick's eyes widened and he shook his head ever so slightly. Molly stared back at him for a split second and a niggle of fear squirmed in her stomach.

'This way,' Chuck said, leading her towards the bus.

Molly caught a last glimpse of Mick's expression and her worry deepened.

There was something going on and she simply knew she wasn't going to like it.

'Take a seat,' Chuck said when they had boarded the bus. He sat opposite and leaned forward. 'This isn't easy, but you leave me no choice. I'm terminating your contract with BeSpoke.'

Molly's mouth dropped open. She'd been expecting a telling off, but not this! 'Why?' she cried.

'You know why. There are good, solid reasons for not allowing support staff to get involved with the riders, and especially not during a Tour. Alex can't afford to have any distractions, and you, my dear, are one big distraction, indeed.'

'Nothing's happened!' she protested, but even as the words left her mouth she knew it wasn't strictly true. They might not have shared a bed or declared their undying love for each other, but they had most definitely kissed, and she suspected Alex felt the same way about her as she did about him. Not that he'd said as much, but she was pretty certain. Wasn't she?

'Yes, it has. Don't lie to me, Molly. I know what's been going on between the pair of you. It's my job to know more about the riders than they know themselves. I realise Alex thinks the world of you, but it's got to stop. I can't have you on my team, taking his focus away from his cycling. Especially now, when he's done so well. You understand that, don't you? You wouldn't want anything to come between him and his chances of winning the Tour de France?'

Oh, that was a low blow, Molly thought. But Chuck was right. Alex was on the cusp of something great, and if her love for him did anything to spoil that...

Her heart dropped to her feet; she'd just admitted to herself that she loved him.

And because of the love she felt for him, she found herself agreeing to Chuck's terms.

CHAPTER 32

'You were wonderful!' Molly exclaimed as the riders filed onto the bus. 'You all were.'

Alex was last on, having been ambushed by Eurosport for an interview. Chuck and Greg followed him on. Greg ignored her. Chuck gave her a level stare.

Molly bit her lip.

While she waited for Alex to shower, she tried to compose herself. It wasn't easy when there was a plane ticket to Heathrow tucked in her bag. At least BeSpoke hadn't made her find her own way home, she thought. And she had another twenty-four hours with Alex.

Or rather, not exactly *with* him, because Chuck had made it perfectly clear that she was to stay away from him except for the physio treatments.

'All done,' she said brightly, putting the equipment away. She'd do more work on Alex later, but for now he was free to go. 'How are you feeling?'

'To be honest, I'm not sure. It's all a bit of a blur.'

'I meant physically.'

'Tired. Very, very tired. But good, apart from that.'

'Good,' she said. Her smile felt as false as Katie Price's boobs.

Alex pulled his T-shirt on and as his head popped through the neck opening, he paused. 'Is everything all right?'

'Fine,' she replied, then, realising he was waiting for her to expand, she added, 'I'm tired, too. And excited and nervous.'

'We all are,' he said, straightening his T-shirt, before getting to his feet.

When his arms came around her, she stiffened. Oh, God, she wanted nothing more than to sink into his embrace and to feel his lips on hers, and it took everything she had to move away.

The brief flare of hurt in his eyes wrenched her heart. She hated doing this to him, but she had no choice. Chuck was right; Alex needed to focus on tomorrow.

'Seven seconds,' she said, by way of explanation. 'Go and make sure you're fully hydrated, or Chuck won't let me hear the end of it.' Seven measly seconds between del Ray and Alex, that was all.

He studied her for a second, then his expression cleared. 'Yeah, I suppose I better had. The pair of them have got their heads together working out my nutrition for tonight and tomorrow, but if they try to get me to eat any more rice…' He ground to a halt. 'Are you sure you're OK?'

'Positive,' she said, desperate to kiss him. She washed her hands instead, and by the time she'd turned around he had returned to the main body of the bus and was taking his seat.

It was all she could do to hold in her tears until she got to her room.

How she was going to get through the next twenty-four hours was a mystery.

CHAPTER 33

*W*ell, here we are, at the penultimate stage of the Tour de France. This stage will be the decider. Del Ray is still wearing the yellow jersey, but do you think he will be able to hang on to it?'

'*Who knows, Norris. Normally at this point, the winner is assured, but I think anything could happen today.*'

'*That's a nice shot of Lake Annecy,*' Norris said as the helicopter showed the view below. '*Annecy, of course, is on the French-Swiss border, only 22 miles south of Geneva, so there are probably more than a few Swiss down there in the crowd. And what a crowd it is, Eamon, all here to see the start of a terrific battle between Oscar del Ray from Team Espanda and Alexander Duvall from Team BeSpoke.*'

'*Let's hope it is a terrific battle and doesn't turn out to be a damp squib. These guys have got to be tired.*'

'*They're bound to be. And to have a mountain stage like this right at the end, is pure evil.*' Norris chuckled and Eamon joined in.

Molly couldn't see anything to laugh at. The tour organisers were sadists, she was convinced of it. Hadn't the riders suffered enough, and yes, it might make for memorable viewing today, but to have 125 kilometres with a summit finish was sadistic.

She was actually fed up with hearing Norris and

Eamon going on about it. They were positively ecstatic with glee. Molly just wanted the whole event to be over, as much for her sake as for Alex's.

Molly watched listlessly as the helicopter zoomed in on a squat grey building with an odd shape like the prow of a ship, sitting half-in and half-out of the river. The shot vanished to be replaced by the seven BeSpoke riders lined up in a row on their turbos, and her heart lurched uncomfortably when she saw Alex's gorgeous face. He looked composed and calm, his expression giving nothing away.

She wished she felt as calm as he appeared to be, even though she guessed he was probably nervous and excited and scared all at the same time.

Molly felt those same emotions, too, but her overriding feeling was loss and a bone-aching, teeth-clenching love. The knowledge that she had just found the man she wanted to spend the rest of her life with, only to have him snatched away from her by the very thing that had brought them together in the first place – cycling – was tearing her apart.

'And they're off. 125 kilometres of cycling, with three Category 3 climbs, one Category 1, and the summit finish at Semnoz,' the TV informed her.

Molly stared woodenly out of the window. Semnoz was less than 18 kilometres from Annecy, (although the riders would be taking a much more circuitous route) so it would only take the car about a half an hour to get to arrive at the finish, but she was barely aware of the steady, gradual rise up through the trees. The thought of tomorrow and what it entailed filled her mind and it took all her self-control to hold back tears.

'You OK, darl?' Mick asked for about the

twentieth time, and for about the twentieth time she nodded, not trusting herself to speak.

Out of the corner of her eye, she could see the soigneur sending her worried glances, but she ignored him. She had no choice. She didn't want to confide in Mick, firstly because she didn't trust him not to say anything to Alex, and secondly because she didn't want to get him into trouble. It was all right for her, she had a steady, well-paid job to return to; cycling and Team BeSpoke were Mick's life, and she didn't want to jeopardise that. Anyway, she was in the wrong, she had known the score, and she was the one who had broken the rules. It was only fair she should be the only one to pay the price.

But what about Alex, a little voice said. Will he be paying the price too, or will the thrill and joy of coming second in the Tour de France eclipse all thoughts of her? For his sake, she hoped it was the latter, because she never wanted him to feel as wretched as she felt right now.

It'll be fine once she got back home, she kept telling herself. Think of this as a little holiday romance, intense and wonderful while it lasted, but unable to withstand the return to normality. Her feelings would fade, and she'd be left with pleasant memories of a man she had a crush on when she was (briefly) a part of the most famous cycle race in the world.

That's what she kept telling herself. She hoped it was true, because right now she felt raw and aching, and the possibility that she might feel like this for the rest of her life filled her with dread. If this was what being in love was like, then she didn't want any part of it.

What she did want was a coffee, and as soon as Damien brought the car to a standstill, she was out of the door and heading off into the growing crowd. She heard Mick call her name, but she ignored him, feeling a bit of a cow for doing so but unable to face his continuing concern. If she could just get through the rest of today and this evening without breaking down, she could cry all she wanted on the flight tomorrow. Chuck had been insistent that she carried on as normal, and she had agreed – she owed it to Alex and the rest of the team not to upset any fragile apple-carts. She owed it to Chuck too, because at least he had been gracious enough to allow her to remain with the team until they arrived in Paris later tonight. She was even booked into the same hotel, but as soon as the riders left for the start at Versailles tomorrow and the final, triumphant stage, she was to leave, too – for the airport. She would be flying home a whole day earlier than the rest of the team.

In a way, she was relieved. She would do her celebrating for him from afar and grieve for what she had lost, without putting a dampener on his astonishing achievement.

Speaking of achievements, it was about time she concentrated on the race and not on her own misery. It was Alex who was important right now, not her, so she bought a coffee and found a screen.

'This pair has been glued together since the start,' Norris was saying. 'If del Ray keeps this up, Duvall's chances of gaining vital seconds will go out of the window.'

'It'll all depend on the next climb. These riders are tired, they're emotional, and they're both fighting for the yellow jersey.'

'I bet the viewers at home are on the edge of their seats, Eamon. I know I am.'

247

'They've been climbing steadily now since Annecy with only a couple of respites on the occasional downhill. Who do you think is the better climber, Eamon?'

'There's not much to choose between them. Del Ray has proved himself time and time again – we've seen him in the Giro d'Italia this year, and the Tour de France last year, to name but a few. But Duvall has always been Tim Anderson's lieutenant. He's dragged him up his fair share of mountains, and although Duvall has won a couple of smaller races, like the Tour of Flanders for instance, he's always been second wheel to Anderson on the grand tours. It took Anderson crashing out for Duvall to come into his own, and he's showing us what he can do.'

Poor Tim, Molly thought. It must be hard for him watching the race from his hospital bed and seeing how extraordinarily well Alex was doing.

'The race is just about at the halfway mark and we're starting to see del Ray attacking already. He knows he has to put some distance between himself and Duval. Every second counts at this point. There he goes, and Duvall is slow to respond. He's letting del Ray get ahead… No… wait… there he goes. Duvall is out of the saddle and standing up on his pedals, but he's not looking as smooth as he was on Alpe D'Huez. What do you think, Eamon?'

'I think he's playing a game.'

'Do you really? If he is, it's a dangerous one.'

'My guess is that he's lulling del Ray into a false sense of security, letting him think he's more tired than he actually is.'

'He likes playing head games, does Alex. We've seen him do that with our own eyes.'

'That's what cycling is all about, Norris. You can be as fast and as strong as anyone but if you can't read the race and read the other riders, then you ain't gonna win. It's all about the tactics.'

248

'Do you think his tactics today will work?'

'They seem to be so far. Del Ray keeps trying to draw away; he clearly believes he has a chance and that sooner or later it will work. Duvall lets him get a few wheel lengths ahead before he reacts, but notice that he does react. Always. He always gets back on del Ray's wheel. And, he's letting del Ray do all the work, too.'

'He is, he certainly is. And there del Ray goes again, but he's slower this time.'

'The gradient is steeper, Norris, but Duvall is keeping pace with him. Who'd have thought that the Tour de France would rest on the shoulders of these two riders and on the very last day of racing.'

Molly's phone rang and she jumped. For a short while she had been fully immersed in the race and had forgotten the outside world existed.

It was Mick.

'Where are you?' he asked.

She looked around. 'Um, near the press tent, I think.'

'What are you doing?'

Despite the pain in her heart, she chuckled. 'Watching the race, of course.'

'Why aren't you watching it with us? Jakob has snacks,' Mick wheedled.

Eating was the last thing on Molly's mind, although another coffee would be welcome. 'I'll join you soon,' she promised. 'I'm enjoying soaking up the atmosphere.'

'Are you sure you're OK, darl? Because you don't seem it.' Mick sounded worried. 'You can tell me, you know.'

No, she really couldn't. It wouldn't be fair of her to burden him, and it wouldn't do any good anyway.

'I'm fine,' she repeated yet again, then went to fetch another coffee.

When she returned to her spot, Alex and del Ray were more or less neck-and-neck at the top of Mont Revard. Unlike Mont Ventoux and Alpe d'Huez, the summit of this mountain was barely noticeable. There was no drama, just a point in the tree-lined road when the up stopped and the down began. Only the Tour banners and the number of spectators lining the road marked it as a summit.

Alex had scraped past del Ray on an outside bend and was hunkered down over his handlebars and leaning into the curves of the road.

Please be careful, Molly pleaded silently, images of him sprawled across the road searing her mind.

She watched as he gained ground on the other rider and slowly but surely he began to pull away.

'Let's see if he can keep this up when he gets to the bottom of Semnoz,' Norris chortled. *'With over 1000 metres of climbing to come, he'll be hard pushed to stay ahead of del Ray.'*

'He only needs to be eight seconds ahead,' Eamon pointed out.

'Eight seconds is a huge amount at this level,' Norris countered.

'He's gained four on the descent,' Eamon said.

Four more seconds. All Alex needed was another four seconds.

From the start of the climb to the finish was roughly 10 kilometres, and Molly agonised through every one of them, willing Alex on, as though her prayers alone could give him wings and help him fly up the road.

'Can you believe that, Eamon? Duvall is off! He's

determined not to get caught.'

'He can't afford to be,' Eamon said.

'Del Ray is being left behind! His legs have gone and he's got nothing left in them. You can see by his face how much he's suffering,' Norris said as the motorbike camera zeroed in on del Ray's agonised expression. *'Del Ray can't keep up with Duvall. His chance of winning the Tour de France this year has well and truly gone.'*

The camera focused on Alex and the determination on his face.

'I think we're looking at the man who'll be wearing the yellow jersey on the ride into Paris tomorrow.'

He passed under the red arch that signalled there was only one kilometre left to go, and Molly held her breath, her eyes glued to the little counter at the top of the screen which told viewers how much time there was between Alex and Oscar del Ray.

Del Ray was several bike lengths behind. It equated to three seconds.

Alex and del Ray were neck-and-neck on time, even though Alex was physically ahead of the other on the road.

'Put your foot down, Alex,' she yelled at the screen. 'Go on! Go on!

Alex powered around a steep bend, taking the inside line. Molly jumped up and down as the road flattened off a little and Alex did as he was told and put his literal foot down. It was almost as if he could hear her shouting. Then the gradient kicked up again and Alex slowed a fraction.

'Don't you dare slow down!' she yelled.

Oh, my God; there is was – the finish line! 'Go on!' she screamed again. 'You can do it! No, no!' The little time counter in the corner of the screen had disappeared. 'Not now, bring it back!'

Then Alex was over the line and Molly had no idea whether the man she loved had won the Tour de France or not.

CHAPTER 34

Desperate for news, Molly dashed to the BeSpoke parking area, stumbling over her own feet and elbowing people out of the way.

'Excuse me, excuse me. Let me through,' she cried, pushing through the milling crowds, who were all heading in the same direction, hoping to catch a glimpse of the winner. Whoever that may be.

She reached the tour bus with the turbos lined up along the side of it and waited. The mechanics were there, waiting to rescue their precious bikes from those pesky riders, but she knew the swannies would be at the finish line to help the riders when they crossed it. She also knew from experience that some cyclists were so exhausted they were hardly able to keep their bikes upright, and she wondered what sort of a state Alex would be in.

While she waited, she turned the sound up on the TV in the bus.

'He's done it. Alexander Duvall from Team BeSpoke is the winner of this year's Tour de France, unless something untoward happens tomorrow. Stage 21 is mostly a ceremonial stage, with fifteen laps of Paris before the grand finale on the Avenue des Champs-Élysées.'

'I'm astounded,' Eamon said. *'Duvall has won by two seconds. He'd better make sure he stays on his bike tomorrow,'* he joked. *'It isn't exactly a decisive victory, is it?'*

No, she agreed, but it was a victory nevertheless, and she defied anyone to take that away from him.

Her heart swelled with love for Alex, it seemed like months and not weeks had gone by since he had walked into her treatment room in Worcester with his newly healed wrist and told her he was competing in the Tour de France. She recalled the incredulity on his face and the disbelief that a boy from a village in the West Midlands was taking part in the most famous event in the cycling calendar.

She could only imagine what he was feeling right at this very minute. He must be so very proud of himself and she was proud for him.

A huge cheer went up outside and she guessed Alex had arrived, and she peered out of the window to see him surrounded by members of the press, other team staff and Tour officials, as well as members of the public. It was chaos out there, and Alex wore a stunned, disbelieving expression.

One of the mechanics leapt forward to grab the bike and Mick led a slightly wobbly Alex to his turbo. There was no sign of either Chuck or Greg and Molly was grateful, but she ducked into the rear of the bus all the same and waited for Alex to come to her for the very last physio session she would ever give him.

It wasn't Alex who slid the partition aside, though, it was Mick. 'Here you are! I wondered where you'd got to. Alex has been asking for you,' he said.

'Where is he?' she asked, gazing past him and down the aisle.

'Meeting his public,' Mick laughed. 'The poor

bloke can't believe it. He's gobsmacked. We all are. He'll be a while yet, what with having to appear on the podium, so do you want to join us for a glass of champagne? Just the one, because we've still got work to do, and Jakob only had enough money on him for one bottle. I dare say there'll be more with dinner tonight.'

'In a minute,' she said. She wanted to have a drink with the others – they'd become almost like family over these last few weeks – but she didn't know if she could hold herself together and now wasn't the time to start sobbing.

'I'll save you a glass,' he promised. 'A paper cup, actually, but you know what I mean.' He turned to leave then turned back again. 'Oh, before I forget, Chuck said you're to travel to Paris with us in the car this evening. There's no need to bother with any physio tonight. Henno will see to the guys and he'll be flying to Paris with Greg and the riders.'

Oh. She hadn't realised the riders would be *flying* from here to Paris and that the rest of them would have to drive. How far was it from Semnoz to Paris anyway?

'About six hours by car,' Mick said when she asked him. 'We won't get there until about midnight.'

So, she'd not be seeing Alex later. Her last real sight of him (apart from on the telly) was two days ago on the pretty little terrace in the hotel in Megève. If she had known then that she wouldn't get a chance to say goodbye—

She murmured something unintelligible and turned away before Mick saw the tears spilling down her cheeks.

CHAPTER 35

To Molly, Paris meant romance and lovers. It was the city of light and love and she had always wanted to go there, but it was the sort of place she had intended to visit with the man she loved, and not on her own.

She sat in a café in Charles de Gaulle airport and fingered the ticket Chuck had given her, a coffee going cold in front of her. The smell of it was actually making her feel a little sick, too rich, too full of flavour and memories. A nice cup of tea, that's what she needed, she thought, but she couldn't be bothered to move.

She had found a note shoved under the door of her (very) small hotel room when she arrived last night after one of the longest and most depressing journeys of her life, telling her that a taxi had been booked for nine a.m. Her flight was at twenty-past twelve. Clearly, Chuck-n-Greg had no intention of letting her anywhere near Alex. The drive to the airport was only thirty or so minutes; she hadn't needed to check out of the hotel until ten-thirty a.m. But she did as she was told without protesting, because what else was she to do?

Wondering if Alex had noticed she had gone or

was too wrapped up in winning to even think of her, she blinked back tears. She was fed up with crying. And having never, ever cried over a man (apart from Ben Gleasedale when she was fifteen, but that didn't count) she couldn't understand why she was feeling so distraught now, or how she had let herself get in such a state in the first place. That's it, she vowed, I'm not getting this involved again. Not if it hurts this much when it goes wrong.

A bitter little laugh escaped her lips, and she glanced around to see if anyone had noticed. It wasn't as though she'd gone looking for love, was it? It had arrived all by itself and out-of-the-blue. And she wished it would bloody well go back to where it came from.

She checked the time. Five minutes past eleven. The gate would open soon, and she would be on her way, leaving France and the damned Tour well and truly behind. The only good thing to have come out of these last three frenetic weeks was that Alex had won. She only wished she could be there when he stepped onto the podium on the Champs-Élysées later this evening.

It was time to go, the BA flight to Heathrow was departing from Gate 26.

Molly had every intention of getting on it – really she did. But when she got to the check-in desk, she hesitated.

Other passengers pushed past her, and still she paused.

This wasn't right; she'd been there at the start and she should be there at the finish. She needed to see this through to the end, no matter how painful it might be. She wanted to be close enough to see

Alex's face, she wanted to celebrate with him, albeit from a distance.

Molly Matthews had unfinished business in Paris.

Turning sharply on her heel, she marched out of the airport and didn't stop until she found the RER station which would take her into the heart of Paris, dragging her case behind her. It was an inconvenience, but if she could find a cheap bed and breakfast for the night, she intended to check in and leave her case there; she would catch a flight tomorrow.

Cheap and Paris were two words which weren't exactly synonymous with each other, Molly discovered, but she eventually found a little pension in the west of the city not too far from the Seine that didn't make her eyes water when she was informed of the price. It actually looked quite cute from the outside, and the little reception area was quaint and old-fashioned, with a bell on the desk and a door leading to a pretty courtyard.

Her room was tiny but it had a Juliet balcony which overlooked the street, a minuscule en suite and a TV. She resisted the urge to turn it on. The final stage of the Tour de France wouldn't start until four p.m., leaving from the palace at Versailles – another place she would have loved to see – so there was ages to go yet.

Deciding she may as well spend the next couple of hours sightseeing, she returned to reception, grabbed a brochure of what to see and do in Paris, closed her eyes and jabbed her finger at it.

She opened them again.

Wow! The Catacombs? Really?

Of all the wonderful places to visit, she would

never have chosen The Catacombs. But maybe it was for the best; she could save the really good stuff, the romantic stuff, for when she came back to Paris. The Catacombs were probably somewhere she wouldn't have gone with a boyfriend or a fiancé, but on her own and at this particular point in her life, it was perfect.

They were also rather more interesting than she anticipated. Her guide, Igor (very apt, she thought) led Molly and a few others down several sets of stairs, explaining that the site was originally a quarry, and many of the older buildings in Paris were constructed of the stone quarried from it. He said that the tunnels stretched for miles and there were many that were still undiscovered.

The Catacombs was a strange relationship between macabre and artistic. Many of the skulls and other bones were arranged along the walls in sweeping arcing patterns, or lined the columns in strangely compelling designs. It was both beautiful and horrific at the same time. To think that the remains of six million people lay in these tunnels and some of them were on show for the amusement of the public, astounded her.

But Igor spoke with such reverence it made Molly think that maybe having your bones line a wall here might in fact be better than having them slowly decay in the earth or be burnt to a cinder.

Oh, God, she was becoming seriously morbid, and although she enjoyed seeing The Catacombs, she was delighted to be in the fresh, warm, summer air again. Blinking in the unaccustomed sunlight, Molly checked her phone.

She'd had three missed calls and a handful of texts

from Alex. She deleted the texts without reading them, blinking back tears. It was over, done with; there was no point in dragging it out. She was going home. He wasn't. That's all there was to it. Speaking to him would only make things worse for both of them.

Squaring her shoulders and reluctant to dive back underground for the Metro, she decided to walk. It was quite a distance to the Champs-Élysées, but straightforward enough, and her route would take her down the Boulevard Saint-Germain and the Seine at the end of it.

Even the name of the famous river conjured up all sorts of connotations.

She wasn't disappointed when she saw it. Glittering in the late afternoon sun, it wasn't as wide as she had thought it would be. She'd imagined something on the scale of the Thames, but it was altogether a smaller, but no less impressive river, with boats chugging up and down and people strolling along its banks. She was also surprised to find the bridge was blocked off to traffic, although pedestrians could still get through.

Her phone vibrated again, and she ignored it, although she guessed that the riders would have departed from Versailles by now and were probably almost in the city. She could see the advance vehicles already, the floats, the trucks, some official vehicles, and the noise was deafening as music blared from numerous loudspeakers, a commentary in French (goodbye Norris and Eamon) over yet another loudspeaker and lots of cheering as each float trundled past.

Molly found a spot on the Rue de Rivoli, and

unable to go any further because the Champs-Élysées was barriered off, she settled down to wait for the man she loved to ride past one last time.

CHAPTER 36

Alex and his team were all in a line at the front of the peloton as they made their final approach to the finish line, after completing several laps of the city, and once more the crowds clapped and cheered. Every single one of the riders had a massive grin on his face.

All except Alex. He was smiling, but with his face bare of the usual cycling glasses or visor, Molly could see his eyes. He didn't look as happy as he should, considering his long-held dream was about to come true. Something was troubling him. Was is Tim, she wondered. She was only guessing, but knowing Alex, he probably felt it should be Tim wearing the yellow jersey and not himself.

She waved frantically, willing him to look up and see her, to know that she was thrilled for him, but he didn't notice her, his focus on the road ahead.

Then the team swept past, turned the corner, and were gone.

It was over.

Done.

She just wished she could have been part of the final celebrations, to see her Tour through to the end.

With a drawn-out sigh, she turned away from the

barrier and wondered what to do now.

She really should try to eat something. She hadn't managed anything since breakfast yesterday, and then she had only picked at her pain au chocolate, the sweet stickiness making her feel slightly nauseous.

There was a coffee shop directly behind her. Assuming it would be pricey, being just off the Champs-Élysées, but not caring, she slipped inside.

All the tables were occupied. Despondent, she was about to leave when a heavily accented voice said, 'Excuse moi? Are you wanting to sit? I will go soon. You are welcome to join me.'

The voice belonged to an elderly man wearing an overcoat. A tiny cup of ink-black coffee sat on the table in front of him.

She smiled gratefully at him and took a seat.

'English, yes?' he asked her.

Was it that obvious? She supposed it must be. 'English,' she confirmed.

''Oliday?'

'Sort of. I'm here for the Tour.'

'Ah, Le Tour.' He nodded and smiled. 'I, too. It is magnifique. You are 'appy that an Englishman won, non?'

'Very happy. Coffee please,' she said to the waiter who appeared at their table. 'And what sandwiches do you have?'

The waiter looked at her blankly.

The old man spoke in rapid French, and the waiter responded in kind.

'Ham, cheese, or the pâté here is good, he tells me,' the old man translated.

'Ham, please'.

The waiter didn't wait for his own translation. He

jerked his head in acknowledgement and stalked away.

'Parisiens, huh!' the old man exclaimed. 'They are all the same.'

He reached into his overcoat and produced an iPad. Molly blinked in surprise as he opened it up and placed it on the table.

'Do you mind if I watch the ceremony?' he asked her, and when she looked blankly at him, he explained, 'Your Monsieur Duvall, when he stands on the—' He lifted his palm to shoulder height and made a downward patting motion. 'He will accept first prize,' he added.

'The podium?'

'Oui. Do you mind?'

'Of course not, I'd like to watch him too,' she admitted, shyly.

So far, she hadn't seen a single TV screen anywhere today, but as she had been watching it live on the street she hadn't needed to. It would be fitting to see Alex step onto the podium and make a speech while still in France, and not have to wait until later to see the highlights.

Molly had eaten her sandwich and had drunk two cups of coffee before the three riders stepped on to the podium.

She watched the man she loved walk across the yellow stage and receive his trophy. She watched him shake hands with Tour officials, and with his fellow riders who had come second and third. She watched him bow his head as God Save the Queen was played. And all the time her heart was so full of love and pride and an all-consuming sadness that she thought it might break.

'I don't know what to say,' Alex began, and she

264

smiled gently. Trust him not to have prepared a speech. He probably thought that if he did, he'd jinx it somehow.

'I never thought I'd be here on this podium. I never dreamt I'd win the Tour de France. No, that's not right – I *did* dream, all the time, but I never thought it would happen. I was just a normal lad, but I had big dreams, and today has proved to me that dreams can come true.' He stared directly into the camera. 'Some of them.'

Alex cleared his throat. 'There are so many people who have made this possible – my parents for letting me loose on a bike and not nagging me too much about being careful. Is this careful enough for you, Mum?' The crowd broke into laughter, and Molly joined them.

'I'd like to thank all those guys I've ridden with over the years – you've all been an inspiration to me. Then there's my team at BeSpoke – thanks for putting up with me and for dragging me up all those mountains. Tim, mate, this should be you up here – maybe next year? I promise to be your wingman. Then there are all the people behind the scenes; Chuck, my sports director, and Greg, the team manager, both of whom believed in me; the soigneurs, who have a damned hard time of it. Sorry for all the sweaty kit you had to wash, Mick.' More laughter. 'The mechanics, the drivers, the chef – no more chicken and rice for a while, eh? And Henno, who treated more saddle sores than I care to remember.'

He paused, his expression serious, and the chuckles died away.

'There is one other person. She's not here now,

but I wish she was, and that's Molly Matthews. She's beautiful, smart, kind, funny… And if you're watching Molly (and I hope you are), I couldn't have done it without you.' He turned to hand the mic over to one of the Tour officials, but hesitated. 'Oh, and I forgot to say, I love you, Molly, with all my heart. Thanks, everyone.'

There was absolute silence for a second, then the crowd went wild.

Molly sat, stunned, as the meaning of what he had just said sunk in.

When her phone rang, she reached for it automatically, and answered without looking at the screen, her attention on the glorious, wonderful man still standing on the podium.

'Hello?' she said.

'Molly?'

The voice was female. It sounded vaguely familiar, but to be honest she wasn't really paying that much attention to it.

'Yes. Who is this?' she asked, absently.

'Gina.'

'Who?'

'Gina Anderson, Tim's wife.'

'Oh, hi. Are you OK?'

'I'm good, thanks, but from what Tim and Mick tell me you're not. And neither is Alex. What are you waiting for, girl? He's already told the whole world he loves you.'

He had, hadn't he? What was she waiting for? Oh, yes, there was the little problem of never seeing him—

'—and don't use the excuse that he'll hardly ever be home,' Gina was saying. 'If you love him, you'll deal with it. It won't last forever, you know. He's going to retire from professional cycling at some point.'

Gina was right.

'I've got to go,' Molly said to the bemused old man, leaping to her feet. She lifted her bag from the back of her chair, pulled out a wad of notes and flung them on the table. She took a step, then turned back, leant down and gave the elderly man a swift kiss on the cheek. 'Thank you!'

Then she was out of the door and fighting her way through the mass of people, most of them going in the opposite direction to her. After a few minutes and more than a few strange looks, she realised she was crying, and she laughed wildly.

Alex Duvall loved her. *Loved her!* He'd just said so on national TV. He'd told her he loved her in front of all those millions of people who were watching the closing ceremony of the Tour de France.

She felt giddy with it, her head spinning, her heart racing.

He loved her!

She had to get to him and tell him how she felt.

Praying that he hadn't been whisked away, she pushed and elbowed, barged and jostled. But she wasn't getting there fast enough so, desperate he might have already left, she hoisted herself up and over the barrier and onto the now-empty road, put her head down and ran up the Champs-Élysées.

After several minutes of headlong flight, she realised that she couldn't keep the pace up, and she also realised something else; she was being followed. Puffing and panting, she looked behind her to see a police motorbike hot on her heels.

The brief wail of a siren made her jump out of her skin and she staggered to a halt, her hands on her knees, winded.

The police officer got off his motorbike and sauntered towards her, one hand on his hip. Molly tried to see if he was about to pull a gun on her, but her eyes were too blurry from tears, and she straightened up, brushing them away with her fingers.

He called out something to her, but she had no idea what he was saying, and when he repeated it, holding out a hand, palm up, she shook her head.

'He wants your ID,' someone on the other side of the barrier shouted at her.

'Oh right. Hang on,' she said to the officer. 'I've got my passport here somewhere.' She delved into her bag, seeing him stiffen, but he relaxed a little when she pulled out her passport with all the aplomb of a magician pulling a rabbit out of a hat. 'Here!' she cried, waving it at him.

He moved closer and took it from her, opened it and stared at it.

Molly wished he'd hurry up, and she glanced over her shoulder, shuffling from foot to foot in her haste to leave.

'Name?' he asked her.

'It's there, on my passport. Molly Matthews. Look, I'm in a hurry, can you be quick?'

The officer studied her face, then looked back down at the passport in his hands.

'Please?' she pleaded. 'I've got to go.'

'Where?'

'There.' She pointed to the Arc de Triomphe in the distance.

'Why?'

'Because Alexander Duvall, the winner of the Tour de France, has just told the whole world he loves me!'

The man narrowed his eyes at her, then reached up to the radio pinned to his chest and spoke into it. She heard her name mentioned and she gritted her teeth, a thought suddenly occurring to her; what if they thought she was some kind of terrorist and arrested her?

Anxiously, she peered at him. He stared impassively back.

'D'accord,' she heard him say, and without warning he caught hold of her arm and almost dragged her towards his bike. Surely, he wasn't arresting her?

Letting go of her, he shoved her passport into her hand and got on his bike. She was about to resume her frantic run towards the Arc de Triomphe, when a police car, sirens blaring, hurtled around the corner and came to a halt.

Oh, bugger, she really was going to be arrested. Wonderful. Then she remembered that Alex had said he loved her, and she couldn't help smiling.

An officer climbed out of the car, and jerked his head indicating she should get in, and she sent a helpless look at the motorbike copper, who gave her a nod and a salute. The cheeky git. Thanks a bunch, she wanted to yell at him, but common sense prevailed.

Instead, she walked towards the car, and the policeman opened the door for her. She had never been so humiliated in all her life when he placed a hand on the top of her head to guide her inside.

The door slammed shut and her stomach dropped to her boots. Wondering just how awful

French police stations were and hoping she didn't have to spend too long in one, she prayed they'd provide someone who spoke English, otherwise she was done for.

The irony when the car drove straight up the Champs-Élysées wasn't lost on her, and as the vehicle drew closer to the podium, Molly craned her neck, twisting her head this way and that as she peered out of the windows.

The car stopped right in front of the podium. The officer got out. He opened Molly's door and jerked his head for her to follow him.

Hardly daring to believe what was happening, Molly did as she was told, trotting quickly in his wake as he approached the barrier and spoke to one of the security guys. She heard her name mentioned, and the man in his high-viz jacket stared at her.

Then she heard Alex's name mentioned, and someone else said "Molly Matthews" and suddenly her name was on everyone's lips. A huge cheer went up and people started clapping, and the man in the high-viz jacket opened the barrier for her. She squeezed through and was about to ask where she could find Alex Duvall, when the sea of people parted, and there he was, surrounded by press, officials, and other riders.

She drank him in, the sight of him filling her heart with so much love she thought it might burst. He looked shattered, totally and utterly exhausted, but he carried on answering questions, Chuck hovering at his side. Greg was conducting his own press conference a few feet away.

Should she walk up to him? Could she? But now that she was here, almost close enough to touch him, her courage left her. She'd made a promise to Chuck – dare she break it?

'Go for it,' Mick said in her ear, and she whirled around and flung her arms about his neck. 'I don't know what's gone on between you and Chuck but I can guess. He's wrong – Alex is a better rider with you in his life. If you love him as much as I suspect you do, don't let anything get between you.'

Molly opened her mouth but Mick hadn't finished.

'I've never seen him like this. He was devastated when he realised you'd left the team. Chuck told us some cock and bull story about you wanting to go back to England and not liking the whole cycling thing, but I don't buy it. Besides,' he grinned at her, 'You wouldn't be here now if you didn't feel the same way about Alex as he does about you.'

He gave her a gentle push in Alex's direction and she took a little step forward.

Then something, some sixth sense made Alex glance in her direction. In wonderful slow motion, she watched his gaze swing towards her. Their eyes met.

For long moments, he stared at her, then his face broke into a huge smile. Pushing through the photographers and various people holding out mobiles and microphones, he dashed towards her. En masse, everyone's head swivelled towards her.

Molly just had time to hear someone ask, "Is that Molly Matthews?' and someone else say, 'I think it must be,' before Alex was in front of her.

Sweeping her into his arms, he lifted her off her feet and twirled her around, before putting her down and kissing her soundly.

Everything faded as his lips met hers, and she melted into him, and all she was aware of was him.

When she finally came up for air (reluctantly she might add, because she wanted to spend the rest of her life being kissed by him) it was to the sound of cheering and clapping.

Just then a microphone was shoved in his face. Molly expected him to push it away, but he took hold of it and cried,' This is Molly! I couldn't have won the Tour de France without her. Tell her, Chuck.'

Molly blanched. She hadn't realised Chuck was standing right beside her, having been too wrapped up in Alex and his wonderful kiss. Please don't send me away again, she pleaded with her eyes as she caught his less-than-pleased gaze. He shook his head.

'I give in,' he muttered. 'Le Tour de France, be damned? It's more like Le Tour de Love.'

Alex laughed and Molly giggled as the mic picked it up and Chuck's words bounced back to them over the speaker system.

'I love you,' he shouted in her ear, trying to make himself heard above all the noise.

'I love you too,' she told him and there was nothing in the world more wonderful than the adoration on his face and the joy in her heart.

A letter from Lilac

This book isn't meant to be a book about cycling; it's a romance, which just happens to be set during the Tour de France. If you want to know more about the nitty-gritty of the sport, there are some excellent autobiographies out there from those guys who actually ride bikes for a living, who will be far more accurate than I have been.

I've taken liberties, many of them and quite often, too. For instance, the Bagnères-de-Luchon to Carcassonne stage is actually cycled in reverse in the book, so for anyone who is familiar with the Col de Portet d'Aspet they will be aware that from the direction Alex et al approached it from meant that the monument to Fabio Casartelli would be on the uphill slope and not the downhill, as I have shown it to be.

Actually, there are lots of little anomalies like this in my novel, and they are deliberate in order to allow the story to flow and not to bog the readers down in too much detail. Take mountain classifications, as another example – there are actually five categories of climbs (not four as in Le Tour de Love), ranging from 4, which is the easiest, although if you cycled up one you'd know it isn't easy at all, through to H, which means 'beyond categorisation'. These mountains, the Col du Tourmalet and Port de Bales being but two, are harder than Category 1 climbs, and although I would dearly have loved to have included all this detail in my book, I left it out, along with a lot of other stuff, because this story is really about Molly and Alex and their love.

Thanks to all the cycling people who helped me with Le Tour de Love – as promised, I've not mentioned any names and I take full responsibility for any errors, both deliberate and accidental. Oh, and yes, I did stretch the realms of possibility a little, too, but I make no apology for that – this is fiction after all!

Love,
Lilac x

About the author

Lilac spends all her time writing, or reading, or thinking about writing or reading, often to the detriment of her day job, her family, and the housework. She apologises to her employer and her loved ones, but the house will simply have to deal with it!

She calls Worcester home, though she would prefer to call somewhere hot and sunny home, somewhere with a beach and cocktails and endless opportunities for snoozing in the sun…

When she isn't hunched over a computer or dreaming about foreign shores, she enjoys creating strange, inedible dishes in the kitchen, accusing her daughter of ~~stealing~~ borrowing her clothes, and fighting with her husband over whose turn it is to empty the dishwasher.

For regular updates and news on new releases check out:
www.lilacmills.com

Lilac can also be found on Twitter and Facebook

Lightning Source UK Ltd.
Milton Keynes UK
UKHW041542300320
361075UK00004B/1295